CW00589584

A Little Different From The Rest

A little different from the rest

Joe James

Text Copyright © 2021 by Joe J. T. A. James

Cover image copyright © 2021 by Joe J. T. A. James

All rights reserved.

No part of this book may be reproduced or used in any manner without written permission of the copyright owner except for the use of quotations in a book review.

FIRST EDITION

In dedication to my Wife Sylvia, my Son Simon and my Baby Girl Sophie

Contents

ACKNOWLEDGMENTS

This book was originally written as a gift to my children 5 years prior to publishing. Since then, it has been through many changes and edits to finally be the novel I always believed it could be.

This is mostly due to my amazingly supportive wife Sylvia and my two children Sophie and Simon. I am so grateful to have you in my life and without you I would never have been the man I am today.

Being Autistic and ADHDifferent is not always easy, but it really is a benefit to humanity to have Neurodivergent people in it. I have only ever struggled in life when people refused to try and understand me. This is what adds to my disabilities and makes things unnecessarily difficult for me. So please find it in your hearts to learn more about Neurodiversity and help make some people feel happy about being a little different from the rest. Thank you.

I would also like give a special thank you to Gayle Allsop and Caitlin Faroo for kindly proofreading this book and giving me some much needed confidence to publish it

Chapter 1

The classroom looked empty and all that could be heard was the faint sound of children playing, coming from the open windows. It was a beautiful day and the sunlight glared through the glass and lit up the room. Dust particles danced like fairies, disappearing and reappearing as they passed from one light beam to another. Chairs and tables were set out neatly facing the whiteboard, which was still covered in various math equations from the lesson before. It was as typical a classroom as you could imagine. Posters about acceptance and diversity filled the walls alongside ones about numbers and environmental awareness. There was even one about how important brushing your teeth was, which had been there for some time and was yellowing and curled at the edges. There was good and bad art from a project about the North Pole and a small wooden cross with a sacrificed half-naked man nailed to it, pinned above the door to the stationery cupboard.

This time of the day for most kids was an escapism from the drudges and hardships of school. It was their time to switch off, play and interact socially with the other children. They played games, discussed important issues, like which one smelled the worst, or which one had the strongest dad, played tricks on one another and gradually found their place within the playground hierarchical system. However, this wasn't the same for all the kids as one little boy sat quivering under the teacher's desk, holding back tears and counting the seconds before this torturous break was over. This was the worst time of day for Alfie. He had never felt like he fit in and hated being subjected to the cruel punishment of being made to interact outside with the children who never liked or accepted him. Alfie hadn't given up easily though and as bad as it was, he had always tried his best, even when it usually ended up with him sitting by himself reading a book or chatting with his best friend that no one else could see.

The reason why he was hiding under the teacher's desk instead of under a tree or in the playhouse was that today was a particularly bad day. He had inadvertently upset some nasty boys during their last lesson, and they had whispered threats and promises of retribution when the bell rang. Alfie had sneaked back into class when no one was looking hoping to avoid them but knew deep down they wouldn't give up easily.

'Don't worry, it'll be ok. Just keep quiet and they won't hear us,' said Stubbs, his voice only a whisper in the little boy's ear.

'But what if they check under the desk?' he asked the imaginary spider sitting on his shoulder.

'They're not that smart, at least I hope they're not,' Stubbs replied
The door to the classroom slammed open knocking several books sideways on a nearby shelf. The sound of footsteps and sniggering violated the room as two boys entered. Alfie curled up and wished he was somewhere, or even better, someone else.

'Where is he?' a small spotty boy asked, his hands bunched into fists.

'Dunno, he came in here so he must be hiding,' the larger boy answered, while half picking his nose.

'Damn, they're smarter than I thought,' whispered Stubbs into his best friend's ear, shuffling nervously.

'Shush they might hear you,' Alfie whispered back to the small seven-legged arachnid. He shuffled his bum into a more

2

comfortable position, without making a sound. Chairs creaked, and desks scraped against the cold shiny floor as the two bullies searched for their pitiful victim. Every sound made Alfie's stomach feel like it was somersaulting.

'He has to be in here, come on ya little git, where are ya? I heard what you said. You think I'm stupid, don't you. Well come on then let's see how smart you are when I beat your sorry ass,' taunted the larger boy whose name was Finley. He had always had it in for Alfie ever since they started school. Before that at nursery, they were like two peas in a pod. Best friends for life, or so Alfie thought. Everything changed when they moved to the big school as Finley quickly realised that Alfie wasn't the same as the other kids and they aggressively let him know about it. Finley figured that it was a safer bet to turn on Alfie rather than get picked on as well, therefore within weeks he had become Alfie's worst nightmare. Alfie never understood why, but Alfie didn't understand a lot of things the other kids did and they rarely understood him.

'Hey! Fin, I bet he's under the teacher's desk wetting himself like a baby again,' sneered Jason, Finley's new best mate and fellow Alfie-tormentor. They had bonded over their dislike for things they didn't understand, as their slow and achingly dim-lit brains could not cope with people acting "weird" as they, and most others, put it.

Alfie's whole body went stiff, and he held his breath. He felt a tear well up but made sure it stayed where it was. He wouldn't give them the satisfaction of crying. Stubbs sighed and they both looked at each other as if to say, "here we go again". The desk was yanked away with deafening noise and Alfie sat there exposed to the bullies, fists clenched and ready to defend himself. Stubbs was by his side, but imaginary friends weren't that useful in fights.

'Got ya,' Snarled Finley, his face screwed up in anger that was half real, and half exaggerated. He raised his fist and brought it down heavily on Alfie's back. Alfie collapsed in a heap, winded and dazed. Finley and Jason laughed as Alfie wheezed out his gasping breaths. Just as he was regaining his air intake,

3

Jason's foot smashed unforgivingly into his stomach, knocking him sideways and unable to inhale. Alfie tried to kick back, but his attempts were weak and ineffective. The boys towering over him just continued to laugh as they delighted in their abuse. Abuse of a fellow human being that was different to them, who they thought deserved this sort of treatment. It never crossed their simple minds what sort of consequences these actions would have on Alfie, then again not much ever did cross their minds.

Snot and tears ran down Alfie's face and he swore to himself that one day he would get them back for this. Alfie was not the easily violent sort of kid. He was sweet and kind, very smart and incredibly altruistic. He was the sort of child that would help an elderly person carry their shopping or give his pocket money to a charity for turtles. But everyone has a snapping point if stretched far enough and Alfie felt that he was close to that point. As angry as he was though, It turned out he wasn't angry enough. It turned out that it was just another day when he would curse his attackers, wish that he was an action hero with huge arms and a chest that could dance and blow them all away using a gun so large it wouldn't look out of place on the front of a tank. Alfie's imagination was vast and he would often get caught daydreaming, lost in another world.

'Stop trying to get up Alfie, you're just antagonising them more and more,' Stubbs begged. He would have loved to help Alfie out but what could an imaginary seven-legged spider do exactly? Nothing was the answer, not one damn thing. Alfie looked up at Finley with pleading eyes and hoped that somewhere inside this oppressor still lurked the companion he once knew and liked. Finley looked back and for a fleeting moment hesitated. A dash of recognition in his otherwise blank eyes gave Alfie a twinkle of hope, just before his foot came crashing into Alfie's abdomen forcing the rest of the air out of his lungs. Another blow came, this time to his knee, which forced him to let out a whine, the sound was barely audible over the boy's laughter. To Alfie's relief, before they could do any more damage, the bell rang and the boys sprinted out of the room almost tripping over each other as they bundled through the

4

door, 'It's not over,' yelled Jason as he disappeared from the room. Alfie believed him, he would be foolish not to.

'It's not your fault Alfie, you know that right?' Stubbs said, sympathetically snuggling up to his shoulder. Alfie didn't reply, he could barely speak. He pulled himself up with the help of the teacher's chair and sat down clutching his stomach. His face was injury-free; the boys knew what they were doing. The first time they had attacked him they had split his lip. Alfie didn't want anyone to make a fuss, so he said he tripped over. His teacher didn't buy it and the boys were questioned, but as there was no clear evidence Mrs Honeywell had to let them off with a warning. They ignored her and continued to make Alfie's life a misery, making sure they only hurt him where no one could see.

Mrs Honeywell walked into the room and stopped dead in her tracks the moment she spotted the beaten and shrivelled form sitting in her seat. She took a sharp intake of breath and released it slowly, preparing herself for the difficult task ahead. She looked down at the little boy. His head was bowed, and his dark blonde hair covered his face. She could see he was shaking, she realised then that she was too. Her deep blue piercing eyes saddened and her thin, but pretty lips, curled up at either side, to reassure her student that she was there for him as she had been time and time again. 'I'm guessing you won't tell me who it was this time,' she stated as kindly as she could, desperately trying not to upset Alfie any more than he already had been.

'It doesn't matter who it was, you can't stop all of them,' Alfie mumbled as he tried to hold back the tears. He adored Mrs Honeywell as she was the only person he had met that bothered trying to understand his odd behaviours. She could see the person he truly was beneath the so-called strangeness that he had become synonymous with.

'Can I get you anything?' she was also holding back tears as she felt overwhelmed by this sweet little boy's plight. She deeply empathised, as she too had been through the proverbial mill when she was his age. She produced a tissue from her pocket in anticipation of him needing it and the plastic packet crinkled as the white sheet was pulled free. She reached out her hand, offering it to him. Alfie shook his head and stood up. Still hunched over he limped towards her, his hair a ruffled mess and his uniform dirty from the dusty floor. He desperately wanted a hug and she equally wanted to hug him. Instead, he smiled at her as he walked passed and sat down at his usual desk, never once looking up from the floor. 'I think you should go to the nurse's office!' she said as she turned and faced him once more.

'If I go, they'll know they hurt me, I can't let them think I'm weak. I won't let them think they beat me,' Stubbs looked at his friend and felt an overwhelming sense of pride. He smiled broadly and affectionately snuggled up to Alfie's neck.

'Ok Alfie, have it your way. But the moment you start feeling ill or dizzy or anything out of the ordinary tell me immediately!' she tried to be firm, but she knew he saw straight through it. She began correcting the chairs and desks, finishing with her own as the students piled in, some eager and some not so much to start learning.

'Hey look! Smarty-pants Alfie is already here, what a teacher's pet,' a ginger-haired girl named Sue proudly announced. She, like a few others, didn't have anything against Alfie per se, but felt, to a slightly lesser extent, the same as Finley. Better to join in with the taunts and jibes than suffer them yourself. Alfie raised his middle finger, a gesture he had seen his father do from time to time when he was driving and stared blankly at her, not breaking his gaze for a second as she walked across the room, 'Miss, Alfie's swearing at me,' she whined to the teacher.

'Maybe you shouldn't antagonise him, Sue. He didn't do anything to you before you insulted him!' Mrs Honeywell barked. Sue smiled at her sarcastically and sat down next to her equally annoying companion Rachel. Alfie could barely tell them apart. To him, they were just clones that said mean things so people would like them and hate him even more. He had told them something like this once in defence of a previous verbal attack but had since learned that it was pointless trying to communicate with these primitive life forms. He often wondered if he was even the same species as most of the people he met and often felt like an alien from another planet visiting barely evolved apes. The rest of the class took their seats and soon the class was full and ready to commence with learning. Just as Mrs Honeywell was about to ask anyone where Finley and Jason were, they walked in full of bravado as if they owned the place, swinging their arms from side to side and trying to look cool.

'And where exactly have you two been?' asked Mrs Honeywell, having her strong suspicions that these were the brats that had hurt Alfie so badly.

'Nowhere Miss, we were in the toilet that's all,' Finley smiled confidently.

'How could you be nowhere and somewhere at the same time?' came the question from a source that may surprise some, but not those who knew him.

'Shut it, Alfie, you smug dweeb,' snarled Jason. He gave Alfie a double look as he could barely believe his eyes that the boy they had seemingly beaten into submission only minutes before, was sitting at his desk as if nothing had happened. Finley almost smiled again as he was secretly impressed by the resilience of his victim, but held it in so as not to show weakness. The two of them sat at their desk together and stared back at Alfie who just looked straight ahead avoiding eye contact and hoping that the two of them would drop dead from some rare and sudden disease.

'They won't stop bothering you if you keep annoying them,' Stubbs whispered. Alfie nodded but avoided answering him. It had been noticed before and he suffered relentlessly being subsequently labelled the freak that speaks to himself. The lesson went on with the usual comments directed at Alfie as the butt of the joke, but it wasn't anything that he couldn't ignore. Well at least on the outside anyway. He had been subjugated with this and other sorts of cruelty all his short life, but it still ate at him every single day. He could never understand why him? What did he do to deserve it? Why was he the sole object of their hatred? Nevertheless, he didn't give in to their attacks and a lot of the time he made it worse by not being able to keep his mouth closed. He couldn't help ridiculing them intellectually; he felt that at least if he went down, he would go down fighting. It was like he had no control over this and it sometimes frightened him. All his attacks were in self-defence of either physical or verbal abuse, but he was always the one who was blamed. He was labelled as a troubled child even though he was the one who was bullied.

Mrs Honeywell had in the past broken through his thick and scarred barrier which is why she sort of understood him, but even she didn't know about Stubbs and their secret friendship. The only person Alfie ever let into his intimate thoughts and feelings was his older brother Ryan. Ryan was everything you could ever hope for in a big brother. He was playful, nurturing and protective. He taught Alfie everything he wanted to know about the world. Ryan was ten years older and acted more as a father figure at times than a brother. Alfie's actual father was aloof, much like Alfie, and the two never seemed to see eye to eye. Luckily Ryan was always there when Alfie needed someone to spend time with and patiently teach him how to behave in general society. Ryan always knew Alfie was different but instead of shunning him like the rest of the family, he had embraced the quirky side of his little bro. Alfie in turn was besotted with him and followed him relentlessly as much as he possibly could. Except whenever Ryan was elsewhere, Alfie would shut himself in his room and play with his Lego obsessively until Ryan's return, when he would immediately, as he did not understand personal space or patience, harass Ryan until he joined him building spaceships or whatever else took his fancy.

The end of school bell rang loudly and as soon as Mrs Honeywell had given her permission, the class poured out into the playground like stampeding wildebeests on the plains of Africa. Alfie was the last to leave, waiting patiently in his seat so he wouldn't be punched or kicked on his way out. Mrs Honeywell smiled and was about to stand and walk over to him when he jumped up and without even looking in her direction left through the open door. She sighed and stared at the space for a while, hoping he would change his mind and come back to speak to her. After a minute or two, she leaned back on her chair and let out a few tears that had been welling up ever since she saw him hobbling across the room. He was so brave, but she feared enormously for his health. Not just his physical health but also and more worryingly his mental health. She had tried explaining to his parents and the headteacher that Alfie was very different.

He was extraordinarily intelligent and didn't take anything at face value. He twitched when he was excited and even spoke to himself under his breath. He was shy but had no issue telling people how he felt or what he thought about them. This inevitably led to the other children bullying him. Nevertheless, it would fall on deaf and ignorant ears, as they believed that he was the one at fault, bringing it upon himself and that she was also to blame for his difficulties because she was encouraging him. She had been told that she must discipline him when he "played up" otherwise it would harm him in later life if he believed others should pander to his negative behaviour. She knew they were wrong; she knew Alfie wasn't trouble, but instead was troubled. She could see beyond the rude questioning and constant interruptions because when she did manage to get him alone and teach him things without any distractions, he would astound her with his ability to understand the most complicated of scientific facts and theories. "At least he has Ryan," she thought and that made her smile.

She at one time, like the others, thought he was just a bad kid. That was until a shocking moment in class pushed her to the very limits of her patience but inadvertently showed her that there was far more to Alfie than she had first seen. Alfie had stated in class that he did not believe in God during a lesson on God's love. Mrs Honeywell found this very upsetting as she was a devout Christian and had never met a child that questioned her faith in any way, let alone such a methodical and fact-based attack on her and others' beliefs. He stated defiantly that there was no way a mystical being existed, but if it did it was not in any way good. He recited line after line and verse after verse all the atrocities that were committed by God and for God as stated in the bible. The other children did not take kindly to his berating of an ethereal being and they started hurling abuse at him. She had never thought about the God she had always loved in the negative and to hear someone so self-assured speaking facts undeniably, had her shaking to the core. She had told him to sit down and shut up, which was completely out of character and she had immediately regretted it. Alfie stormed out of the class throwing his chair across the room, luckily not hitting anyone. After much searching, she found him muttering to himself inside the play castle. She could have sworn he was speaking with someone but when she peered inside he was alone. They had sat together all lunch and he had explained to her why he felt the need to say things that sometimes upset people. She discovered that it was never intentional and instead he was, in his way, trying to help people by teaching them facts that he had read and become interested in. He was genuinely surprised by the incessant negativity towards him and surmised that others must just be ill-informed and therefore he would try and teach them even more. This vicious circle ended up with him being a very lonely child and her heart reached out to him as she sympathised with his problems.

She never again lost her temper with him and instead became his biggest fan as the two of them sat at lunch breaks teaching each other and learning new and exciting things about the world around them. But despite her friendship with young Alfie, he still would not trust her fully with his secrets. She wiped away the moisture from her cheeks with the back of her hand and began packing away her books. Without any warning, Alfie ran back through the door and grabbed hold of her. He squeezed tightly and she hugged him back. As quickly as he appeared he was gone and this made her even more upset, 'oh Alfie if only they knew how precious you are,' she said to herself.

'Was that Alfie I saw running out of here?' the headteacher Mr Pratt asked, peering into the room. He was a tall, pale man with a large and uncomfortable looking midriff, who constantly scowled as if he hated everything, but secretly he just hated children. He had a long scruffy brown beard that he would constantly stroke as if it were a pet and he was soothing it. He also had the annoying habit of standing far too close to her and she would often have to take at least two steps back to avoid smelling his rancid breath.

'Yes. He was picked on again but refuses to tell me who did it. I think he's afraid that if he does it will get worse,' Mrs Honeywell picked up her bag and walked towards the door. 'I'm sure it was Jason and Finley again,' she sighed.

Mr Pratt watched her predatorily and grunted like an excited pig when she drew close to the door, 'where are you off to now? Do you fancy going for a drink with me?' he raised his arm across the door blocking her way out.

'No thank you, Mr Pratt,' emphasising the word Pratt, 'I must get back to my husband, we are meeting with friends tonight and I don't want to be late,' she ducked under his sweaty armpit stain, cringing inside.

'I still haven't met this man of yours, I'm starting to think he doesn't even exist,' he turned and faced her staring unapologetically at her bum while stroking his beard.

'Think what you like Mr Pratt but if you continue to behave in this manner, I will bring it up with your wife next time I see her,' she continued walking away.

'I don't know what you're talking about woman. I know you like them simple-minded just like that little weirdo Alfie. I'm not mental enough for you?' his eyes narrowed while he grinned waiting for her to react, knowing that if she did, he would be able to discipline her for it, or at least threaten to if she didn't behave herself. She paused and he thought he'd got her, but instead, she turned around, looked at him up and down as if he was nothing more than dog mess on her shoe and walked away. He grumbled under his breath and waddled away defeated.

Alfie had seen and heard all of this from his hiding place behind the bookshelf in the open library outside his class. He wanted to rush out and heroically protect Mrs Honeywell but instead, he cowered in between the fantasy and science fiction sections. He put a new book from the fantasy section in his bag and when the coast was clear he dashed for the exit.

Chapter 2

Alfie could see Ryan was waiting by the gate. He didn't look best pleased as he was the last one left waiting, so he ran as fast as he could to get to him. Ryan's frown soon turned into a full-blown grin when he saw little Alfie sprinting like a gazelle being chased by a cheetah. Alfie crashed straight into the gate and fell over backwards, 'Slow down there little dude you're going to hurt yourself one of these days,' Ryan laughed.

'Sorry Ryan, I was just imagining I was a Supermarine Spitfire pilot and a Nazi Messerschmitt BF-109 pilot was attempting to gun me down with its 13mm MG 131 machine gun,' Alfie blurted out losing breath towards the end of the sentence.

Ryan blinked slowly trying to take in all the information and said, 'how fascinating, I always thought they were just called Spitfires. Well, thanks to you, I learn something new every day,' Ryan knew better than to question Alfie as he was almost certainly correct when it came to facts. He just soaked them up, or immediately forgot them, depending on how interested he was in the subject. Alfie could be discussing football one minute, which was more on Ryan's level of understanding, and particle physics the next. It could catch you off guard if you weren't prepared for it. But Ryan was always prepared for whatever Alfie could throw at him and at times he literally threw stuff at him, but he never meant it.

They began the walk home together, occasionally shoving each other, Ryan gently and Alfie as hard as he could which still wasn't enough to budge his beefy brother. They took a long way home preferring to take their time and chat about the day. They passed the playground where Alfie was too afraid to play ever since some boys had made him eat the sand under the swings because he told them they were stupid for smoking. They passed the local shop where the owner loved Alfie because he was so polite and was able to greet him in his native Indian tongue. They passed the allotment where Alfie and Ryan were growing tomatoes because Alfie had decided one day they should be self-sufficient or at least tomato self-sufficient, so Ryan had set it all up for them. Ryan looked down at Alfie and inwardly sighed, 'I know they've been hitting you again,' he said calmly, his eyes darting to Alfie's leg that occasionally limped as he walked. Alfie looked down at the path unable to make eye contact, 'did you tell Mrs Honeywell?' Alfie shook his head still looking at his own feet, 'I thought we agreed that you would,' Alfie remained silent, 'Ok little Dude, I'll sort it out for you. Don't worry they won't do it again I promise.' Alfie didn't look up but smiled to himself. He didn't know if Ryan could stop the bullying, but it was enough for him that he was willing to try. He was happy in the knowledge that someone was on his side when most people he met seemed to misunderstand him and therefore, in his mind, be against him.

A man with a big black fluffy dog waved to them from the opposite side of the road and Ryan waved back. Alfie didn't react to the man but instead just looked directly at the dog and beamed at the wagging tail, which meant the dog was happy. They stopped and waited for the man to cross over and Alfie's stomach cramped up with a mixture of happiness and terrified anticipation of this random interaction with someone he didn't know. The man approached and the dog lunged excitedly at Alfie who jerked backwards and nearly fell over. The man pulled on the dog's lead and he was forcefully stopped inches from Alfie's face, 'sorry about that mate, he's just a puppy you see. He doesn't know what he's doing just yet but don't worry he's as soppy as a marshmallow on legs. Worst he'll do is lick ya ta death,' he chuckled at his own joke and turned to Ryan with his free hand outstretched.

13

'Alright Dave, I haven't seen you in the gym lately,' Ryan said, shaking the man's hand. Alfie glanced at the dog eyeing him suspiciously before looking at Ryan. He was in awe of his big brother and how he could speak with people with such confidence. People respected him and Alfie loved being around him because those people would be nice to him just to impress Ryan.

'Can't do anything with me knee in the state it's in,' replied Dave who was shorter than Ryan by at least half a foot and nowhere near as broad, 'still the doc says it'll only be another week or so then I'll be back giving you a run for ya money,' he laughed again at this attempt at wit and absentmindedly loosened his grip on the lead. The dog bounded forward and knocked Alfie to the floor and began licking his face.

'Alfie,' Ryan cried out in horror, not knowing how his little sibling was going to react to this seemingly harmless situation. To his relief and the relief of Dave, who had gone white with fear, Alfie was giggling and ruffling the dogs head as it gleefully treated him like a human lollipop.

'I'm fine,' he spluttered breathlessly. Dave gripped the lead tightly and gently eased the dog away from Alfie so he could get back to his feet. 'He's so funny,' Alfie said wiping the sleeve of his coat across his mouth.

'Glad ya likes him', Dave said with relief evidently present in his voice, 'you can come over and play with 'im whenever ya wants. As long as that's ok with ya Brother,' he looked at Ryan and Ryan nodded his head.

'Would you like that Alfie?' Ryan knelt to catch his eye line.

'Yes please,' he answered not once looking at Dave, 'what's his name?' he asked.

'Bear,' Dave said proudly and ruffled the dog's hairy head.

'I like that name' Alfie said reaching out and stroking Bear between his ears. Bear tried to lick Alfie again, but Dave held him back.

'Cheers. Well, mate I better get goin' or the other half will have my kneecaps for breakfast,' Dave smiled and went to jostle Alfie's hair and then drew his arm back quickly and looked apologetically towards Ryan as if remembering something he had been told that he almost forgot. Ryan smiled and mouthed that it was alright. Dave gave Alfie a thumbs-up instead and Alfie responded with one back.

'See ya later. I'll give you a call,' Ryan put his hand to his ear making a sign like a phone and the group went their separate ways, Bear less eagerly than the rest as he had taken a liking to Alfie and wanted to carry on playing with him.

'I thought you were going to flip out when the dog jumped on you,' Ryan said tentatively as they neared the road that led to their house.

'His name is Bear and I knew he was going to jump on me because Dave wasn't concentrating, but I didn't realise how strong he was, so that's why I fell over. But I liked him he was funny'.

'Who, Dave?' Ryan snorted obviously not agreeing with Alfie's sense of humour.

'No wally! Bear,' he shoved Ryan who didn't move, 'why would Dave's wife have kneecaps for breakfast if it is almost dinner time?' He asked straight-faced.

Ryan smiled, 'it's just a phrase little dude, it means he'll be in trouble.'

Alfie shrugged, 'I don't get it.'

'One day you will, believe me,' Ryan laughed to himself, which confused Alfie even more, but he was used to people thinking the things he said were strange and didn't take offence.

They walked a little further and Alfie pulled on Ryan's jacket. He looked down, 'do you think Daddy will let me have a dog? You know a small one like a Yorkshire Terrier or a Bichon,' he looked up to Ryan expectantly as if his brother could make anything happen if he just wanted it bad enough.

'I doubt it, little Dude, you know what Dad's like. He isn't exactly Mr Nice from Friendly Town at the best of times, but after the incident in the supermarket the other day he's been practically unapproachable,' he stopped and knelt beside Alfie again, 'I know it wasn't your fault but Dad refuses to believe or is too ignorant to understand, that you aren't like most kids. You have your own unique, and in my opinion, an amazing way of looking at the world and I know that sometimes places like the supermarket can become scary and make you panic, but in his mind, you're just misbehaving.'

'He doesn't love me, does he?' Alfie said almost whispering.

'Of course he loves you Alfie he's just confused, especially since Mum left him'.

'She left because of me, didn't she?'

'No,' Ryan said a little louder than he had meant to and deliberately lowered his voice and continued, 'no Alfie she left because that git of a man pushed her away every chance he got and she just wanted to be happy. You were too young to remember but believe me when I tell you she wouldn't have left us if it wasn't for him.'

'Why doesn't Carol run away? He always shouts at her especially when she's nice to me,' Carol was their step Mum whom Gary, their Dad, had married about seven years ago. Carol had always struggled with Alfie but not through lack of trying. Ryan resented her for taking his Dad's side during many arguments about Alfie but if she hadn't she would have felt Gary's fury when they were left alone.

'Carol's pathetic,' he grunted as if this alone was a good enough answer.

'No she's not Ryan, Carol is my Mummy and she reads to me sometimes and takes my temperature when I'm ill and loads of other stuff. She bought me that Space Station Lego set for my birthday,' Alfie tended to judge people on what sort of Lego they gave him. he clenched his fists in anger but unclenched them when Ryan's face became sad.

16

'I'm sorry little dude, sometimes I forget how much you love her. My problems are mine and I shouldn't force them on you. Just remember that I've always got your back no matter what ok,' he stood and opened his arms. Alfie fell into them.

'I love you, Ryan,' Alfie muffled his head pushed up against Ryan's stomach.

'I love you too Alfie.' They continued walking until they got to the front door of their end-of-terrace three-bedroom house. It had a slightly overgrown front garden and shabby window frames that needed a lick of paint.

'You forgot your key didn't you,' Alfie said rolling his eyes and fiddling in his pocket before pulling out his set of keys.

'I don't have to remember them, I can always rely on you for that,' Ryan shrugged. Alfie opened the door, and they entered the hallway. He threw his bag in the cupboard under the stairs but not before taking out the pilfered book. He would always return them, but he couldn't be bothered with all the form filling in as it gave him too much anxiety. Instead, he just became his own librarian. 'What's that one about?' Ryan had spotted the book under Alfie's arm as he was just about to head up the stairs.

'Dragons,' he twitched his head slightly. An involuntary movement he occasionally did when he was excited.

'Cool. Did you fill the paperwork in properly this time because you know you got in trouble last time when they caught you reading a stolen book in the playground,' Ryan had to go down to the school and listen to the lecture from Mr Pratt about disciplining a tearaway properly and then gave him a letter to give to his Dad which he threw in the nearest bin on his way home.

'No,' Alfie bowed his head as if to say sorry, but he was only sorry because he thought he had upset Ryan and not for taking the book. He felt his way was better than the school's and therefore he was justified in taking it.

'Take it back on Monday without them catching you and please don't do it again Alfie, I don't want you getting told off by that Pratt,' he smiled, and Alfie laughed.

'He is a pratt, isn't he Ryan. Stupid pratty Pratt,' he turned to go but Ryan put his hand on his shoulder, he pulled away involuntarily and faced his brother.

'You want something to eat?' he nodded in the direction of the kitchen.

'No thanks' he turned on his heels and ran up the stairs almost slipping but regaining his composure just in time. Ryan shook his head and smiled to himself. He couldn't help but feel sorry for his younger brother after their mother abandoned them and he vowed that he would always look after him no matter what. He would constantly put himself between his dad and Alfie when Alfie would push Gary to his very limits with his questioning and constant undermining. He was always pointing out his dad's mistakes when it came to facts, but the most annoying of these corrections was when it came to computers. Alfie could shockingly run rings around his father when it came to IT knowledge and instead of Gary embracing this akin fondness for technology, he would feel threatened by a nine-year-old making him feel stupid. He would think that Alfie was doing it deliberately and would lose his temper with the poor kid. Ryan took his father on and the two of them, despite having a good relationship when Ryan was younger, would clash and Gary would lose. This made Alfie even more despised by his father as he blamed him for falling out with his favourite son.

Ryan headed to the kitchen to grab a snack and pondered what he was going to do about the little scumbags who were picking on Alfie. He decided that he would first speak to Mrs Honeywell, whom he had a crush on, and see if they could deal with the situation amicably but if not he would take things into his own hands and sort the boys out himself with a few carefully chosen words when no one was looking. He hoped it wouldn't come to that, but it's not like they wouldn't deserve it. He took a packet of crisps off the shelf and pulled apart the top to reveal the crunchy treats inside. He sat down and began munching.

Alfie reached the landing and peered in on Carol as she ironed in the master bedroom, 'Hi Mummy, how was your day?' he grinned stupidly as this is what he thought she wanted to see. He had been told many times that his Mummy loves his smile, so even when he didn't feel like smiling, he would try his best to make her happy.

She looked up from the shirt she was working on and melted inside at the sight of her little man looking so happy. "Why can't he be sweet like this all the time?" She thought and that just made her feel sad. Her face couldn't hide it and she almost began to cry, the emotion of her rollercoaster life bearing heavily on her shoulders. She tried her best, she really did, but was always caught in the middle of Gary and Ryan like a volleyball being smashed to and fro, 'my day was lovely thank you, Sweetheart, how was yours?'

'Some boys didn't like me, and I hid under the desk until the teacher came. Don't worry they didn't hurt me I'm invincible,' he spun around and trotted off to his room.

Carol let out a sob, 'if only he was normal! He wouldn't have to go through all this crap, why can't he just be normal? Why?' she muttered to herself, fiercely ironing the stubborn creases on Gary's shirt.

'He is normal Carol it's you flipping lot who are messed up and what's normal anyway?' Ryan had come up the stairs still chomping a crisp and had overheard her. As usual, he jumped two feet in to defend his brother, 'just because he's smarter than you idiots doesn't mean there's something wrong with him. He's special, his teacher sees it, why can't his so-called Mother. Maybe because he's not yours you don't give a crap,' he knew how to hurt her and, at times, he knew he took it too far. He was just so fed up with everyone judging Alfie when they just didn't understand him, and if they could only be more patient, they would see him for the amazing kid he was.

'Screw you, Ryan, at least I'm here unlike your actual mother who ran off because she couldn't live with you two anymore. You drove her away and now you want to drive me away too. Well, I'm not going anywhere so maybe it's time you got out of my house,' Carol also said things she didn't mean in the heat of the moment, but she was sick of being blamed for Alfie's behaviour by every sodding know-it-all in the neighbourhood or at the school. She was always being told how she needed to discipline Alfie properly and that she was lazy and weak. She had tried so hard with her baby boy but just couldn't get through to him as Ryan could. In a way, she was envious of their relationship, but she was never bitter about it.

'Fine,' he roared, 'I'm going if that's what you want?' he waited for her to fold and apologise but she had had a nasty argument with Gary that lunchtime and was still fuming.

'Do what you want Ryan, you always do,' she barked uncharacteristically and folded her arms across her chest in defiance.

He looked her straight in the eye with so much hate she took a sharp intake of breath. Then said through clenched teeth 'as soon as I get a chance, I'm coming back for him,' he pointed at Alfie's bedroom door. He went to his room, grabbed a few items of spare clothing as if to make a statement and stomped down the stairs. He paused on the last step, reconsidering his actions. He decided he needed to cool off and would be back later to apologise. The whole thing with his dad and Alfie was tearing their little family apart and he knew the burden was his to bare on his broad but tired shoulders. He took the last step and swiftly left through the front door. Carol began to come to her senses and looked over to Alfie's room. She couldn't let Ryan leave, what was she thinking? Why did they argue so much when all she wanted was to love them both? Before she knew what had happened, she heard the front door slam shut. Carol looked out of the window regretting what had been said and hastily opened it. She called out to him to come back but he was too far away to hear her. She watched helplessly as he drove away, wheel spinning the tyres of his VW Golf and speeding off from the estate. She sat on the bed with her head in her hands sobbing and wishing she had just kept her mouth shut. She always wished she just kept her mouth shut.

Alfie was oblivious to all of this as he was building a dragon from Lego blocks listening to his music through his headphones while chatting away to Stubbs. He loved Elvis and bopped his head up and down while constructing his fire breathing creation. Once he was focused on his task it was almost impossible to distract him. By the time Carol had made him dinner, after having a blazing row with Gary about Ryan and how it wasn't all Alfie's fault despite Gary blaming him as usual, she found him fast asleep surrounded by bricks and books. She looked down at the dragon he had made and couldn't help but be fascinated at the exceptional detail he had put into it using nothing more than plastic bricks. He was amazing, she could see it, 'Ryan is right,' she said to herself, 'I need to stop listening to all the others and try harder with him,' she covered him with a blanket knowing better than to wake him up and turned the light off as she left. A big cat darted into the room before she shut the door, 'Sorry Monty, I forgot you like to sleep with Alfie. Take care of him. You're probably better at it than I am,' Monty meowed as if to say yes and settled down snuggling up against Alfie's arms. Alfie smiled, lost in a dream where he was the hero, and everybody loved him.

Chapter 3

It was about two o'clock in the morning when the doorbell rang. Gary nudged Carol in the back to wake her, 'I think someone's at the door Luv,' he grunted, his voice still half asleep.

'Go and see who it is then, why are you waking me up? You're the man of the house, aren't you?' she put the pillow over her head as a statement that she wasn't going anywhere.

'Fine, I'll look out the window,' he got up and peered into the garden, 'It's the police Carol what the hell do they want this time of night?' he thought for a second then asked, 'did Ryan come home last night? I can't see his car outside,' it was raining heavily and his view was restricted by the downpour.

'I don't think so. I just presumed he went round to his girlfriends. Jessica or Jenna, something like that. Why? Do you think he's got himself into trouble?' she switched on the bedside light and a sick feeling rushed over her body as she suddenly began to wake up and realise the seriousness of the situation.

'I'm going down to talk to them,' Gary stated.

'I'm coming too, just let me put my gown on,' Carol quickly pulled her dressing gown down from its peg behind the bedroom door and wrapped it around herself. Together they descended the stairs, Carol holding tightly onto the shoulders of Gary. She felt something was very wrong and she hesitated halfway down.

'Come on Sweetheart, I'm sure he's just got himself into trouble. We'll sort it out no matter what,' he was being kind for once and she felt a rare feeling of being loved but the dread and anguish didn't allow her to enjoy the moment. They got to the front door and Gary opened it slowly, his breath held firmly in his lungs.

Chapter 4

The funeral was on a Thursday. It was, as you'd expect, a sombre affair held at the local church within walking distance from Alfie's house. It hadn't stopped raining since the night of the accident, but that's nothing out of the ordinary in England. Umbrellas and raincoats littered the cloakroom of the tiny rented hall and people clambered over one another to get to the adequate spread of food on the rickety tables. Carol sat in the corner of the room surrounded by her friends. Gary was already drunk and working on getting completely hammered with his mates from the local pub, drowning his sorrows with shots of whisky. Ryan's girlfriend Jess was sobbing in the arms of her supportive father, her shoulders shuddered as the tears fell against his hefty chest and he patted her back soothingly. Gary's mum who lived in Spain had come over to take care of Alfie so he would not be a burden on his parents in their time of distress. She was chatting with the local priest about how bad the weather was when she turned around to find Alfie nowhere to be seen, 'where's he gone now? Seriously I turn my back for a few minutes and he's off. Maybe I should get him a lead and collar, that'll teach him,' she was as compassionate as her son when it came to Alfie, as she also presumed that all he needed was a good telling off.

'Now, now Barbara the boy has just lost his older brother, you cannot expect him to be behaving properly,' said the priest trying to show his compassionate side but agreeing with Alfie's grandmother. He had his grievances with Alfie after he had been subjugated to a verbal attack by the nine-year-old about how he was indoctrinating the innocent by telling them bald-faced lies about Jesus and the Holy Bible.

'What that boy needs is some tough love!' Barbara sipped on her glass of wine, spilling some down her chin, 'now where the hell is he?' she looked apologetically at the priest for saying the word hell in front of him.

He looked away embarrassed, 'perhaps he's with his friends,' the Priest suggested.

'That boy has no friends and it's hardly surprising the way he rants on about facts and nonsense. He always thinks he knows better than anyone else. Who wants to be friends with that?' The priest shrugged his shoulders and took a bite of his sandwich. He looked out of the window and wondered if Alfie was outside despite the downpour.

In the opposite corner of the shabby wooden hall Gary was slurring his words 'typical of my luck,' he lent on a chair for support. 'It had to be the good son,' he sipped another shot of Whisky and slammed his glass in the plastic foldable table next to him. 'Keep em coming,' he pointed at the empty glass, his finger almost knocking it to the floor.

'That's enough mate,' said one of his friends. Keith took the glass off the table and placed it on another further away. 'And keep your voice down about what's fair, if Alfie hears you what do you think that will do to the poor kid? I know you're hurting but so is he, Ryan was everything to him and you know that.'

'I don't care if he hears, it's his fault anyway,' Gary stumbled as he reached for the bottle of dark alcohol, he didn't need a glass to drink he thought.

'DON'T YOU DARE BLAME HIM!' Carol screamed. She had overheard her husband from across the room, in fact, everybody had overheard him. They all stared at her like in a western when the lone stranger walks into a bar.

Gary's hand hovered in mid-reach. He looked sheepishly at her for a split second before he saw everyone staring, then he scowled, 'shut your trap woman, it's your fault too.' Carol stared at him incredulously then broke down. She ran into the toilets and slammed the door behind her. A couple of her friends gave Gary evil stares and followed her.

'Nice one!' Keith snapped, 'very classy Gary, what are you going to do for an encore, punch a baby perhaps?'

'Keep out of it Keith, she's my wife, I'll talk to her however I like,' it was clear the alcohol had loosened his tongue but he meant every word and everyone knew it. He grabbed the bottle and staggered out of a fire exit into the rain. Keith looked around for Alfie but couldn't see him anywhere. He hoped the poor boy hadn't heard any of that but feared he had and had run off just like his useless dad.

'You see what that boy causes even when he's not around!' Gary's mum spat to no one in particular. The priest and the other guests didn't know where to look, so in the typical British style, they ignored it and talked amongst themselves. Mostly about what had just happened and their own opinions on little Alfie.

Up the hill, away from all the drama, Alfie stood soaked to the bones next to Ryan's grave. Ryan was the only one who understood him, the only one he could rely on. He loved his mummy and daddy, but he had never felt so alone, 'I'm so sorry Alfie,' Stubbs shed a tear that dripped onto Alfie's shoulder and soaked into his jumper. It made no difference as it was already wet through from the rain.
'Maybe he went to heaven Alfie?' Stubbs tried to cheer him up.

'Stupid spider, there is no heaven, there is no afterlife. We are all just cells with deoxyribonucleic acid, so how could there be an afterlife for just us and not every single living being including every blade of grass and every extinct animal that has ever existed?' Alfie finished his monologue with a huff.

'I guess there's no answer to that Alfie, I was just trying to make you feel better,' Stubbs looked at his friend and wished that he could be real, so he could embrace this now lost boy. The church loomed over Alfie as he stood silent and sodden, the grave did not yet have its stone but it had been filled in while the family walked back to the hall. Alfie had decided to take one more look at the coffin before it was gone forever but by the time he had run back, the diggers had just finished filling it in. They didn't see him as they laughed away making jokes about his mum's big breasts and as soon as they had tidied up they left in their truck. Alfie had cautiously approached the grave as if he was walking over a shaky bridge, he was still in shock from the night his life changed and had barely said more than a sentence since.

He had woken to find himself on the floor of his bedroom covered by a blanket with Monty laying on his hand. He pulled it out from under the cat and removed his headphones, the music of which had stopped many hours ago. He placed his MP3 player on his desk and looked around for Stubbs. Where had he gone this time? Alfie knew the cat had scared him off, but seeing as Monty was as sweet a cat as you could imagine he was hardly going to blame him. Instead, he picked up the heavy ball of fur and squeezed him, most cats would have hated this but nothing ever seemed to bother Monty especially when it came to Alfie. Still holding his feline companion Alfie walked across the hall to Ryan's room and knocked on the door. He had made the mistake of just walking in before and had caught his brother and Jessica almost naked and kissing. Ryan didn't shout at him but he could tell he was angry and the last person he ever wanted to upset was his hero. He promised to always knock and had stuck to that promise ever since. This time though there was no answer. Alfie knocked again, 'Ryan are you awake?' he put his free hand on the door handle but took it away immediately just in case he made a mistake again. He shrugged and decided to get some breakfast. He had no idea what the time was, this was trivial to Alfie, as far as he was concerned he was up and no longer tired and as he felt peckish he would eat. He flopped down the stairs making as much noise as he could. The sound of the carpeted steps being stomped on was a pleasant noise and he jumped the last ridge much to Monty's surprise. He meowed to show his annoyance but didn't bother trying to escape Alfie's grasp. He walked into the kitchen and to his disbelief both his parents were sitting at the table, cups of tea in their hands and sobbing. He

27

wondered why they were even up as it was still quite dark and neither of them were usually early risers. 'Hello Mummy, hello Daddy. Why are you crying?' he stared at the ground, uncomfortable with making eye contact even with his parents. This is something else his father had told him off for because it is apparently disrespectful, but as best he had tried he had always struggled with it.

'Come over here Alfie and sit down,' Carol pointed to a chair, remembering to be specific as it seemed to make Alfie happy.

Alfie sat opposite his parents and his dad trembled, his tea cascaded over the edge of his cup and splash landed on the tabletop, 'I can't do this Carol,' he stood up and walked out of the back door into the garden. Carol watched him leave then turned to face Alfie who had become distracted by the tea stain, now spreading through the table cloth. The dark liquid forced its way through the cotton fibres and Alfie watched intently not giving a second thought as to why his father had stormed out.

'Alfie sweetheart,' Carol gently tried to get his attention.

'Where's Ryan Mummy? I knocked on his room like he said to do but he didn't answer. Do you think he's still sleeping? I wanted to show him the Lego dragon that I built. I based it on the dragon we saw in the film last week,' Carol knew if she didn't interrupt he would carry on speaking for as long as he had words to say.

'Alfie, listen to me,' she paused and waited for him to look at her, 'Baby, I'm so sorry but Ryan isn't coming home. He was driving in his car last night and he had an accident,' she waited to see his reaction but there was no change in his facial expression.

'That's silly Mummy. Of course, he can come home. Why would you not let him home because he had an accident? That means it wasn't his fault so you shouldn't blame him. Please let him come home I really want to show him the dragon,' Alfie shuffled in his seat and his head compulsorily twitched.

'No Alfie that's not what I meant. He can't come home Baby because he went to heaven to see Granddad,' she bit her top lip so as not to burst out in tears. She couldn't risk upsetting him any more than she had to.

'There's no such thing as heaven,' Alfie stared impassively at the tea stain.

'What?' Carol was taken aback. She didn't know what to expect but she expected something more than that.

'I said there is no such thing as heaven so Ryan could not have gone there,' his voice was raised this time and Carol recognised the signs of him losing control. She composed herself and strangely felt a little better because even a bad reaction was better than none. 'Granddad is dead Mummy so Ryan cannot see him, so where is Ryan? Where is Ryan? WHERE IS RYAN? He crashed his hands down onto the table and quickly jerked to his feet sending the chair toppling backwards and scaring the life out of Monty, 'where is Ryan? Where is Ryan?' Alfie demanded repeatedly, his voice raising every time he spoke.

Carol desperately wished Gary would come back and help her, but she knew the cowardly git was probably sitting in his car, hiding from his "problem-son" as usual. Ryan would always be the one to calm Alfie down but with him gone how was she going to cope? 'Please Alfie stop shouting you're upsetting Mummy. Sit down and we can talk about it,' her tone wreaked with desperation and she physically shook.
Alfie picked up an apple from the fruit bowl above the fridge and hurled it at his mum. It hit her square in her face and she lashed out slapping Alfie across his cheek. He screamed and ran upstairs, 'Alfie, please. Mummy's sorry, please come back. I need to talk to you. Please Baby,' she begged but it was too late. She had already lost control and now she knew she had to suffer the consequences. All on her own and without any support.

Alfie crashed through his bedroom door. He understood that Ryan was dead, but he wasn't angry about that. He was mad because he couldn't show him the dragon he had made. From the moment he finished it he had wanted to show him, but now he would never get the chance. He hated any sort of unexpected change and at this moment, not showing Ryan the dragon was his main concern. He punched the wall as hard as he could until his hands were weak and sore. He kicked his door continuously only stopping when he heard a crack and a large hole appeared. His attention settled on his dragon sitting proudly in the centre of his room. 'Alfie no. Don't do it,' pleaded Stubbs, 'you know you'll regret it,' but Alfie couldn't stop himself, he kicked out and caught the beast right in its neck. The head flew off and shattered against the wall. Alfie realised what a huge mistake he had made, but instead of calming down this just made him angrier. He picked up the remaining body and hurled it at the window which happened to be open. It flew gracefully through the air before inevitably landing hard on the garage roof and exploding into countless pieces. Alfie fell to his knees and wept. He dropped to the floor, curled up in a ball, punched the air a few times and then lay still, completely bereft of energy. Monty peered into the room but decided now was not a good time for a cuddle and lay down next to his scratching post on the landing.

Carol approached the landing but waited until Alfie had stopped screaming and smashing. Perhaps she was also a coward but what else could she do? She had no idea what was wrong with Alfie, only that whatever it was could not be fixed by simply telling him not to do it again or threatening some sort of punishment. This was not her boy this was some sort of little monster living inside of him. Why did she have to tell Ryan to go? She blamed herself even though she wasn't driving the lorry that had hit him as he waited sensibly at the lights. The driver hadn't seen him and ploughed into the back of Ryan's car completely devastating it. Her eldest didn't stand a chance and he was immediately killed. At least he didn't suffer, at least it was quick, she thought to herself. That wasn't going to help Alfie understand why his brother wasn't coming home and she dreaded having to be the one to step up and look after him. She decided to leave him, not for his sake but selfishly for hers. She hated herself for thinking like this but she felt weak and she acted accordingly. She descended the stairs and went into the living room to call her parents and Gary's mum.

In the following days, Alfie had been a shadow of his normally vibrant self, but that was to be expected. Gary had pretty much ignored him and had taken solace in alcohol. Carol had been so busy organising things she'd forgotten to make sure he was alright and Gary's mum didn't know the first thing about being a compassionate human being. This is how Alfie ended up alone, at the graveside of his fallen hero, cross-legged and staring at the freshly made muddy mound.

'Are you ok buddy?' asked Stubbs.

'No, I want Ryan,' Alfie sobbed, his bottom lip trembled.

'I know, I know. Do you want to go on an adventure with me Alfie? Maybe we can find Ryan there?' Stubbs and Alfie often went on adventures together. At times, it was Alfie's only way of coping when things became too overwhelming.

'Can we go and get my dragon back?' he asked, sniffing back the tears.

'Of course, buddy that's a great idea. And I know exactly where to look for it,' Stubbs climbed on Alfie's shoulder, 'now close your eyes,' Alfie did as he was instructed, 'ok Alfie open them,' Alfie lifted his lids and the light almost completely blinded him.

Ragaland

1

The forest was damp. It had rained the night before and the remnants of water glistened off the vast array of different coloured leaves that covered the trees as far as the eye could see. The smell of fungus wafted up Alfie's nostrils and he crinkled his nose. He put his palms flat against the sodden, muddy ground and pushed himself to his feet. He felt by his side and was pleased to find his sword still around his waist. He checked his back and touched his fingers to the quills of his arrows, snug in his quiver. By his feet lay his bow and he leaned down to retrieve it. Just as he did an axe flew over his head and landed with a thud in the tree behind him. He dropped to the ground and writhed around on the floor desperately trying to pull his sword from its sheath.

'What the kraal are you doing you ridiculous fool?' Ryan the Barbarian stomped over to the tree and without any effort pulled out his axe.

'You almost killed me! What do you think you're playing at?' Alfie quickly stood up and brushed the mud off his thick leather armour.

'Oh, stop whining Sir Alfie, it barely skimmed you. I could hit a swallow's beak off in full flight with Emily if I wanted to,' Emily was the name Ryan had given to his axe, as she was as precious to him as his sister whom he named her after.

'Well, that may be the case you giant oaf but I am no swallow and believe me I would not fly away from you,' they stared each other down but neither could keep up the game for long and they both burst out laughing at the same time. 'How long was I asleep?' Alfie asked as he pulled on his boots.

'Not long, a few hours. I kept myself busy though, look at these beauties,' he produced two large hairs from the leather pack on his back, 'we can cook these up with the thyme we found earlier. I told you it would come in handy at some point,' he patted the herb pouch he kept on his belt.

'Thank you Mr Know-it-all,' came the sarcastic remark from a tree branch above their heads, 'I don't suppose you brought back some firewood while you were at it?' a huge spider as big as a grizzly bear, climbed down and took his place by Sir Alfie's side. Stubbs was loyal to his master and proved to be a valuable bodyguard when things heated up as they tended to do in Ragaland or at least ever since the Gored took control of the Haranto throne.

'Of course, I did,' Ryan said smugly as he pointed to a pile of timber already flickering with signs of heated life. Ryan the Barbarian and Sir Alfie had been on the road for three months. They had been sent to find Braken the dark dragon of the East when word came of the impending attack on the Kingdom. Queen Honeywell had given them strict instructions, as her two best warriors, to search out the infamous dragon and return with him to vanquish the Gored. They left with heavy hearts as they desperately wanted to stay and protect their home. The queen knew in her heart they would not win the fight even with her mighty fighters by her side, so she made the decision, which was the hardest she had ever made, to send them for help no matter how long it took. She would surrender to her enemies, only to rise again from a stronger position. The Gored had been more ruthless than anyone could have imagined even in their worst nightmares. They had devastated the beautiful land and destroyed any sense of hope. Or so they thought.

'What are you waiting for?' said Alfie, licking his lips. 'Let's cook them up, I'm starving,' he grabbed the rabbits from Ryan's clutches and headed over to the fire. He pulled his knife from his belt and began to skin one, the noise made Stubbs cringe.

'I should know better than to come between you and your meal,' Ryan laughed. He sat down beside Sir Alfie and started skinning the other rabbit. 'Not far now,' he remarked as he yanked at the fur of the hapless bunny. Sir Alfie didn't answer, he was lost in his thoughts of home. The fire crackled and small sparks jumped onto the mud, desperate to escape the blaze. 'I miss it too,' Ryan said. He knew what Sir Alfie was thinking, it's all they had been thinking about since they left. They sat in sombre silence, pinning for their loved ones and mourning the many dead friends they had lost. Stubbs rested by a large redwood tree and watched the two warriors as they cooked and ate their food. He wondered how they coped with such a burden and vowed to do whatever he could to help them.

After they had eaten, they made sure to cover any traces of their presence. The Gored had been looking for them and they had narrowly missed their clutches on several occasions. They were not afraid of the fight, but they understood their mission was far too important to even risk being killed before its completion. They were not going to let down their queen and they sure as kraal weren't going to let down the Kingdom. Over the last couple of months, they had seen the landscape become darker and more rotten as the Gored imposed their evil throughout the land. Once green, luscious hills and fields were now putrefying, and the people were being slaughtered or used as slaves. The blood of the slain was used to fertilise the repulsive crops of the sickening swill the Gored consumed. They were the vilest of Ogres, a race of violent hate-filled beasts whose only purpose in life was to serve their queen. Like a colony of ants, they mindlessly followed her instructions only ever wishing to please her every whim. Srokesh had taken a fancy to Ragaland after she had finished decimating the last Kingdom she had conquered. They had used up every possible resource and therefore needed somewhere new to build a home. She had to feed her family after all and no creature would ever stand in her way. It was not the first land to be pillaged, and over decades they had perfected the art of war. Before they moved on, they would transform any remaining slaves, who had managed to survive the most impossible hardships, into Gored, which is how their numbers had grown exponentially over the many years they had been destroying nations.

Much to his surprise, the hills of Aronate were still green when Ryan the Barbarian set eyes on them. He was scouting ahead making sure the way was clear for his companion and captain. He had sworn an oath to protect Sir Alfie and even if he had not, he would have died for the man he called brother. He understood more than anyone how important Sir Alfie was to win the war, but many others had doubted him in the past. He had championed Alfie, as he was known at the time, to the late king and was proven right as Alfie showed his worth time and time again in the defence of his kingdom. The king on his deathbed knighted Alfie and made him captain and lord protector of Ragaland. It crushed Sir Alfie's soul when he was ordered to abandon his post and go in search of Braken, but ever the loyal servant to his royal masters, he obeyed without question.

As Ryan climbed the highest of the hills to gain a better lay of the land, he could see the darkness spreading around him. Fires burned in every town, in every direction. The smoke billowed up from the helpless communities and filled the air with a smoggy haze. Even from this distance Ryan could smell and taste the embers of once happy places, now shattered by unstoppable hatred. He wondered if he would ever see his fellow compatriots again. Before they left, Queen Honeywell had told them of a group of two hundred soldiers that she had sent to the Raincloud Waterfall and explained that they were to mount their attack from this stronghold. He hoped beyond all hope that they had managed to make it and were ready for the triumphant return of their leader Sir Alfie. He reached the peak and sat down on a huge rock facing south towards Jargred. It was far beyond his sight but he could still see it in his mind's eye. The bustling streets and busy markets. The theatre where he had spent so many a night drinking and making merry with his friends and family. He loved the plays and in his younger days had dreamed of being an actor, spouting lines written by the great Henrik Figaro the most famous playwright in Ragaland. The first Gored attack came on one of these pleasant nights. He remembered it as if it happened yesterday. He was sitting in the front row as usual, wide-eyed and fascinated by the latest story, when a colossal explosion crushed the tranquil atmosphere like a boulder landing in a puddle. The noise was deafening but Ryan the Barbarian was ever ready for battle even when relaxing. He brought forth his mighty axe from its resting place in his belt and rushed outside. The main gate was in flames and several soldiers lay strewn across the ground, some dead and others dying. He spotted Sir Alfie, sword in one hand and a bucket of water in the other, gallantly running towards the fire. Sir Alfie threw the water on the gate but it had very little effect. Ryan joined his captain's side 'nice to see you!' Sir Alfie bellowed over the crackling cinders.

'You too, Sir. Do we know who did this?' Ryan hoped it was just some bandits trying their luck, but even for them, this was extreme.

'Not yet but I wasn't planning to wait around and find out,' he then proceeded to jump through the fiery gap in the gate, sword first with every warrior following him fearlessly. He made them believe with his bravery that they could win no matter what horrors lay ahead. The battle that ensued was bloody and riddled with death. Many creatures lost their lives that night and many more would do so in the months to follow. Sir Alfie had been injured but never stopped fighting until the last Gored was either dead or retreating. Ryan the Barbarian had found him lying in a pool of his and several Gored's blood. Their bodies were cut to pieces and spread over the battlefield. He had carried his leader back to the palace where the Queen herself cared for him. She had always held a spark for Sir Alfie ever since he first dined with the king. She was ten years his junior, but age meant nothing to her. She pined after him for years until finally he took notice and in the shadows they began a secret love that matched any star-crossed lovers. Ryan was the only one who knew and had promised to keep it hidden from the king. His Highness would probably have approved of the union but the couple never wanted to risk it. After the king died Sir Alfie had broken away from the princess, who was now the Queen, out of respect for his master, but never stopped loving his soul mate. She understood but continued to hope that one day they could be together again. In the meantime, she had a Kingdom to take care of and he had an army to lead. The two barely had time for friendship, let alone rebuilding a broken romance. Despite his injuries, it wasn't long before Sir Alfie was back on his feet and the short time that the two had been together was enough to rekindle the stuttering fires. They had made love several times and it was almost as if they had never been apart. But news soon came to them of the evil that was spreading, and many towns and villages had been destroyed by this new, impending threat. Sir Alfie left with half the army ordering the other half to protect the Queen. They had fought off the hordes of Ogres as best they could, but the numbers were far too overwhelming in the end. The sheer force of the Gored's army was no match for mere mortals and retreating to the palace was the only option. Sir Alfie had hated this decision, but he was as smart as he was brave, and retreating would be the only way he could carry on the fight from a more secure position. This was never to be the case as over thirty thousand Gored marched upon Jargred. A mass of hatred that was built for one purpose, to kill and plunder.

'What do you see?' Sir Alfie had grown impatient and had climbed the hill after his friend despite the concerns of Stubbs.

'I told him to wait but he is stubborn and doesn't know what is good for him,' the arachnid complained. They had met Stubbs early on in their journey. He had been hurt badly fighting off some Gored who thought that he might taste good on a spit roast. He managed to kill all five of them but lost a leg in the fight. Sir Alfie had found him half-dead and nursed him back to health. The spider had not left his side since and as previously mentioned, protected his master many times. As he had no name Ryan nicknamed him Stubbs due to his missing leg, the spider didn't like it but seeing as Sir Alfie loved the barbarian so much, he decided not to argue.

'He knows what he is doing Stubbs, this is the greatest warrior I have ever had the privilege of fighting beside. I'm positive a hill will be no challenge for him,' Ryan stood up and walked over to the pair. He removed his helmet and held it under his arm before scratching his head, 'I can see Druin Gorge. It's about half a day away if we hurry.'

'Good, the sooner we get there the sooner we can return. We have been away far too long as it is. The Queen will not have lost hope and I am sure the army is waiting for us,'

'What if the dragon is not there or just as likely he will not help?' surmised Ryan to himself but accidentally out loud.

'He will be there, do not worry about that and if the lazy thankless beast will not come willingly then I will make him,' Sir Alfie had a tone to his voice that would fill the biggest coward with the strength to fight and that is why the king chose him to lead, not only because of his fighting skills.

'Dragons are notoriously stubborn Master,' Stubbs pointed out.

'So is Sir Alfie,' Ryan chuckled and patted him on the shoulder. Sir Alfie smiled but quickly stopped when he saw a Gored patrol at the base of the hill in the direction they needed to head in. They had stopped to rest and were fighting amongst one another over a deer's head. They were between eight and ten feet tall, built like rhinos with dark green leathery skin which acted as a giant plate of armour. This made them notoriously difficult to kill as they could repel most blades and arrows. Their faces were contorted with a hatred that made them so ugly if you looked at one for too long, you might die of fright if they hadn't killed you already. They wore large cloths covering their genitalia and some had helmets and armour they had stolen from the bodies of men they had killed. It didn't really fit them properly and almost looked comical if you didn't know the previous owners were dead. Alfie had gotten wise to their defences and had forged weapons from Diamond Steel, the hardest and sharpest substance known to man or beast for his army. This made the fight more even despite the difference in numbers. 'We could wait until they leave but who knows how long that would take? Or maybe we could go around. It would add a few hours onto the journey but at least it would be safe,' Ryan suggested. He hoped Sir Alfie would not want to pick either of these options but he had to give them nonetheless.

'We have wasted enough time avoiding the fight if it can be helped and I am done with playing it safe. Our destination is just beyond our fingertips and I will not let these filthy monsters stand in my way any longer,' his voice shook with anger, 'these devils have killed and raped in our land for long enough and now it is time for some payback,' Sir Alfie lifted his bow from his shoulder, took a diamond steel headed arrow between his two fingers and pulled it from his quiver. He placed it snuggly in the taut string and drew. After a few seconds, he released the projectile towards his enemies striking one dead as it stood laughing at its comrades. Its bulbous body crashed onto the ground like a felled oak and the surrounding Gored stood stunned. A second arrow flew through the head of another unexpecting Ogre and he also fell lifeless at their feet. The remaining seven drew their clubs and axes readying themselves for an assault. The Gored were never frightened as they did not fear death, only disappointing their queen. One more arrow came but only stuck in the arm of the pack leader. Alfie could tell who he was, as he had a helmet with crow feathers protruding from it. He snorted and pulled out the annoying stick, showing no signs of pain.

Ryan bolted towards the group, Emily in hand and swung ferociously cleaving the head off a Gored's shoulders, sending it hurtling through the air. Stubbs jumped onto the back of another and sunk his fangs into its neck, ripping its throat out. Sir Alfie was the last to charge as he had been firing the arrows and his sword came to rest in the belly of the pack leader. The Ogre did not appear bothered by this and punched Sir Alfie in the face. He was slightly dazed but undeterred, he twisted the blade before ripping it out. The Gored leaned over in pain and Sir Alfie dropped to his knees and thrust the tip upwards into the forehead of the beast. The pack leader toppled over beside Sir Alfie who then swung around, chopping the leg off another Gored. He sprang to his feet and plunged his sword into its throat. Ryan the Barbarian dodged an erratically swung club and sliced open the chest of its owner before throwing his weapon swiftly through the air. It aggressively landed in the unsuspecting Gored's face and he too met his end. Stubbs finished the last one off, but not before the Ogre took a swipe at him with her axe. It dug in his side leaving the Gored known as Yank completely exposed.

Stubbs seized his prey and using his stinger punctured her stomach incessantly even after she was dead. 'I think that one is worm food Stubbs,' Sir Alfie approached his friend gently so as not to startle him, 'let me get that for you,' he pointed to the axe poking out of Stubbs' body. He looked up at his master with love in his eyes and Sir Alfie, as smoothly as he could, pulled the axe out and threw it to one side, 'Better?'

'Better,' answered the spider shaking the oozy green sticky Gored blood from the tip of his stinger.

'Good, now let us not waste any more time on these things,' Sir Alfie emphasised on the word 'things' with a hissing contempt in his voice, 'we must reach the Gorge as soon as we can. We shan't stop for night or food. We can rest when we are dead,' he wiped clean his dripping green sword with his sleeve and placed it back in its sheath before collecting his arrows from the deceased.

'Damned things are easy to kill in small numbers but there are few that travel this light,' said Ryan cleaning his axe and looking around as if expecting more to show up.

'This was a seemingly rare occurrence but perhaps they are getting overconfident, after all, they have not faced much of any opposition for quite some time. These were soft and fatter than we are used to. Perhaps they believe their fighting days here are done?' Sir Alfie had a keen sense of observance and barely ever missed anything even amidst a battle or, in this case, a fight.

'If that is the case then this is truly the time to strike back before they decide to reinforce themselves,' Stubbs weighed in.

'Exactly my faithful friend, so let us do just that,' Sir Alfie nodded at him and the three of them headed off as fast as they could towards the lair of the Dragon known as Braken.

2

Druin Gorge was many miles long and at least a mile in width. It was the perfect dwelling for an aloof dragon who wanted only to be left alone and not bothered by the problems of others. A long scaly tail protruded out from behind a gargantuan boulder. It twitched and swayed, the light bouncing off from its gleaming shards. Attached to the other end was a creature so huge that a Tyrannosaurus rex would have barely reached its knees. This colossal beast was as old as the gorge itself and had lived through many ownership changes of the Kingdom. He had heard from his feathered friends that an invading force had conquered Ragaland, but as long as they left him alone, he would not bother with such trivial things. He was well fed by the wildebeests and deer that were unlucky enough to roam too close to his lair and would spend most of his days lounging about, soaking up the sun or enjoying the shower of a rainstorm. The weather was of no consequence to this thick-skinned reptile as there was no substance known to man or beast that could penetrate his outer shell. He was a mightiness of which tales and songs had been written but never exaggerated, as there was never a need. Braken had fought in his fair share of battles when called upon to do so, but the last was over a hundred years ago and he had become content in keeping it that way. The tail swished upwards and crashed down causing the ground to shake. The boom echoed through the gorge and the tremor could be felt over a mile away.

'Did you hear that?' Sir Alfie asked.

'Hear it! I damn well felt it,' Ryan's hand was on the handle of his axe readying to use it if need be.

'Well, at least we know Braken is here. I don't know if he will be pleased to have visitors though,' Stubbs cautiously continued walking in the direction of the thunderous noise.

'Perhaps, but he has them all the same,' Sir Alfie steadfast in his stride, led the way down into the valley. The others followed slightly less enthusiastically.

Braken yawned. Two rows of razor-sharp fangs, each one the size of a fully grown man glinted like diamonds under the sun. His long snake-like tongue rolled out of his mouth and overhung his chin. It quickly retracted back inside like an elastic band and his giant claw covered foot reached up and scratched behind his left ear. He was like an enormous dog to the passer-by, but his brain was as sharp as his teeth despite his old age. He snorted and smoke shot out from his nostrils. He lay flat on his stomach and stretched all four of his legs out and reached as far as he could with the ends of his toes. After that, he lifted his wings out from their folded position on his back and beat them twice. The wind force that they created could have blown a castle down, 'time for lunch I think,' he said to himself as there was never anyone else around to talk to. He stood up on all fours and strolled over to the edge of the gorge. In one graceful movement, he leapt in the air and beat his wings into flight. He reached the top of the cliff within seconds and perched on the edge. Searching his gorge for any signs of movement, he saw something, or was it several somethings coming his way?

He looked more carefully and saw that there were two men and what seemed to be a Lethanreal Spider of the South plains. He knew every single species of creature that had come, gone and remained in Ragaland over his lifespan and this strange group of companions must have been a first. The Lethanreal Spiders were notoriously distrusting of people and often ate them if given the chance. So, to see one walking alongside humans and not trying to fill its belly was outrageous if not impossible. Was he going mad in his old age? Perhaps he had begun seeing things? He squinted and looked again, no he wasn't seeing things it really was the oddest of events. 'Well this I must see up close,' he muttered to himself and flew off the cliff deep into the valley towards the group.

'I guess we will not have to look for him, he is coming to us,' Sir Alfie pointed as if the others might miss the dragon racing towards them. The gale from his wings was enough to have them on their knees.

'I hope you know what to say, Master, he looks as if he wants to eat us,' said the terrified arachnid as it inched behind Sir Alfie.

'Shall I prepare for attack?' shouted Ryan over the ear-splitting noise of the hollering winds.

'No. We came to ask him for help, not for a fight. If he attacks then so be it, but I must have faith that the old alliances still stand with this king of beasts and that he will do what is right for Ragaland.'

Braken was slightly confused as to why the tiny beings were not trying to run away but he thought at least if he was going to eat them they would not provide much in the way of a challenge. He no longer craved the thrill of the chase, preferring to get a meal with as little effort as possible. He landed not far from Sir Alfie and stretched his long neck out until his nose was only a few metres away, 'my eyes do not deceive me, these humans are travelling with a Lethanreal Spider of the South plains. Well then, that is interesting. Is he your captive or have you just adopted him as a pet?' sneered the dragon his voice booming and echoing around them like someone shouting in their ears.

'The spider's name is Stubbs and he is my friend,' stated Sir Alfie boldly.

'Is that right? Well, that is even more interesting. Why do you follow these humans spideraseradicus?' Braken knew the ancient tongue of Stubbs ancestors and decided to speak it to him.

'I do not follow Sir Alfie, I protect him. He cared for me when I was done for, I owe him my life,' he proudly stated stepping out from behind the knight.

'Sir Alfie you say, the lord protector of Ragaland rescued a Lethanreal. Perhaps had he not been busy protecting Spiders he might have been able to protect his Queen?' Braken's words were spiteful but he loved to antagonise and rarely had the opportunity.

'What do you mean? The Queen is being held by the Gored surely?' Sir Alfie felt a sickness surge through his gut.

'I am afraid not, brave knight, she was killed months ago or so I am led to believe,' he eyed Sir Alfie carefully to read his reaction to this news. He wanted to know if this was really the Lord Protector or just an imposter wasting his time.

'What?' his voice buckled but he remained composed. Sir Alfie rubbed his eyes. He could not believe it, she was gone. His one love had been torn away from this existence and he was not there to stop it. This lazy, sorry excuse for a dragon was coming with him even if he had to drag him all the way to Jargred. 'I was tasked with recruiting you by the Queen. This, as it turns out, was her last wish. She surrendered to the queen of the Gored under the agreed conditions that she would be a prisoner, but it seems they never intended keeping their word,' even as he said it, he knew how ridiculous it sounded. He had suspected for some time that his Queen was dead but hearing the news, and in such a spiteful way, was beyond a hurt he had ever experienced.

'You mean, you know what is happening to our lands and you hide here and leave us all to suffer. People and creatures alike are being slaughtered in their thousands and you swan about your gorge like a cowardly snake,' Ryan lost control.

'Careful tiny morsel or you will be my entrée. I have no wish to involve myself with yet another skirmish. I have had my fill of such things, consider me retired if you like,' the dragon snorted and smoke covered the trio.

'Enough, Braken. Enough of this childish sneering. You are impressing only yourself and our expectations of you are only diminishing the more you spit your bitter words. You have known we are in trouble and have remained here concealed from our enemies whilst they destroyed the lands you call home. I do not know what you have been told by your flying spies, but I can only assume they have not been seen or heard of for quite some time.' This was true, Braken last had word that the Kingdom was overrun but that was more than a month ago. He had lost track of time and had not realised that his spies had not been visiting.

'It cannot be worse than the Kanision Wars? They ravaged the land for over a hundred years but Ragaland managed to recover, it always has,' the dragon's demeanour shifted.

Sir Alfie saw this slight change and saw his opportunity to strike his verbal blow, 'a long time ago Braken, you made a promise to protect this land and all who reside in it, just as I have. Centuries may have passed between that day and this, but an oath has no end date. No timescale to which it no longer becomes valid. You are a dragon of the ancient order of Trinasia Rolandia the most feared beings to have ever roamed or flown over this or any other Kingdom. Your name is known throughout every land and your battles are legendary, but these Ogres do not care. They do not care about how you fought the army of ice bears in 1751. They do not care about your quest to find the golden bird of Umbrian. It makes no dent in their mind that you killed the Babilanion sea monster. These feats of bravery and heroic triumph do not influence their decision to destroy our home. They have but one goal and that is to bleed dry every last resource we have until we have nothing more to give, then move on to the next Kingdom to do the same. They have done it before and they will not stop until someone stops them. Their numbers are without question intimidating but if we do nothing if you do nothing there will be no more Ragaland for you to hide in or eat in or even speak your name.' Ryan had heard this great leader say the most amazing rallying speeches on the battlefield that had men baying for the blood of the most fearsome of foes, but this was beyond anything he could have ever imagined.

Braken closed his huge eyes slowly, carefully. The three creatures dwarfed in his enormous shadow inadvertently held their breath and tensed their muscles. He shuffled his feet then said, 'what are we waiting for, its sounds like you have been gone too long Lord Protector,' he bowed his head in respect as he had never in all his years been spoken to in such a way. Sir Alfie's words had reignited the fire inside him he had but long given up on. He felt ashamed that he had become so cut off and promised himself if he was to survive, he would never again hideaway. He reached out a foot as an invitation to climb on it.

'Thank you,' Sir Alfie bowed his head in respect and Ryan did the same. They then climbed up onto Braken's foot.

'I do not like this one bit,' complained Stubbs as he crawled over a claw.

'Fear not Stubbs, save it for when we return. There will be plenty of time to be terrified I assure you,' Ryan settled down in a crease in the palm of Braken's foot.

'You will see I speak the truth as we fly over our once green and fertile lands,' Sir Alfie stood and held on to one of Braken's toes,' we need to head to the Raincloud Waterfall, we have a hidden cave behind it where my soldiers should be waiting.

'Hold on,' Braken curled his toes so they would not fall out and launched himself into the air. He flew up out of the gorge and high into the sky. He had not been up this high for a long time and he immediately saw the devastation that Sir Alfie had spoken of. It was far worse than he could ever have imagined and he cursed himself again for being so lazy. Anger boiled inside him. This was no war, no conquering of another's lands, this was pure destruction of everything in sight. No living thing, creature or plant would survive if this was left to continue. The Lord Protector was correct they had no intention of staying as there would be nothing left to stay for after they had finished. His stomach rumbled and his white underbelly glowed orange. He opened his mouth and expelled a gust of fiery lava. The heat could be felt by the companions and it seared the hair on their skin.

'I think he is angry,' the Barbarian stated jovially patting out a stray ember that had landed on his shoulder.

'Let us hope that is enough. Even with his help the task at hand is treacherous,' he replied and managed to smile but inside he had died a little. He would never see Samantha again and even though he would not stop until every last Gored was dead, he knew that in the end, nothing would bring her back. He regretted leaving her, not just before the Gored took control but when her father died. He could not bear the thought that he had been dishonest to his king and out of respect he had done what he thought at the time was the honourable thing. He was stupid and wished he had shouted from the rooftops how much he loved her and that he would have died for her. The people would have been happy to see the two together, alas he had made the biggest mistake of his life and now it could never be corrected. Just then he had a thought. It had occurred to him before but he never had a way of making it a realistic possibility. He looked up to the dragon, cupped his hands around his mouth and shouted as loudly as he could, 'Braken, I have an idea,' his voice was barely audible above the rushing wind but Braken had superb hearing and nodded his acknowledgement. 'I think I know the Gored's weakness but we must make a short detour to the Kingdom of Shangrasio to confirm my suspicions.' The enormous, flying behemoth once again nodded his acknowledgement and shifted his body slightly to the left to change direction. He straightened up and flew full speed knowing there was no time to lose.

3

The water crashed onto the rocks as it cascaded from the river above, bursting into clouds of colour as the light bounced off it. The pool below the waterfall was crystal clear; every fish and stone could be seen beneath its surface. Behind the thunderous aqua was a small tunnel invisible to those on the outside. The entrance was just about big enough for a large person to fit through, its sides were damp and slippery and glistened throughout the day. About fifty feet down a gradual slope the tunnel opened out into a huge cave where the soldiers lay in wait for the return of their Captain. Fires were scattered in every available place to keep the soldiers warm, in light and fed. The refuge had several months worth of supplies so the secret army never had to leave their hiding place.

The most senior of the soldiers and Sir Alfie's second in charge was a knight by the name of Elsa the Crusher of Dreams, otherwise known as Ely to her friends and Lady Elsa to the rest of the army. Sir Alfie had convinced Queen Honeywell to knight her after a particularly foul battle in which Lady Elsa had crushed the heads of over fifteen attacking bandits when out on patrol in Galdarof Forrest. She had saved the lives of the Kingdom's most famous actors Gerald Smokey and Herashio Albertson the Third. The two were travelling to a show in a nearby village when the bandits attacked. She and two other soldiers, who were sent to protect the actors, fought off a group of twenty men but Lady Elsa had used her club and knife to kill many more than her fellow fighters. The tale of her bravery was spread far and wide by the two celebrities and it was not long before a play was written in her honour. Sir Alfie was already aware of this fearless and talented warrior, much to his and the queen's delight this new-found fame meant the people loved Elsa and rejoiced when she was given the knighthood. Many battles later against the Gored and the army had lost over half of its knights. By default, but more than worthy of, Lady Elsa had become second in command and was tasked to hide this small group of men behind the Waterfall. She begged the queen to let her take more, but not only was there not enough room or supplies but the Gored queen would have surely noticed half the army missing when she entered the gates. This army needed to be small so it could go under the radar and act as the only hope in an almost hopeless situation. 'Lady Elsa,' a soldier approached her by the mouth of the tunnel shifting nervously and rubbing his hands together.

'What is it?' she continued to stare out into the visually impenetrable water and mist.

'The soldiers are getting anxious about food supplies. They are almost depleted and we were wondering if a small group, no more than ten, could perhaps go hunting and bring back some fresh supplies?' he shuffled his feet against the rocky floor.

'Impossible,' she replied still staring straight ahead, 'we are the last hope this kingdom has and if any of us are spotted it puts this whole plan into jeopardy. I am sorry Jake we just cannot risk it,' she knew who it was just from his voice. They had been cooped up for so long they had got to know each other more intimately than most would care to admit. She had given in to becoming friends with the soldiers in her command, which can be a precarious position to put one's self in. But this much time spent inside a cave will break down most barriers and in a way the closer they all became the more determined they were to fight alongside each other.

'I know you're right Lady Elsa but what if Sir Alfie does not return? Are we to starve to death?' he was pushing the boundaries of their friendship and hovering very close to insubordination.

'Sir Alfie will not fail. He has never failed. He does not know how to fail,' she paused for a second as she thought she heard a noise but must have been mistaken, 'if it comes to more dire circumstances then I will evaluate the situation, but until then we wait.'

'As you wish Lady Elsa. The army is with you, I just hope your right,' he turned around and headed back down the tunnel.

As he did there was a loud boom and the earth shook beneath his feet. Small rocks fell from the ceiling and he covered his head.

'Jake!' called Lady Elsa.

He looked over his shoulder brushing off the dust from it, 'Yes Lady Elsa.'

'Prepare the soldiers. Our Lord Protector has returned,' she smiled as she had never smiled before and Jake ran down the tunnel to spread the joyous news.

Braken landed beside the waterfall and gently put his foot through the falling water where Sir Alfie had instructed. He spread open his toes and the trio stepped out onto the ledge that led to the tunnel entrance. Alfie saw Lady Elsa standing with her jaw almost hitting the floor and jogged over to her. 'Am I glad to see you Ely,' he reached out his arms and hugged her.

'Likewise, Sir,' she squeezed him back, 'I knew you wouldn't let us down,' She looked over his shoulder nervously at the massive spider that crept behind Ryan towards her, 'is he with you Sir?'

He stepped back and laughed, 'Yes Ely, he is with me. His name is Stubbs and he is my friend and bodyguard. There will be plenty of time later for the story of our journey but for now, we have a kingdom to win back and there is no time to lose,' he touched her on the shoulder, 'I have some grave news,' her face dropped.

'What is it Sir? Is it about the Queen?' he nodded. 'I understand Sir and may I say I am so sorry, I know how much she meant to you,' her voice cracked slightly as she spoke.

'She meant a lot to all of us,' he held back the tears. This was no time for mourning.

'Yes, Sir. May I suggest we do not tell the army just yet as I think it would be damaging to morale? They have been on a knife's edge for a few weeks now, cooped up in this stinky cave and, if they still think they have someone to fight for, it will spur them on.'

'Agreed. Let's get inside, we need to discuss our strategy,' they all headed down the tunnel in a line with Stubbs upfront so the others could help him squeeze through.

There were more than a few shocked faces when Stubbs popped out from the tunnel entrance into the cave but when they all saw Sir Alfie and Ryan the Barbarian they immediately settled down. Swords were sheathed and arrows were placed back into quivers, panic was soon replaced by joy and the whole cave became a murmur of hope. Jake had run in moments before with the good news, but until they saw it for themselves, many had doubted the soldier.

Sir Alfie stood on a rock so everyone could see him, 'the time has come,' he bellowed, his voice echoing from wall to wall, 'I have returned triumphant!' A cheer erupted, sending a tingle down his spine. He waited for the noise to subside then continued, 'we now have a great ally and with his help, we will retrieve our land and homes from the scum who dared take it from us. We will avenge our fallen and drive this virus from Ragaland,' another cheer roared from the crowd. His voice rose above them again, 'we have gained valuable information on our journey here from another land the Gored have destroyed. The only way to defeat this force is by killing its heart; its queen. By killing her, the others will not be able to follow, becoming useless and without direction. It will leave them weak and easy to kill. This is our only option, there is no plan B. Tomorrow we will return to Jargred and there we will destroy the killer of worlds queen Srokesh,' an even louder cheer reverberated from the army and every last man and woman believed without any doubt that Sir Alfie would lead them to victory.

Ryan the Barbarian lifted Emily high in the air and shouted, 'death to queen Srokesh and long live Ragaland,' every soul repeated what he said several times before Sir Alfie jumped down and was surrounded by jovial folk. He was their hero but ever the modest man he made sure Ryan and Stubbs got the credit they deserved.

After some food and a strategy meeting with his head knights, Sir Alfie headed outside to speak to Braken who had been waiting patiently by the pool. 'Sorry it is taking so long. I have not seen them for a long while and we needed to form a plan of attack,' Sir Alfie sat on a rock at the edge of the pool and stared down at his reflection. He noticed that he looked weathered and barely recognised the war-torn face scowling back at him.

'These things take time and time is something we are running out of. I assume you have told them about the queen's hold on the Gored and the consequence of killing her?'

'I have. It is the only thing that truly gives us hope,' he paused and looked up at his gigantic accomplice, 'can I tell you something?'

'Of course,' the Dragon blinked and nodded.

'I feel empty inside,' he hunched, bowed his head and leant his elbows on his thighs.

'What do you mean?' Braken looked confused.

'Without Queen Honeywell, I am struggling to feel the strength in my heart. I know what must be done and I am not afraid to do it, but a part of me feels that now she is gone there is nothing left for me,' he stared down at the pool once more.

'Sir Alfie you have much to live for,' the dragon spoke with a gentle and soothing tone, which had never been witnessed before, 'love is hurtful, there is no denying it. It hurts when you first feel it and the thought of losing it crosses our minds. It hurts when we come close to losing it or, from time to time, when it begins to fade. Most of all though it hurts when it is taken from us and there is nothing we can do. This pain is impossible to cure and will leave a scar that runs as deep as the gorge I call home. But the thing about scars Sir Alfie, is that they fade and with time they might even become barely visible. It will always be there and you will never forget that love but there is a lot of flesh on your body, more than enough room for more scars. Love will rise again but not if the Gored have their way. You must fight for your love. The love of the people, the love of your friends and the love that has been taken from you. Tomorrow you will kill the destroyer of love and love will once again be possible in Ragaland.'

Sir Alfie was left speechless by the dark dragon's kind-spirited words. He touched his hand to Braken's foot next to him, 'thank you. You are a noble creature and I will be forever in your debt. I will see you in the morning and together we will have our revenge,' he stood up and ambled back up the path at the side of the waterfall, disappearing down the tunnel. Braken looked up at the stars ubiquitously filling the sky. He said a silent prayer to Borashak the great dragon God of hope and another to Esmerandon the dragon God of war, then curled up in a clearing he had made for himself and slept with one eye left open. Through that eye, he swore he saw a creature scuttle away from the cave, but decided it was a trick of the light and settled into sleep.

4

Beyond the hills, the light was seeping into the blackness of the night. The green grass was no longer vibrant and full of life but dark and rotting like old seaweed. The sun began to appear and the world was introduced to the day, but these days were almost as dark as the nights and even the mighty sun could not brighten Ragaland during the time of the Gored. Shadowy clouds covered the sky and darkened the air. The Gored hated the light and this cover was perfect for their survival. A young and stupid Gored named Noovis was perched with both legs dangling over the edge of the wall that surrounded the City of Jargred. His helmet was too big for his head and wobbled around when he moved. He had asked for one in his size but had been told that it was just for show as there was no chance of a rebellion as the queen had crushed all opposition into dust and they were free to do whatever they liked without repercussions. He looked out over the Kingdom and cackled when he saw a slave girl being hacked to death by her captor. He knew this evil Gored who went by the name of Tanger. He was well-known as a ruthless killing machine and was liked by the queen. She, in all her infinite wisdom, had put him in charge of slave gathering and he was unforgiving in his brutality. He would push every last slave through the boundaries of impossibility, and any that survived would be sent to the pits to be tortured and twisted into Gored for the continued building of the queen's great army, 'that'll teach the pathetic slime who is boss,' he called out.

'She won't give me lip again, that's for sure!' Tanger took his knife and sliced off her lips and held them up victoriously.

'Can I have them? I've been up here for hours and I'm starving,' Noovis begged.

'Fine, but don't tell anyone else or they'll all want some. As it is, I'm running out of slaves. They just aren't as tough as the last lot, they keep dying on me or getting themselves killed by trying to escape,' Tanger kicked the dead girl as if to make the point.

'Thanks,' he reached down and Tanger threw up the lips. He caught them but immediately dropped them.

'What the kroll are you doing you stupid...' before he could finish his lambasting, a fireball smashed into the ground eviscerating him without even a scream. Noovis fell backwards and hid behind a turret.

'DRAGON!' he squealed, 'DRAGON!' Other Gored had also spotted Braken flying towards them with what looked like a man riding on his neck holding his sword high in the air. Weapons were grabbed and many Gored stumbled over themselves and others trying to prepare for battle. They were not the well-disciplined army that had taken this land, but a slower and fatter version of it. They were a true reflection of the queen herself, who in her victory had become lackadaisical. She heard the commotion from the window of her throne room and called out to one of her personal guards, 'what is going on? You there, go and find out,' she waved her slender hand in the direction of a burly Ogre who nodded and obeyed. He opened the door to the grand hall and his eyes almost popped out of his head.

'We're under attack your highness,' he looked terrified.

'By whom? Who dares stand up to the Gored in this weak and defeated land?' She did not show an ounce of fear for she arrogantly thought there was no match for her army.

'A Dark Dragon and a small army of Ragaland soldiers, your Highness.'

'What? Impossible! Why would a Dark Dragon help these pathetic creatures?' the question was asked to herself but others were close and could hear the sudden panic in her scratchy voice.

'My Queen, you must hide. We'll protect you with our last breath. You're the only thing that matters,' her personal guard stood tall and gave her his hand to take.

'I will not hide from my enemies Harrak. I will summon your brothers and sisters and we will wipe this lizard off the face of our land,' she closed her eyes and lifted her arms to the imposing ceiling above, 'I call you here to me my family, my children. Protect your Mother and you will be forever rewarded in the endless beyond,' she sat back in her stolen throne, crossed her fingers on her lap and confidently grinned with rows of razor-sharp teeth bared.

'I can see the city walls,' cried out Sir Alfie over the beating wings of Braken.

'Watch this,' Braken breathed in deeply and expelled a fireball of lava at a ferocious velocity. It hit a credulous Gored and left nothing behind to remember him by.

'That is one way to say good morning,' Sir Alfie chuckled, 'remember Braken do not damage the city, we still need a home to go back to. Your job is to keep the Gored out, allowing us to get to the queen.'

'Yes Sir Alfie, I understand,' he landed hard just before the wall to the city and bent down so Sir Alfie could leap off.

His tail acted as a ladder and the rest of the army, four at a time, led by Ryan the Barbarian and Lady Elsa, ran up his back following their leader. Sir Alfie jumped at a hapless Gored whose helmet had fallen off and split his head in two. Ryan the Barbarian cleaved the heads off two others who were fighting over a club laying on the floor, 'death to Srokesh,' he called out and the army roared behind him. One by one they killed their way through the vast hoard of Ogres. The Gored desperately flung themselves at the soldiers, occasionally taking out one with them. As they fought, a particularly fearsome Gored named Halnark steadied her throwing arm. She aimed carefully at the head of Sir Alfie, knowing if she killed him, the others would waver. Just as she was about to release, her arm was sliced away at the shoulder. Lady Elsa stood firm, her sword in both hands. Halnark was about to speak when Lady Elsa's sword came down on her head. Sir Alfie looked over and nodded his thanks before finishing off his foe.

The relentless beasts sacrificed themselves over and over with one purpose, to slow the attackers down. This was giving the rest of the Gored who were deeper into the city time to prepare, and prepare they did. Axes, shields and clubs were being handed out efficiently making sure that every Gored was fully ready for battle. They did not run into the fight but lined up in rows of twenty across and fifteen deep. They were building a blockade and would not be moved easily. A scout who had run the rooftops came back with a gaping wound in his side. With his dying breath, he informed Sir Alfie of the barricade ahead and left the living knowing he had done his Captain proud. Sir Alfie rested the scout's head on a nearby pile of hay and rose to face his men, 'there is a barrier of Gored up ahead in the heart of the city. It is deep and wide and will stop us if we falter. We must not falter, we must not pause and we must face them head-on and crush them like they have crushed our families and friends. They will not survive this day I promise you that,' he raised his blood-covered sword, 'FOR OUR QUEEN!'

'FOR OUR QUEEN!' The soldiers boomed in response. Then they ran without a moment's hesitation.

Braken was busy outside. From the woods, an army of thousands had appeared and without a stutter had attacked him. He could see now how despicable these vile beasts were as they were using human children as shields, carrying them under one arm as they bombarded him with axes and clubs. He had to make the decision that would haunt him for the rest of his days and attacked back despite the consequences. These poor little innocents would be killed at his hand or the Gored's but he would try his best to save as many as he could. He let loose a spray of flames behind him blocking the entrance to Jargred. They were not getting in and he just had to hold them off until Sir Alfie could kill Srokesh. He readied himself and beat his wings powerfully in the direction of the oncoming army. It blew them backwards, all but a sturdy few were on their backs scrambling to get back up. He wished he could be nimble and collect the children but his size was not always to his benefit. They were picked up again and the Gored attacked once more.

The Ragaland soldiers led by Sir Alfie Lord Protector of Ragaland reached the blockade. A fearsome sea of viscous beasts stood between them and Srokesh. Failure would mean the end of the Kingdom and that was not something any fighter was willing to let happen. But what could they do? pondered Sir Alfie. There was no way their small number, now even fewer with many left dead in their wake, could defeat this vast amount without some help. Braken had his hands full trying to stop thousands more from attacking so Sir Alfie had to think. Or did he? He raised his bow and fired an arrow into the sky. It soared upwards and all the attention was set upon it. A loud sound of scuttling could be heard from the walls on either side of the Gored. It turned into a barrage of scratching getting closer and closer. Stubbs appeared at the top of the wall and jumped into the blockade. Hundreds of giant spiders poured over the walls after him and savagely ripped through the sea of beasts turning it green with Gored blood. They had never fought this kind of foe and at such close quarters could only scream and cry out in defence. Stubbs' family made quick work of the barrier and Sir Alfie with the rest of the knights and soldiers finished what the spiders missed. They reached the huge double doors and Sir Alfie pushed them open.

Braken was slowly becoming overwhelmed as he continued to beat the Gored back. They had spread out and were trying to flank him, with some managing to get close enough for him to crush with his feet. He tried not to think about the tiny ones they carried but could not help feeling pain deep inside every time a Gored fell. He used his claws a couple of times when he could and picked off the Ogres with accurate precision. On these rare occasions, the youngster could run away but most were grabbed and killed by the advancing beasts. It was an impossible task but he kept on trying.

Sir Alfie ducked as an axe flew over his head. He rolled forward and thrust his sword into the attacking guard's chest. He swiftly pulled it out and continued walking towards the queen. She sat unmoved and unafraid of the approaching threat still with her fingers crossed, still grinning. This was the first time Sir Alfie had seen queen Srokesh and had to admit she was not what he had expected. She was a divine and beautiful looking woman. Her long black hair flowed like silk over her svelte shoulders, spilling down her back. Her face sparkled in the sunlight coming from the open door and her eyes were soft and not cruel as one would expect. Her slender body was voluptuous in all the right places and to see her was to love her. He fell to his knees. 'You are Sir Alfie and I have been waiting for you,' she grinned wider, her sharp teeth only adding to her foreign beauty, 'you were not here when I arrived and presumed your Queen had sent you away for a purpose. This was no concern to me as you have no way of beating me, but I was disappointed not to meet you. The tales of your exploits litter this land and I was in awe of your heroism. You would make a fine king to serve at my side,' she licked her lips seductively and drew him in with her mesmerising gaze. He looked at her and felt weak. He trembled in her presence and she loved it. Another creature she had taken under her spell. He would be a fine addition to her army. She beckoned him over with a single finger, 'come to me and kiss my hand. You are part of our family, now nothing can harm you again,' he crawled nearer to her as his soldiers looked on helplessly, also entrapped by her spell. He reached her feet and she bent down. She touched under his chin with her hand and lifted his head.

Behind her on the wall, there was a picture. It wasn't the biggest or the grandest, and many said it should have been removed, but queen Srokesh liked to keep it up as a reminder of the monarch that she conquered. Sir Alfie's eyes fixed on the face of his lost love, and his fists clenched tight. He could hear her voice in his head, 'come back to me Alfie, come back,' he trembled as his mind fought against the hypnosis, 'I will always love you, Alfie, come back,' his body stiffened. In a move slicker than oil, he launched himself at the seductive queen, grabbing her throat and with a single twist, he snapped her neck. She fell to his side, still grinning, and the spell was broken.

Braken had done all he could to stop the Gored without killing them, but he was out of options. It was kill or be killed, and he took a deep breath. His stomach glowed orange, and just as he was about to cover the beasts with lava, they all dropped the children and stood still, staring blankly towards the city. Braken swallowed the flame, which was not easy to do and stared at Jargred.

The spiders outside the grand hall were still fighting when all the remaining Gored stopped and stared at the open double doors. The whole city went into a stunned silence.

Sir Alfie carefully stepped over the queen's dead body. He walked over to the painting of his lost love, kissed his fingers and placed them gently on her cheek.

'Sir Alfie,' Lady Elsa spoke softly, her voice trembled. He turned around to face his brave Knights and soldiers. His eyes welled up with tears as he saw where the wayward axe, which had barely missed him had landed. Ryan was laying on the ground, the axe protruding from his chest. Sir Alfie ran to his friend's side.

Ryan reached out and touched Sir Alfie's shoulder, blood trickled from his mouth, 'for Ragaland Brother.'

Sir Alfie put his shaking hands on Ryan's cheeks and looked deeply into his eyes, 'for Ragaland,' he replied. He wanted to say more, but he knew he hadn't the time.
Ryan smiled, then his hand dropped. Sir Alfie pulled him close and wept.

'What now, Sir Alfie?' Elsa wiped her tears from her eyes.

'Now we rebuild,' he said it with no emotion, just cold fact. He could not celebrate the victory, too much had been taken away from him. He had a job to do, and that's what he focused upon. With all the strength he had left, he lifted Ryan's lifeless body and carried him outside. Stubbs cried out in pain, not from a wound but his heart, as Sir Alfie appeared carrying his dead brother in arms. He scuttled to his master's side, and Sir Alfie rested Ryan on his back. Together with the remaining soldiers, they walked through the city and out into the field. Braken bowed down in respect for Sir Alfie and his fallen comrade, and Sir Alfie nodded his thanks. The battle was over, but it had come at a cost. There would be a time to grieve for the lost souls, but now was the time to free the slaves and return this great land to its former glory.

5

In the months that followed, Sir Alfie had done his duty. He, alongside Stubbs and Lady Elsa, had rescued the slaves and organised the building of new towns and cities. The remaining Gored had become docile and, to the horror of some, Sir Alfie had forgiven them and let them help with the work. He understood, having felt it first-hand the spell of the queen, and if it had not been for his love of Queen Honeywell who knows what might have happened.

After a year, the kingdom was well on the mend and the people called out for Sir Alfie to take the throne. They adored and trusted him and he knew there was no getting away from it. He was crowned King Alfie and Lady Elsa was given the title of Lord Protector. Braken was left alone as King Alfie had promised, but found it was not to his liking and he would visit often. He felt the pain of the lost children and would spend days giving the orphans left from the war, rides around the kingdom. His compassion for the children was to be his legacy and the name Braken became synonymous with child care. Ryan's grave became a shrine to all who died during the dark times, and whenever he got the chance you would find King Alfie standing head bowed silent and in mourning. A lonely figure in a world full of loved ones.

'He died,' Alfie didn't move.

'He died a hero Alfie, he died for the Kingdom,' Stubbs patted his friend on the back. They were back at the graveyard and Alfie was shivering from the cold.

'I know, but it hurts in my tummy,' he lay on his back staring at the darkening sky which was now clear as the rain had stopped. The first few stars had begun to appear and he wished he could be there, far away from all of this pain.

'You're feeling the loss little dude, it's part of the grieving process,' for a moment Stubbs sounded just like Ryan, but Alfie dismissed this knowing that he was hearing his imaginary friend in his mind and therefore he had himself sounded like Ryan.

'It's not fair, life is never fair,' Alfie heard tyres on gravel and looked around him. He saw lights from a car pull up next to the church. They momentarily blinded him so he put his arm across his face and shut his eyes to avoid the intense light. The brakes squeaked and two doors opened. Alfie curled up into a ball to warm himself, he heard footsteps close by and knew they had found him.

'He's over here Carol, I've found him,' Keith called aloud, 'don't worry Alfie your Mummy's coming,' he bent down and touched Alfie gently, he was shivering uncontrollably and Keith had to stop himself from grabbing him and trying to warm him. He knew Alfie would more than likely freak out if he did, so he waited for Carol.

After the argument at the funeral, Carol had wept for a good ten minutes before Katy had convinced her to come out and that's when she had noticed Alfie was missing. Gary was nowhere to be found and she didn't care. She was solely focused on making sure her little boy was alright. Keith had come to the rescue suggesting that Alfie may have gone back to Ryan's grave and the two of them had rushed to his car.

'Oh thank you, Keith, you were right, you said he would be here and you were right,' she was overwhelmed with emotion, from the funeral, from her fight with Gary, from the alcohol and now from finding her son who she thought had run away for good. She sprinted to his side, almost slipping on the wet grass.

'He's okay Carol, we just need to get him in the car and warm,' he turned to Alfie, 'would you like that buddy?' Alfie nodded his head ever so slightly.

Keith knew Carol wouldn't be able to carry him and decided to just take the plunge and hope for the best. He picked Alfie up and to his and Carol's surprise, he didn't have a fit. He just lay in his arms like a rag doll.

'Oh baby, what's wrong with me? I'm so sorry I wasn't with you. Grandma was supposed to watch you,' she scowled and felt so much hatred towards her mother-in-law. 'Should we take him to the hospital he looks awfully pale?' Carol panicked.

'I don't think that will be necessary,' Keith answered, 'all this young man needs is a warm bed and some hot chocolate,' Alfie wondered what medical school Keith had attended to make this assumption, but remained silent.

'Okay. If you're sure,' she followed Keith to his car. She opened the back door and climbed in. Keith rested Alfie on her lap along the back seats. She held him close, all the time feeling self-hate and regret. Keith started the car and turned the heaters to full power. He drove but the house was only a few minutes away and the car didn't have time to warm. He parked outside and rushed around to the car door. Carol had already opened it and was trying her best to get out while still holding her son. Keith put his arms out and she nodded in silent agreement. Once again Alfie let Keith carry him and Carol felt a hint of warmth at the sight of this gentle man being so caring towards her baby boy. She looked at the house wondering if Gary had come home, secretly hoping he hadn't and even more secretly hoping he never would. The lights were off, so she assumed he hadn't.

The three of them entered and Keith took Alfie upstairs to his bedroom. Carol followed and the two of them carefully undressed him and helped him into his Pyjamas. Alfie was completely submissive, which concerned Carol even though it was making things easier. He lay on the little bed and she tucked him in. She sang him a song, "You are my sunshine" and he was fast asleep within minutes. Keith thought twice about the hot chocolate but decided he would still make it just in case Alfie woke up later. He would make them all hot chocolate and headed downstairs to start on the drinks. Carol was about to go with him when Monty appeared by her legs. He rubbed himself on her ankle before jumping on the bed and snuggling up to Alfie, 'you take good care of him Monty, he needs you now more than ever.' Monty purred and rolled onto his back. 'Silly cat,' Carol smiled and went downstairs. She sat at the kitchen table and put her head in her hands. She was exhausted and was struggling to keep herself together.

Keith boiled the milk for the hot chocolate, 'don't blame yourself, Carol,' he looked tenderly at her.

'I don't,' she snapped, 'I blame that twisted mother of his. She was supposed to watch him. She's never liked Alfie and I half suspect she let him go deliberately,' she shook with anger.

'You know that's not true. She might be many things, but she's not that bad,' Keith rummaged through the cupboards looking for the chocolate powder.

'Fine, but I'm never letting her look after him again. I must take care of him now Ryan's gone. Before, it was just easier to let him deal with Alfie but now who has my baby got? It's all my fault!' her head shook in her hands and her body convulsed as she sobbed.

'Enough of that. You know it wasn't your fault. But we do agree on something, Alfie needs you. He has always needed you, you're his mother. He might be difficult but that's no reason to give up on him and I know you're stronger than others think you are,' he found the choco powder and spooned it into the mugs.

'Not that one Keith, he'll only drink from his tiger mug. Don't ask me why but last time I tried giving him a different mug he threw it against the wall,' her eyes saddened even more.

He looked in the cupboard and found Alfie's mug, then poured the powder from the wrong one into it, 'it cannot be as simple as he's just a bad kid Carol. That's not normal naughty child behaviour. There must be something more to it. Perhaps he has some sort of disorder? I heard about some other kids like Alfie who had something wrong with them. Maybe you should consider it?' he poured the hot milk into the mugs, stirred and went to hand her Alfie's and hers.

She didn't take them. 'There's nothing wrong with him!' she shouted. 'What's normal anyway?' she said under her breath, remembering what Ryan had said in their last ever conversation. How she wished she could go back and do it all over again.

'Sorry,' Keith paused. 'I didn't mean to say that, I bet you're fed up of hearing people put him down. All I'm saying is maybe you should think about taking him to the doctor,' he tried again to pass her the mugs.

'Gary would never agree to his Son being tested,' she used air quotes with her fingers on the word "tested". 'He would look at it as some sort of failure at being a man,' this time she took the mugs on offer.

'I love the guy but I could strangle him sometimes,' he stared at his friend's pretty wife. 'He should treat you better, you deserve better,' he moved closer to her. He wanted so badly to kiss her. He lent down to meet her lips.

'Stop, we can't do this,' she had felt the tension between them for a while now, but resisted her temptations. 'I'm flattered Keith and thanks for helping with Alfie but you need to go. I'm married and you're his friend,' she turned her face away from him.

'I'm sorry,' he straightened up and his cheeks went crimson. 'I don't know what came over me.'

'It's ok, it's been a difficult day. Let's just forget this ever happened,' she didn't want to forget but she was too scared to pursue it. She put down her mug and stood up. She gently touched his shoulder then without saying another word, left the room and climbed the stairs. Keith stood for a moment staring up after her. He took a deep breath and sighed. He wished he could take it back. He wanted her and had done for such a long time. The only reason he was still hanging out with a loser like Gary was to get close to Carol. He felt he could be the better she and Alfie deserved. He cursed himself for making the move, he knew it wasn't the right time but got swept away with the moment. He wouldn't give up though, he wouldn't let her or Alfie go.

Carol heard the front door open and close and almost wished Keith had followed her up the stairs, but was relieved he hadn't. Her life was complicated enough now without adding an affair into it. 'Alfie baby, Mummy brought you some hot chocolate. It's in your tiger mug just how you like it,' she opened his door but he was still fast asleep. She had somehow forgotten this and she inwardly cursed herself for almost waking him. She checked his head and was happy at least to find he didn't have a temperature. She picked up his wet clothes, put the chocolate down on his chest of drawers, turned the night light off and closed the door behind her.

'Are you awake Alfie?' Stubbs whispered, but his friend was asleep and couldn't be woken, not even by his own imagination.

Chapter 5

Three days passed and Alfie had barely said two words. This once happy, talkative and bubbly little boy was nothing more than a shadow of his former self. Gary had been drinking non-stop since Ryan's death and was mostly at the pub or on a park bench somewhere drowning his sorrows. Carol continued to make excuse after excuse for him in her mind but she just couldn't forgive him fully. The argument at the funeral had driven a huge wedge between them and neither of them was trying that hard to repair it. She decided instead to try to get through to Alfie who hadn't left his room since that fateful night. She sat with him and he cuddled up to her, she sang him songs and stroked his head. She hated thinking like this but she had never felt closer to him. Nevertheless, she worried greatly about his lack of speech and knew she would have to address it sooner or later. For now, she was just enjoying being his mummy and having all his attention, as docile and out of character as it might have been. He would often stare out into space not looking at anything in particular and she would wonder where he had gone. He would occasionally whisper something too quietly for her to hear and she would keep hoping he would snap out of it. Mrs Honeywell had phoned a few times to check in on Alfie, but even for her, he wouldn't speak. Carol liked her a lot and the two of them chatted about how best to help him. She was so glad to have an ally in what felt like the beginning of a long battle.

It was late and Carol was in the kitchen preparing Alfie's dinner. She carefully chopped tomatoes sideways just how he liked them and put them on his dinosaur plate with some chicken ham and a side order of salt and vinegar crisps and salad cream. She had lost track of time trying to get him to build some Lego with her, but he just pushed the bricks aside and watched her as she clumsily built a little mismatched coloured house on a green base. She surprisingly enjoyed it and she even saw Alfie smile when she'd finished. She'd looked up at the clock and panicked when she realised she'd missed his dinner time but to her disbelief, Alfie wasn't angry. He had forgotten his strict routine.

A scratching noise came from the door and Monty the cat stirred from its foot and stretched out wide. He yawned and looked up. The noise came again then a bang that made the cat leap up and dart underneath the shoe rack. 'Carol,' Gary yelled, 'the bloody doors stuck, my key won't work,' his speech was slurred but that wasn't unusual. He banged on the door again, 'Carol, open the f-' it opened before he could swear and she stood with Alfie's plate in one hand the other on the door.

'Drunk again!' she said turning her back on him and heading towards the stairs.

'Off to feed the little prince, are we?' he sneered, swaying on the doorstep. She ignored him and began walking upstairs. 'I hope you made me some food, I'm starving,' he entered and stumbled into the kitchen. The table was bare as she hadn't even made herself any food, then again she barely ate since the accident anyway.

She reached Alfie's door and could hear Gary swearing at her from the kitchen, something about her not loving him and being a bad wife, but she didn't care. She just wanted to be a good mother and could worry about the marital consequences later, 'here you go baby, Mummy made you your dinner,' he sat up from his bed and she handed him the plate. He ate heartily, obviously hungry, and she felt a pang of guilt that she hadn't given it to him earlier. After he'd eaten he lay on his bed in his

Mother's embrace holding tightly to her arms, muttering to himself. She gently stroked his hair. She could still hear Gary crashing around downstairs making himself something to eat, making a show of it to prove some point that only he understood in his drunken mind. He kept shouting and swearing and Alfie cringed every time he did, holding on to her a little tighter each time. His daddy was more like an angry zombie nowadays, slurring and shouting. He wished he would leave them alone.

'How are you feeling little dude?' Stubbs said copying Ryan's nickname for Alfie.

'Not good, Stubbs, not good. Mummy is sad cos I don't talk to her but I don't know what to say. She doesn't understand that I just want Ryan, she just doesn't get it,' he scrunched up his face holding back the tears, 'and now Daddy is mad cos Mummy gave me food and not him and he hates me cos I'm not normal.'

'Shall we go away again? I found a new adventure,' Stubbs enticed Alfie.

'Okay, Stubbs lets go,' Alfie closed his eyes and his mummy squeezed him tighter.

'Did you say something sweetheart?' she asked, but it was too late, he was lost in his own little world again and she desperately wished she could follow him.

Journey through the dead

1

'Run, damn it Alfie, run!' Ryan screamed in his face and Alfie jerked out of his daydream.

'Where are they?' he asked quickly, franticly looking left and right.

'They're coming up the stairs and this time we don't have enough bullets to stop them,' Ryan grabbed Alfie's hand and pulled him to his feet, 'follow me and stay close. We'll make it if we head up to the roof. There's a gangway at the top that we can use to climb across to the next building,' Ryan's dirt-caked and bleeding face went stony. The door at the far end of the warehouse crashed open, his heart skipped a beat. A mangled hand, attached to a half-severed arm, reached out through the gap. 'Come on!' Ryan cried out. The brothers ran across the wooden floor, dust kicking up under their feet. They reached the fire exit and pushed through. The light almost blinded Alfie but he held on tight to his sibling as he was led up the fire staircase on the outside of the building. He could hear the trampling sound of dozens of feet scuffling in their wake. His eyes adjusted as they reached the roof, but they weren't out of danger just yet.

'Where do you think you're going, Ryan?' Cillian had his gun pointed at them. He had been waiting for this moment to betray them and take the antidote for himself.

'You can't be serious? You know this is the only vile,' Ryan did his best to control his nerves but he could feel the metal stairs shake as the zombie mass climbed up towards them.

'Deadly serious,' Cillian's eyes narrowed. ' Sarah needs it, she's almost turning and I don't have the time to wait for more to be made,' the sweat pouring down his face gave away his nervous disposition.

'But if you use it you're condemning the whole world. Can you really live with that? Can Sarah live with that?' Ryan pleaded.

'My mind is made up Ryan, now hand it over or I'll kill Alfie,' he pointed the barrel directly at Alfie's head, his hand shook but he quickly steadied himself. He was serious but he was also sorry.

'I'm sorry Cillian but I'm not letting you kill us all. You're going to have to shoot,' Ryan held the railing as tightly as he could and then squeezed Alfie's side holding him close. He could almost smell the rotting flesh it was so close.

'Just give me the vial god damn it,' Cillian's hand trembled again. He had never shot anyone living before, but he was willing to if it meant saving his precious wife.

'Fine, fine,' Ryan gave in, 'here it is', Cillian's hand dropped by his side thinking he had won and just being glad he didn't have to shoot a kid. 'Sorry Cill,' Ryan leapt over the side of the railings with Alfie under one arm and the other hand clinging onto the bannister. The zombie horde poured over the top of the stairs onto the roof towards Cillian. He stumbled backwards from the surprise and began shooting wildly at the undead wave. A few hit the rooftop but there were far too many and within seconds Cillian had been engulfed. He screamed but only for a few seconds before his throat was consumed and his face torn from its skull. Ryan waited until the last zombie had past and dropped down to the landing below, 'we can't go that way now but maybe we can find a way back through the warehouse,' Alfie nodded still in shock as he thought Cillian was his friend. The two had become close over the past year since they met at the military camp. Cillian and Sarah had become almost like a mum and dad to him and Ryan and knowing both of them were gone broke his heart.

'What about Sarah?' asked Alfie, his voice cracking.

Ryan looked down at his little brother, 'I'm sorry but there's nothing we can do. I have to think about you and this cure, it's our only chance of getting this world back to how things used to be,' Alfie nodded reluctantly and Ryan placed him back on his feet. They headed down the stairs the zombies had come from as slowly as they could so as not to make any noise. Guns out they descended into the darkness hoping that there were no surprises to be found. They reached the main reception and Ryan checked the street outside, 'It's clear. I think we can make it to the car and hopefully we can get the hell out of this stupid town.'

'I liked it here Ryan, I thought we could make it our home,' Alfie looked out the glass doors and spotted the car Ryan was referring to.

'I know little dude but sometimes things just don't work out the way you plan them. Besides, we need to get to London and find Dr Darwin. Hopefully, he can make more of the cure,' Ryan held the door open, 'go, now.' They ran as fast as possible and jumped in the car. The zombie horde had come back down the stairs and had appeared at the reception door. Ryan turned the key and the car muffled and squealed, 'flipping car, just start!' he yelled. The zombies heard and began walking in their direction. Ryan turned the key again and the car gunned into life, 'thank smeg,' he put his foot down and the car bolted off up the road, the tyres spinning on the tarmac. A woman, whose name had been Fay, looked on after them. The skin from her face hung loosely under her eye and her top lip was missing. Her teeth clunked together as she bit the air, a reflex rather than a choice. She sniffed like a bloodhound and her body swayed from side to side. Her clothes were stained with the blood of human food, some of which belonged to her own children. She hobbled along the road with her fellow flesh-eaters, searching for their next fresh meal, a mass of decay and sadness.

The world had become a place of death and misery or at least it had become a world with slightly more death and misery than before. A single virus had spread from the far reaches of Peru to every inhabited place on the planet, over the last year. The news had first reported on this mystery disease as something that was being managed. It was a faraway issue that would barely register in the minds of the Americans let alone the British. It wasn't until a single Christian volunteer snuck back on a plane from Brazil after being scratched by a child at the makeshift medical centre, that it became a reality for the Brits. He turned a few days later while sitting in his chair watching Huntington House on Channel 04. He hadn't wanted to go to the hospital as he was worried they were going to quarantine him. His wife had seen he was sick but just gave him some lemon drink and prayed to her god that he would get better. It didn't work, and that evening as she knelt by her bed, hands together pointing at her ceiling, her husband feasted on her shoulder followed by the rest of her plump physique.

It was like a fire spreading across dry grass and there was no way of stopping it. The army tried but was soon overrun by the sheer mass of undead tearing the country apart. No one was safe and no one was immune. The zombie apocalypse had wiped out most of the humans and turned them into flesh-eating monsters. The Fenix brothers were two of the lucky few who were still left uninfected and it turned out they were mankind's last hope. 'Are you okay?' Ryan glanced at Alfie as they sped along the abandoned motorway.

'Yes,' he looked out of the window and watched the town disappear over the horizon. He thought about Cillian and Sarah, Giles and Abed. He welled up when he remembered Victoria who he had fallen head over heels for and her mum Kate, who had encouraged their relationship. All of them had been killed because of the antidote, either trying to protect it or trying to use it. It had been given to them by a Dr Nuala, whom they rescued from the school in the middle of the town. She had been on her way to London to give the cure to her mentor Dr Darwin at the University of Specialised Sciences. Only he, according to her, could formulate a worldwide cure and put an end to the virus. They had agreed to get her out of the town and Abed even wanted to go all the way with her, but a herd of zombies had passed through their camp two nights before and killed half their group. The rest had escaped thanks to Sarah's quick thinking but she'd been scratched as she made sure every last person alive had gotten through the gap in the fence that she'd prepared in case of an emergency. Alfie had been that last person as he was lagging due to him looking for his backpack which Ryan had always told him to put by his bed, but he had once again left it in Victoria's tent.

He blamed himself for Sarah, but soon forgot as one by one the rest of the group were picked off by savage attackers. Victoria had been killed when she slipped as they climbed a ladder, she'd fallen heavily but was still alive. Her mum climbed down as quickly as she could but by the time she got there the zombies had overwhelmed her daughter and pulled her down too. Ryan had dragged Alfie kicking and screaming as they were torn limb from limb and he had barely spoken since. When the Doc had been bitten, she gave the vial to Ryan making him promise to get it to London. She'd refused to let them take her any further, saying that the cure was the only thing that mattered and at least she would die for a reason not just for lunch. She had kept her spirits to the end and Ryan did the kind thing and ended her life quickly. It hadn't been the first time he had done it but it never got easier and he would feel their pain for weeks after. They had held up in the warehouse and Sarah and Cillian had gone to the roof to get a better view of the town. Alfie had tried to get some rest, but as usual, there wasn't any time. Now it was just the two of them and Alfie felt lost and empty of hope.

'How far is it to London?' Alfie asked staring out of the window. He saw a small group of zombies mulling around a phone box as if they were waiting to make a call. He sometimes wondered if they remembered anything about their previous lives as he would often see them doing things that almost looked normal.

'About six hours, try and get your head down,' they were up North as they'd figured the Lake District would be a good place to get away from the virus. It turned out that others had thought the same and by the time they got there it was overrun with zombies. There seemed to be no escape from them and now Ryan was heading into the most populated city in Britain, the exact opposite of where he wanted to go. He wasn't going to let a little thing like over eight million zombies stop him from fulfilling a promise, especially one as important to the survival of the human race as this one was. He knew, inside, how impossible it was going to be but how could he live with himself knowing he hadn't even tried? He just had to think of a way into London that wouldn't mean immediately being overrun. Could he just drive in and hope the streets were clear? Not likely, and even if they were clear of the undead the chances were that they would be blocked with vehicles abandoned by their desperate, and now probably deceased owners. Perhaps going through the sewers might work, but they were more likely to get lost and die from starvation than reach central London and be eaten. However, underground did sound like the best option. He paused and then it hit him. Underground… the underground! They could walk the railway and get into London safer than any other way he could fathom. It would still be suicidal but it was their best and only hope.

He rubbed his stinging eyes and cleared his dry throat. He looked at Alfie sound asleep and thought of his responsibility to his little brother. He was supposed to keep him safe but so far, he had done anything but that. He'd tried his best but still felt disappointed with himself. At least Alfie was still alive, but for how long? He could leave him outside London but the little dude had become a dab hand at zombie disposal despite his size and age. He learned pretty quickly that to survive you have to learn how to kill. Either the flesh rotting monsters hobbling around or an innocent animal that must become a nourishing meal. Kill or die, that's the world they lived in now and if they did nothing it would remain like it forever. Several hours went by as Ryan drove past cities and towns. Luckily the main roads were mostly clear of abandoned cars, but occasionally he would have to slow down and manoeuvre his way through vast volumes of traffic. Even after a year, he couldn't get used to seeing his country in this state. He missed the old world so much, which is why he was now willing to risk everything to get it back. He daydreamed of what it might be like to rebuild from this apocalyptic wasteland

and hoped that his parents were still able to be brought back from the hell they were trapped in, that is of course if they hadn't been disposed of. He wondered how many of the zombies he'd killed that could have been saved and even worse, how many of the people he had put out of their misery could have been cured. Then he asked himself the ultimate question, the one that ate at him ever since he first held the antidote in his hand. Could he watch Alfie turn and still not use it? He still hadn't convinced himself that he could, even though he had condemned others to a fate worse than death when he could have saved them. Was it selfish to think he would be so hypocritical or was he just saving the vial for Alfie and was willing to let others die so he could keep him alive? Perhaps both were true, but none of this was going to change what had happened so he just did what he could and kept driving forward.

2

'Where are we?', Alfie woke with a start as the dream he was having turned into a nightmare much like the reality he resided in. He looked out of the window and could see the grey houses and dark streets that made it clear they were not in the countryside anymore.

'We're getting close. I thought the best way into the city would be the train track, then use the underground to get around,' Ryan explained.

'Sounds good, well not good obviously but...' Alfie trailed off.

'It's okay Alfie I know what you meant. It's the best option but I warn you the risk is still enormous. We're going to have to fight our way to the University there's no way of avoiding them completely,' Ryan said reluctantly.

'I'm ready Ryan but I am a bit scared, is it okay if I'm a bit scared?' Alfie looked at him with his big green eyes.

'I wouldn't have it any other way, little bro. Fear is what heightens our senses and makes us more acutely attuned to the environment around us. It's what keeps us safe when danger is near. Those who are not afraid often end up dead as they have no way of judging fight over flight. Trust me fear is good, just make sure you own your fear because if you let it own you, it can control you and that's more dangerous than anything,' Ryan's words instilled themselves in Alfie's brain and he soaked up every drop of his Brother's advice. It's this sort of wisdom that had kept him alive for this long and the one time he didn't listen to Ryan it got Sarah scratched, all because he was lackadaisical with his approach to camp safety. Ryan was his mentor and his hero and now was the time to step up and show him what he was made of. 'We can stop here and resupply,' Ryan pulled into the shop car park and turned off the engine, 'Grab the bag from the back seat and don't forget your gun.'

'Okay, Ryan,' he did as he was told and opened the car door. No sooner had he stepped onto the tarmac when a skinny man appeared from behind another car and snarled while lunging towards him. Alfie raised his pistol but Ryan's words from a past lesson rung in his head. Keep it quiet if you can. 'Ryan, there's a zombie.'

Ryan had already spotted it and had crept around the back of the car. The skinny man's clothes were not ripped at all but his throat was completely torn out. You could see to the oesophagus, but the blood had all but dried up. At this moment, a strange but relevant thought crossed Alfie's mind. If the cure worked how would this man ever survive? It's not like his throat would rebuild itself so what possible cure could cure the zombies? It was then he realised that the cure would only be for those who had not already turned and therefore his parents and everyone else he ever loved would not be coming back. This blow made him sick to his stomach, especially when he thought that Cillian had been so stupid as to think that he could bring Sarah back. His anger boiled over and he momentarily lost his head just as Ryan was about to crack the man over the head with a brick Alfie kicked his legs out from underneath him and the zombie crashed to the ground. He stamped as hard as he could on its head and felt it turn to mush under his foot. He stamped again and again until Ryan picked him up, pulling him away from the mushy pulp and squeezed his arms, 'it's okay Alfie, it's okay. He can't hurt you anymore,' or anyone else for that matter he thought to himself as he looked down at the heinous mess by his feet.

'They ruined everything! They killed Mum and Dad. Why do they always want to kill? Why can't they just stop?' Alfie burst into tears.

'I don't know little dude, all I know is we're going to stop it and that one day all this will just be a bad dream,' he held his little brother tight and felt him shake as he cried.

'You know it can't cure them. It can't bring Mum and Dad back. You can't cure the dead.'

'What do you mean?' Ryan asked.

'They're beyond saving. Look at them,' he nodded towards the pile of flesh at their feet, 'how would that come back to life? You cannot cure death you can only stop it from happening.'

The revelation was crushing, so crushing in fact that Ryan let go of Alfie and stumbled backwards. He looked at him incredulously, 'you're right' he said under his breath, 'you're bloody right.'

'I know I am,' Alfie said confused as to why this was so surprising to Ryan. Most of the time he was right.

'Why didn't I see it before? How stupid I've been. How stupid we've all been. We were fighting over what we thought was a cure when all this time it was a flipping vaccine,' he shook his head in disbelief.

'It's no one's fault. We were a bit distracted by all the monsters trying to eat us so I think we can be forgiven for our lack of foresight.'

Ryan couldn't help but smile at the sarcasm and he too shook away the feeling of disappointment, 'come on let's get some grub. I bet you're starving.'

'Famished!' Alfie agreed.

'OK stay frosty and watch my back.'

'Yes, Ryan,' Alfie followed him to the supermarket doors. Ryan prised the doors open as quietly as he could and the two of them slid through the small gap. The fresh fruit and veg section had become not so fresh and the smell was overwhelming but not as repugnant as the odour coming from the mass pile-up of dead bodies that littered the shop floor. The rotting corpses of ex humans were putrefied and full of all sorts of busy little animals feasting on their nutrients. Alfie had seen so much in the last year but this was different, these people were never zombies, they had never turned. They had no obvious bites or scratches and it was clear from the offset what had happened to them. It was mass suicide. These poor creatures had culminated in this one place to seemingly hold up for as long as they could, but when they had given up on the hope of survival or rescue they had decided that this was the only option. Wrists were slit, pills and alcohol had been consumed and in some cases, children and the weak and elderly had been strangled humanely by their loved ones. Throats had been slit in the more extreme circumstances and the dried blood stuck to the boys' shoes wherever they walked. They both held their hands over their mouths to help with the smell but it had little effect and they were soon close to vomiting.

'Christ, this is beyond messed up,' said Ryan.

'I don't feel hungry anymore, that's for sure,' Alfie whispered.

'No need to be so quiet little dude, if there were zombies around, this lot would show the signs of being chewed on. Looks like we're in the clear, for the time being at least. Let's grab as many cans as we can and get the hell out of here,' he started by picking up some beans and placing them in his rucksack.

'Okay, Ryan,' Alfie did the same but with some peaches. They made their way through the mass grave, filling their bags with as much as they could carry without overburdening themselves. Every decision you made in this world could cost you, so you always had to keep in mind the risk versus reward of your actions. It might be worth the risk to carry a lot of food so you can feed yourself but that heavy bag could slow you down when you were trying not to be food. Everything had a consequence the only question was, is it worth it? They left the way they entered, the images of the dead burnt into their minds to haunt them for the foreseeable future. They had to shake it off otherwise it would consume them. Luckily, they had a coping method for this and that was to sing. They sneaked back to the car unhindered and sat quietly with the doors locked staring out of the windscreen wishing things were different. Ryan began, 'always look on the bright side of life.'

Alfie whistled.

Ryan continued, 'always look on the light side of life.'

Alfie whistled again and both burst out laughing. It worked almost every time and it was the only thing that ever did. Ryan turned the key, and they were off again.

3

Signs for Central London began to appear and Alfie knew without having to ask, that the time was almost upon them. They pulled up at Southfields train station near Wimbledon and sat staring at the disarray that surrounded them. Cars were abandoned and some were overturned. Shop windows had been smashed and a few of the buildings had been burnt to a crisp. Alfie could see a train in the station over a small brick wall. There was blood on some of the windows, he didn't want to know what was inside. Their Nan used to live in one of the high rise flats nearby but she had died some time ago. Still, Alfie could vividly remember her as the sweetest and most kind-hearted lady he had ever known. Every time they would visit, she would take them to Wimbledon common and hunt for Wombles whilst eating a bag of sweets. They would play mini-golf and paddle in the huge pond. They never did find a Womble, but their Nan would always say that that didn't mean they don't exist. Alfie pointed out that it probably meant that they didn't, but he enjoyed the game all the same. They both took a deep breath, then released simultaneously. 'Time to go,' Ryan opened the car door.

'Cool' Alfie opened his. They stepped out and grabbed their weapons. Ryan couldn't believe their luck. There didn't seem to be any zombies around here. It crossed his mind that perhaps that just meant there would be more somewhere else, but he would deal with that then and for now he would just bask in the glory of the day. The sun was shining and the clouds were few and far between. There was a foul stench in the air but with the insurmountable amount of death about that was hardly shocking. They made their way into the station and hopped over the barrier. They descended the stairs to the platform and stopped next to the train.

'There could be something useful in there,' Ryan nodded to the giant metal coffin.

Alfie looked up at a blood-soaked window and shuddered, 'I'd rather not find out. Let's just go, please?' He begged.

'Perhaps your right,' he ruffled Alfie's hair playfully and jumped down onto the track. They knew this area better than any other in London, so it seemed the obvious place to start their journey. They kept close to the middle so as not to be snuck up on from the sides but there didn't seem to be anyone or anything to oppose or hinder them.

They walked for almost a mile before either of them spoke. Long silences weren't uncommon in the post-apocalyptic world. It wasn't like they could discuss the latest football transfers or what some daft wig-wearing politician had done or who got voted out of some rubbish reality show. Their world was death and survival. Long gone were the days of chatting for the sake of it. Now it was all about making a plan and executing it without perishing. They could talk about the old days but mostly that just made them sad.

A tunnel loomed in the distance and the two brothers slowed their pace, 'What now?' Alfie asked without taking his eyes off the entrance.

'Don't know 'till we get a little closer, but we'll probably have to go through it,' they continued with their senses heightened. Ryan stopped near the entrance and squinted his eyes as he peered into the black abyss, 'maybe we should go around or over? It doesn't look safe in there,' he couldn't see anything but that didn't mean there wasn't anything in there.

'I'll go up the slope over there and take a look,' Ryan nodded and Alfie climbed up the grassy bank to scout ahead. He reached the top without much of a struggle and ducked down immediately, 'Holy hell,' he whispered to himself. The entire road as far as the eye could see was jam-packed with the walking dead. All the shapes, sizes and colours you could imagine were huddled together like sheep on a cold, winters night. They shuffled around, mulling in between each other sniffing the air and biting their teeth. They lamented in unison each more miserable than the last. Their suffering had been long and Alfie, again, wondered if perhaps there was anything left of the people they once were. He shook with fear as a large portly man turned in his direction and made a deafening cry. The chubby git looked as though he had eaten his fill in life, and in death, he was just damn greedy to keep going. Flesh of an indescribable nature hung from his mouth and his hands were covered in blood, up his arms to his elbows. Alfie didn't wait to find out if he'd been spotted he just turned and slid down the bank, using his hands to slow himself down.

'What's going on Alfie?' Ryan asked looking over Alfie's shoulder half expecting to see a zombie in pursuit.

'We can't go that way. It's heaving with them,' He wiped his hands on his jeans.

'Tunnel it is then,' Alfie nodded. They held each other's hands and entered the blackness. The smell was horrendous. They could barely breathe it was so bad. They couldn't cover their mouths as they had their guns in one hand and each others hand in the other. They weren't about to let go, it was the only thing keeping them together. They kept to the side so Ryan, who was next to it, could reach out with his pistol hand and touch the brick surface to help guide them.

'Stop' Alfie whispered, his voice echoed off the walls.

'What? Did you hear something?' Ryan looked forward but couldn't see anything.

'Yes, I'm sure I heard moaning or talking. Yes, I think I heard talking,' his grip tightened on Ryan's hand.

'Zombies don't talk so if you did hear something it must be people.'

'But what if they're bad people?' They'd met a few of them in the last year. Scum who wanted to rob them or rape the female members of their group. People who only thought of themselves and were willing to sacrifice their humanity to survive. Ryan had killed them to protect his brother and he would do it again and again especially with the human race's survival in the balance.

'Then I'll deal with them. Let's keep it quiet and we might even be able to sneak past,' Ryan wanted to avoid all confrontation if he could, just to be on the safe side.

They approached as silently as they could and the voices became clearer, 'if we don't eat soon we're going to die, then the infected will have an easy meal anyway so we might as well risk it. I would rather die trying than die starving,' Amanda stated in her husky Scottish accent.

'Well I wouldn't and that's that,' Neville whined.

'Who made you the boss?,' Harry barked, 'just because Dad's gone doesn't mean you just get to take over.'

'Yeh it does, I'm the oldest and that means I'm the boss,' Neville huffed and folded his arms.

Ryan could see all this going down as they were sitting around a fire they'd built. The light of the flames flickered off the walls like waves rippling in a pond making his and Alfie's shadows dance on them.

'Na way Neville. Dad always depended on Amanda and me for decision making. He thought you were a wee idiot,' Harry sneered.

'Enough of the bickering. We're family and Dad always said family stick together nah matter what,' Amanda stood up and brushed herself down. Ryan liked her sentiment and felt the same way, that's why Alfie had always come first. 'Can I help yous two?' Amanda turned and faced their direction, 'there's nah point in hiding back there, the shadows gave you away. Do ye come in peace or do ye wanna fight?' She wasn't to be messed with.

'Peace,' said Ryan firmly, 'we come in peace,' they stepped out of the shadows and revealed themselves to the trio.

'Those weapons dinnae look peaceful,' Neville pointed out.

'I assure you they're just for our protection. There is a zombie problem if you hadn't noticed.'

'Zombies. That's a funny word for a bunch of sick people,' Harry chimed in.

'They're not sick, they're dead,' Alfie explained, 'they died when they got bitten so technically they are zombies.'

'Someone's a know-it-all aren't they!' Neville scoffed.

'He knows more than you could possibly imagine so back off!' Ryan jumped to Alfie's defence as always.

'Calm down pal, no one's picking a fight with your wee man there, my Brother's just a plonker. He dinnae know how to hold his tongue,' said Amanda.

'How long have you been down here?' Ryan changed the subject.

'About two days,' Amanda answered, 'we came down here to hide from that lot up there,' she pointed upwards, 'we were hoping we could sneak out the other end of the tunnel but that's blocked with them as well. They're flipping everywhere and we're trapped like rats in a lab. We were hoping they would move on and we could go and find some food, but so far they haven't budged.'

'Do you know what the City is like? Is it as bad as here?' Alfie asked peering around Ryan who had stepped in front of him protectively.

'Nah. The city has a lot of them, but they're all spread out. You can hide from them easily or kill 'em off one by one. That's the problem though, this lot are in the way,' Harry stood up and approached the brothers, 'I'm Harry, by the way, this is me Sister Amanda and that scrawny piece of ass is me Brother, Neville. Who might yous be?'

'My name's Ryan and this is my Brother Alfie,' Ryan walked over and shook Harry's extended hand.

'That explains why yous defended him like that,' Amanda was impressed at Ryan's family loyalty.

'We need to get to the city centre. We need to meet someone at the London University of Specialised Sciences,' Ryan said, warming himself by the fire.

'Well, until this lot move on, you're bang outta luck pal and besides, there's nah one left alive in the city, so chances are your friend's long gone,' said Harry mournfully.

'I know how to move them,' Alfie stood tall beside his brother and confidently explained, 'if we can distract them at the other end of the tunnel where we came from they might come down the bank and into the tunnel behind us,' he smiled confidently.

'And how will that help us having a bunch of ravenous flesh chewers on our ass?' Neville scorned.

'Because, Neville, that means that the exit should be clear because they all tend to follow one another much like people in a supermarket queue,' Alfie calmly replied.

It was Ryan's turn to smile this time and he wasn't the only one. The siblings also found it funny seeing this little kid put their brother in his place, but they certainly weren't surprised.

'What's so important about meeting up with your friend? Surely it'd be more sensible them coming to yous?' Amanda asked.

'He isn't my friend. He's a professor at the University and I have something for him which could lead to a possible cure for all of this,' Ryan told it straight but didn't give the finer details. He had decided that these bickering siblings were their best bet to make it into the city and at the very least he could use them as protection for Alfie.

'Jesus, are ye kidding us. You have a cure?' Neville sounded so excited his voice quivered.

'I don't know exactly what it is or what it does, but as far as I'm concerned this is the best bet we have of ending this plague and perhaps giving the human race another chance,'

Ryan could hear how dramatic he sounded but the moment had called for it. Alfie believed strongly that he knew what it did, but he kept it to himself as the others might not agree with the obvious solution to this global problem.

'Okay Ryan,' Harry said, 'let's get you and your wee man to the University and save the bloody world.'

4

The night was drawing in, so they decided to get some valuable sleep before starting the zombie riot the following day. They hunkered down and did their best to forget the nightmare of reality. Neville took first watch, much to Alfie's concern, but his siblings reassured him that Neville, though a little simple, was still very vigilant as their Dad had taught him well. Alfie decided to keep his opinion that, had their Dad been so good at being vigilant, perhaps he would still be alive, but instead just nodded and smiled. Ryan was not taking any risks and the two brothers had, in private, agreed to watch each other's backs during the night as they had always done. They slept a little way back from the fire after deciding that if a stray flesh-eater happened to stroll into the tunnel, he would be drawn to the flames first, giving Ryan a chance to protect Alfie.

Two hours passed and Neville had nodded off to sleep. A scratching noise approached at a slow pace and the noise echoed gently off the tunnel walls. It gradually got louder and transformed into dragging and scratching followed by a moan. Neville shifted his body slightly but remained in the land of nod. The moaning was getting closer and still Neville didn't wake until it was too late. He screamed as the pain shot up his leg and immediately attempted to push the hungry attacker away. This just gave the creature something else to feast on and it sunk its rancid teeth into his fleshy forearm. Blood squirted out from either side of its mouth like an orange bursting in a juicer. Neville screamed again and Amanda and Harry ran over to his rescue. Ryan stayed back with Alfie. There could be more and, if there are, the others would be the perfect distraction. He hated feeling like this, but he had to think practically and not with his heart. 'Get off him ye bastard,' Amanda shouted. She used her crowbar and smashed the zombie in the head. It flew backwards taking a lump of Neville's flesh with it.

'Aaagh,' cried Neville as he held his open wound and sobbed violently from the pain and the knowledge that his life was over.

'Finish it,' Harry barked. Amanda lifted her crowbar in the air and brought it down on the snarling beast's cranium as hard as she could. The metal ruptured through bone and brain with pieces flying off in every direction.

'I think there's more of them coming,' Ryan joined them, and Alfie hid in the shadows, 'we'd better get going, this wasn't the way we wanted it but it looks like they'll be heading down here after all that noise'.

'What about me?' Neville cried holding up his arm.

'Sorry mate, but you know how it ends,' Ryan was cold but he had seen it so many times and he had no love loss for this useless idiot.

'Wait for a second friend, we canny leave 'im. He might be foolish but he's still our Brother,' Amanda pleaded.

'What about that thing you have? Canny we save him if we get to the University?' Harry looked desperately at Ryan hoping he had all the answers.

'Listen! I have no idea what this thing is or what it does. All I know is that right now they're coming, and he doesn't have long. He'll bleed out in a matter of minutes-' BANG, Neville slumped forward and presented a hole in the back of his head.

'Neville!' Screamed Amanda as her head darted from side to side looking for where the shot had come from. She spotted Alfie standing close by with his gun still held up, pointed in their direction.

'Put it down Alfie,' Ryan told him. Alfie dropped his hand to his side but held onto the gun.

'Ya wee psycho, what the hell did ya do?' Amanda started marching towards him.

'Stop!' Harry grabbed her and held her tight, 'he did the right thing,' even though he was angry at Alfie he knew that Ryan would kill them both if they went near him. They didn't have guns, so they didn't stand a chance. He also knew that this was a better end for Neville and at least he didn't have to do it.

'Alfie, what were you thinking?' Ryan was careful not to raise his voice too much but was annoyed all the same.

'He would have turned. We need to go. They're almost here,' Alfie stood calmly and waited for the others to make their move.

'I dinna get a chance to say goodbye,' Amanda barked holding back her tears.

'Would it have saved him?' Alfie asked moving his head slightly to the left absentmindedly.

'Of course not!' She shouted, her voice echoed down the tunnel and it was answered by blood-curdling screams that the four of them knew only too well.

'Then what's the point?' he really had become hardened to this post-apocalyptic hell they called life.

'Listen, Amanda, I'm sorry about Neville, I truly am. We've all lost someone and for most of us we've lost many, but right now is not the time to mourn. There is a crap ton of hungry zombies making their way towards us and if we don't go, then we're all screwed,' Ryan grabbed Alfie's hand and started to make his way out of the tunnel. 'Stay if you want but don't whine if you come with,' he called back.

'Come on,' Harry begged, 'we need to go. He's right we have to keep moving forward. That's what Dad would have wanted.'

'Fine but keep that wee creep away from me or I'll nah be able to control myself,' she kissed the palm of her hand and touched Neville on the shoulder, 'sorry Neville, I loved ya always ya silly get,' then they ran.

As Alfie had predicted the tunnel exit was clear, as was the rest of the track as far as they could see. They could hear the horde behind them snarling and groaning but they were out of sight and safe for now. Amanda kept back as they walked briskly towards the city centre and Ryan kept an eye on her. He didn't trust that she wouldn't try and get back at his brother and he could hardly blame her if she tried. Alfie had shocked even him with his cold attitude to killing his first living person, but everyone deals with such things differently, he just thought Alfie would have struggled over such a decision. Alfie trotted along as if he was on his way to the park, but inside he felt sick at having to kill Neville. Nevertheless, his conscience was clear. He didn't want to kill the stupid man but he knew if he didn't then someone else would have to and he knew that Ryan would eventually be the one to be burdened with yet another mercy kill. He didn't want him to go through it again, not when they were so close to ending it all. He decided to take the load this time, as Ryan was weighed down with enough guilt to crush a blue whale.

The small group made sure that every station they passed was scouted first and their luck was holding out because every one of them was abandoned, at least by the track. They passed through tunnels expecting the worst and were surprised every time to find them empty. Alfie had figured out that the zombies would generally stick together and only stray in desperation. He knew that had the tunnels been infested, they would have been able to hear them from a great distance as the sound would have echoed through. He decided to keep his calculations to himself as it seemed everyone was mad at him and he felt it was better just to stay quiet. Eventually, they arrived at the University train station and climbed up onto the platform. 'So, what now?' Amanda asked snappily.

'We go up. We don't have any other option,' Ryan looked at the sign that pointed to the exit, 'Alfie and I will scout ahead and come back for you.'

No way pal,' said Harry, 'we do this together as a team.'

'I agree,' Alfie eventually spoke.

'Me to,' Amanda agreed.

'Alright then. I guess we're all going,' Ryan headed cautiously towards the static escalator. The others followed, staying alert and checking all around them. They reached the top of the stairs and Ryan knelt, holding his hand in the air with the palm flat facing up. 'There are three station guards by the barriers just standing there, I'll get a little closer and see if there are any more.' Harry nodded and Ryan, staying low, snuck closer to the rotting railway workers. He could tell they'd recently fed as fresh blood dripped down their chins whilst they sniffed the air and hissed. He looked around and noticed the victim lying on the floor near the second staircase. She was torn to shreds but still twitching, this meant that she was turning so soon there would be four to deal with. He snuck back, 'there's one more about to turn at the bottom of the stairs, other than that it's all clear.'

'Amanda and I'll sort them, we can do it silent like,' Harry presented his iron bar and Amanda gripped her crowbar. Ryan shuffled aside to let them pass and watched carefully ready to help out if need be. They split up and approached the zombies from either side. Amanda whistled and the guards looked at her simultaneously. They tried to get to her but the barrier was blocking their way and they just walked into it like blind men. She walked close, in unison with Harry who was behind them, and together, like they had done it a hundred times, they swiftly ended the misery of these ex-humans. It was a sight to behold seeing such precision and Ryan was especially impressed with Amanda. She disposed of two of them with one blow each. Ryan shook off any feelings he was having and cleared his throat. Alfie stood up and hopped over the barrier. He turned his gun around and used the handle to smash the skull of the twitching woman. It took him several goes but eventually, she stopped moving. Amanda looked on and softened a little towards him. She knew all about the pain of taking a life and she couldn't imagine how hard it was for someone so young to be ruthless in this real-life horror film. She was also happy that at least she didn't have to finish off Neville as she had done her father. She'd promised him, sometime before, that she would do it but it had been the hardest thing she had ever done, so in all honesty, Alfie had done her a favour.

Ryan walked up behind her, 'he's seen it all you know. Before all of this, he was the sweetest kid. Nothing was ever too much trouble, the neighbours bloody loved him, everyone bloody loved him. I know somewhere inside him that innocent child is there, but who knows if I'll ever see it again.

'I'm sure you will. I dinnae blame him I just wish he'd let me say goodbye,' she looked at Ryan with glassy eyes.

'Sometimes that's even harder but I agree he shouldn't have done it. Please forgive him, he was just trying to help.

'I already have,' she smiled slightly and brushed her hand over her ear pushing her long dark hair behind it.

'Thank you,' Ryan said tenderly. He liked her a lot but continued to repress his feelings for the time being.

'Right, yous two, have you finished your therapy session because me and the wee man here would like to save the flipping world,' he held Alfie on the shoulder and gave him a slight shake for encouragement as he was also impressed with the way Alfie finished off the woman.

Ryan ignored the comment and walked over to the stairs, 'once we get to the top there's no going back,' there was a sign for the university on the wall pointing up, 'hopefully we don't have far to go but be prepared for anything and you won't be surprised,' he walked up the stairs with the group in his wake. The streets were packed, one zombie knocking into another with no space to move freely around. They were moaning and gnashing their teeth like hungry wild dogs. The strangest thing that came to Alfie's mind was that with so many different ethnicities it was nice to see that they were all getting along, so to speak. There was no judgment about each other's old selves, just a unity that sadly only death could bring. 'Right, any ideas guys?' Ryan asked desperately.

'Only one,' Harry without waiting for deliberation ran out and screamed at the top of his lungs, 'COME ON YA BUNCH OF JESSIES, TAKE A BITE IF YA THINK YA TOUGH ENOUGH,' his Scottish burr rang throughout the streets. He winked, blew a kiss to his sister and ran as a savage mass came tumbling towards him.

'No,' Amanda muffled through Ryan's hands over her mouth as he stopped them all from being a meal. She tried to struggle but Ryan's hold was firm, and she didn't want to run she just wanted to want to run.

94

'Go,' the gap was there and it wouldn't be for long so Ryan took the opportunity that Harry had possibly sacrificed himself for, and with each hand, he pulled the other two with him and made a break for the huge steps in front of the University entrance. They almost made it undetected but for a slow child that only had one arm and an almost chewed off leg. He hobbled after the others instinctively but failed to keep up. He fell to the ground and his leg broke away at the knee. He almost looked confused when he tried to stand and fell back down. If he wasn't a flesh consuming monster you might have felt bad for him. He tried again to stand but this time he saw shapes running for the steps and cried out in a deafening pitch. A few of the others stopped in their tracks and turned to face the noise. They also saw the small group and decided that three was better than the one they were after so they began making their way towards the steps.

'They've seen us. They're coming this way!' Alfie shouted in panic. Just then a zombie dressed in a postal uniform grabbed hold of Alfie, he screamed and Ryan jumped into action. The ex-postie snarled and bit down, but just as his teeth were about to dig into Alfie's flesh, Ryan pulled him off his little brother. The two of them wrestled on the ground, writhing around, Ryan desperately trying to avoid the biting and a scratching maniac. Amanda's crowbar made quick work of the zombie's head and Ryan fell back breathing heavily.

'No time for laying down ya Jessie,' she helped him to his feet and they all made a run for the University.

Ryan pulled the handle of the big wooden door, but it didn't budge, 'come on you piece of crap just open,' he pulled again but still, it refused to move.

'LET US IN!' yelled Amanda. She yanked on the handle and fell over backwards as it opened.

'Well done Amanda,' Alfie helped her up and they all ran inside just seconds before the zombies could get them. Ryan was last in and slammed the door shut.

'You might want to lock it so they don't get in,' long bony fingers held out a key and Ryan grabbed it, locking the door behind him. He looked up into the face of an old man. His hair was grey and his cheeks were gaunt, he had large saggy bags of loose skin underneath his eyes and his teeth were stained yellow and black. He wore a brown suit with a bowtie and a chequered red and white shirt which was worn away at the corner of the collar.

'Are you Dr Darwin?' Alfie asked his eyes wide and hopeful.

'Yes young man, and who might you be?' he smiled oddly.

'I'm Alfie and this is my Brother Ryan. The nice lady is Amanda and we came here to save the world although we don't know if we actually can, but we are hoping you can help us,' he stood up proudly and took a breath.

'Is that correct? Well pray tell exactly how are we going to do that,' his voice was posh velvet and Alfie thought he could be an excellent radio presenter.

'With this,' Ryan produced the vial from his pocket and showed it to the professor.

'Is that what I think it is? Oh my heavens it is, isn't it? No, it can't be, she would have brought it herself but that means, oh god no, no, no, no,' he dropped to the floor and sat with his head in his hands.

'She died getting this to you, she was so brave. I'm so very sorry,' Ryan put his hand on the old man's shoulder, 'we have come a long way so please tell me this isn't a load of rubbish, is this a cure?'

'No,' he muttered.

Ryan's face screwed up in anger, as did Amanda's, but Alfie's expression remained the same, 'It's a poison for the zombies,' he stated.

'What do you mean poison, Alfie?' Ryan almost yelled, 'how do you know what it is?'

'I figured it out before. There is no way anyone can come back from the dead, it's scientifically impossible. If it was to stop the apocalypse then it must finish off the ones who have turned, thereby stopping the virus from spreading any further,' they all looked over to the professor and he nodded.

'He's correct. You can't cure it you can only stop it. This poison is genetically designed using the mutated genome of the infected to work against itself and thereby destroy the body completely. Whatever is left of them will turn to pulp and they will simply biodegrade within a few hours. It won't affect us as our DNA has not altered in structure,' he held out his hand, 'I can make it but I need the sample.' Ryan handed him the vial and stood shell-shocked. The professor carefully placed it in his pocket and looked at Alfie, 'you remind me of my Son. He was very smart as well.'

'Yes, I am,' Alfie replied unfazed by the compliment.

'Follow me,' the Professor walked over to a set of stairs. All four of them made their way towards his lab, 'the place was abandoned not long after the outbreak, but the two of us remained here to work on a cure,' he explained as they walked through the grand corridors of the ancient building. 'When we discovered that there was no cure I began work on a super virus to battle the epidemic. She didn't agree with killing them all and ran off with my only sample. I couldn't recreate it because she destroyed all my work. I never blamed her, she was doing what she thought was right, but I always hoped she would change her mind and come back to me. She was my best friend you see and after she went, I was all alone. Just then a three-legged dog came trotting around the bend and barked, 'well except for Stubbs here,' Dr Darwin stopped and stroked the Jack Russell in between his ears. The little dogs tail wagged like crazy. Alfie loved dogs, but he had more important things to do than play with this one. 'The only thing that kept me going was the thought of her coming back, but now she's gone it's all a bit pointless.'

'Nah it's not Professor, the point is we're still alive and with ya help, we can save this planet and everything on it,' said Amanda.

'You're quite right young lady, all is not lost and if you're here maybe others survived as well,' he quickened his step and they were soon at the door to his lab, 'I could do with a hand,' he looked directly at Alfie.

No chance,' said Ryan standing in front of his little brother.

'Please Ryan, I'm very good at science. I can help,' he looked up at his older brother and opened his eyes as wide as he could.

'Oh fine, but I'll be right here,' he stood with his arms crossed and feet slightly apart.

'Thank you,' Alfie chirped, visibly excited by the prospect of being a real scientist. The professor and his new assistant entered the lab and Amanda put her arm around Ryan.

5

Two hours went by and still, the professor and Alfie worked away, running scenario tests and mixing various chemical compositions. Ryan and Amanda were sitting in the hallway on the floor with their backs against the wall trying to stay awake just in case they were needed at any point. Ryan spotted the tears trickle down her cheeks and wanted to comfort her, 'he'll be fine, he's a tough dude your Brother and brave. I wouldn't have baited those zombies like that,' he could see the worry in Amanda's face, she had already lost one brother today.

'So was my Dad, but they still got him,' she closed her eyes and bowed her head remembering her beloved father. Stubbs approached her cautiously and she patted him on the head, the dog immediately took a liking to her and snuggled up to her lap.

'Hopefully, this will put an end to it,' he looked up at the lab window, 'still, I never thought that the cure would be to kill everyone. I guess I hoped they'd be able to come back, but deep inside I knew it was impossible. I thought it might have been a vaccine for us but now I see that would be pointless too. There's too many of them and even if we were immune to the virus, we're not immune to blood loss.'

'Who's to say it isn't possible? This is just the solution we have now. There could be some scientist somewhere else in the world who has made an actual cure but there's no way of him or her communicating that to anyone else. We could be releasing this killer virus on those sick people and never giving them a chance to get better,' she looked up at him with her wide brown eyes that glinted from the reflection of the fluorescent ceiling lights.

'It wouldn't matter. Most of them wouldn't survive even if they were cured, as Alfie said, you can't cure death. I tend to believe pretty much everything he says. I don't love it but I also don't want to be one of those things,' he put his arm around her and she snuggled up against him. They sat in silence eventually falling asleep in each other's embrace.

6

'We did it,' Alfie burst into the corridor yelling. The two asleep on the floor woke with a start and Stubbs barked in surprise.

Ryan jumped to his feet, 'Damn it, Alfie! You scared the crap out of me,' Ryan was shaking.

'Sorry Ryan, but we've done it. We have replicated the virus successfully to a stable state in which it can be functionally distributed to the living dead population. The sample we had would never have killed them, but this will.'

'That all sounds great Alfie, but does that mean they will all die out?'

'Maybe, eventually,' Alfie shuffled from one foot to another impatiently.

'What do you mean "eventually"?' asked Amanda.

'Well, it's a virus that will spread through their populace just as the original virus spread. So, it will take some time for it to pass around, and in some cases, it might never reach some of them. So, at its best it will greatly reduce the numbers which will give us a huge chance of survival,' Alfie monologued.

'So, after all of that, it's still not over?' Ryan punched the wall in frustration.

'Come on Ryan that's not helping. Alfie's right, at least there'll be a lot less of them and all we have to do is stay in London. Any of them roaming near here will catch the virus and die. So, we're safe here,' Amanda patted Alfie on his back. Was it really over? Could they start thinking about building a new life for themselves? The three of them walked along the corridor and over to the window overlooking the street. Below the zombies had swarmed around the building with barely an inch between them. This would spread through them like wildfire, and it wouldn't be too long before they had a whole new problem on their hands, what the hell were they going to do with all the mess?

Ryan felt a tug on his jacket sleeve, 'look Ryan,' Alfie pointed out of the nearest window. He looked and saw what Alfie was pointing at. A figure was waving his arms around from the top of the building opposite and he was unmistakably recognisable.

'Hey Amanda, your Brother's saying hi,' Ryan grabbed her and they hugged. They had a new world to build and this was just the start. He tightened his arms around her and thought about how he hadn't felt this happy for a long time.

Amanda gasped and pulled away from him, 'oh Ryan, no'.

'What?' he asked.

'Your back, you've got a scratch on your back,' her eyes went glassy.

'Wait, no. That's not...' then he remembered the scuffle just before they got to the door. He hadn't felt the scratch but his adrenaline was high and he was focused on his task.

Alfie ran over to take a look, 'she's right Ryan,' his eyes too, glassed over.

'I'm so sorry little dude,' Ryan took his brothers' hands and looked him in the eyes. 'You're going to have to do this without me, Alfie.'

'No,' Alfie's tears streamed down his cheeks coming to a rest on his chin.

'We almost made it, but at least I'm gonna die saving the world and most importantly you, little dude,' he was being brave but inside he was screaming. He had come so far only to fall at the last hurdle. Who would protect his little brother now? He was angrier at the thought of Alfie being alone than the thought of himself dying.

'Dinnae worry, I'll look after him,' it was as if Amanda had read his mind.

He smiled and nodded.

'What now?' Amanda's eyes darted towards Ryan's gun.

'I'll do it,' Alfie sobbed.

'No way little dude, this one's on me,' Ryan knew he could never ask Alfie to live with it and Amanda was already destroyed because of having to end her own father.

'I feel it,' Ryan twitched, he felt hot and sweaty, like he had just eaten a spicy curry. He realised he hadn't been feeling well for a while but had put it down to anxiety and exhaustion, 'I've got to go,' he knelt and he and Alfie hugged one last time.

'I'll show you to a room', Dr Darwin said solemnly. He gestured towards a door at the end of the hallway. Ryan began to walk, but his sleeve was caught on something. He looked down to find Alfie gripping him tightly.

'Don't go, please don't go', Alfie's cheeks were red and blotchy.

'I love you so much Alfie, I know you can do this without me. You are so strong, they all need you,' Ryan looked at the others. Alfie let go and dropped to the ground, Amanda sat beside him. Ryan continued towards the room pointed out by the Professor. Every step was heavy, every second was like a minute. He didn't look back; he couldn't look back. He entered the room and closed the door behind him.

While Alfie sat on the floor, Stubbs pushed himself under his armpit. He held the dog loosely, then he heard the bang of the gun, he tightened his grip on the cuddly canine, who despite its discomfort, did not pull away. Alfie new this world was on the mend, but his life was never going to be the same.

103

Alfie found himself back in the real world. He knew Ryan was gone, but for some reason, his heart hurt a little less. Stubbs stroked him on the shoulder, 'how do you feel?'

'Sad, but not as sad as before.'

'What did you say baby? I didn't catch that,' Alfie looked up at his mother and Carol stared back at him with love in her eyes.

'Oh, nothing Mummy', he didn't want to upset her by telling her about Stubbs.

'Where do you go baby? It's like you're in another world,' she gently stroked his hair away from his eyes.

'I was saving the world with Ryan,' Alfie whispered.

Carol was so pleased he had said something that it almost didn't register what he actually said, 'did you do it? Did you save the world sweetheart?'

'Yes,' he answered bluntly, then closed his eyes and drifted off to sleep. Carol's arm ached from being in the same position for too long. She gently lay him down and then lay beside him. She couldn't face going downstairs to Gary, so instead just fell asleep next to Alfie.

Chapter 6

'I think it's about time he went back to school,' Gary said before stuffing his mouth full of bacon. 'It's not good to let him mope in his room all day.'

'It's only been a week; I don't think he's ready. He still isn't saying much and he just sits in his room, playing with his Lego and reading,' Carol opened the fridge and peered inside looking for something to eat.

'My Mum says we need to be tougher on him and we shouldn't wrap him in cotton wool all the time. She says we are the reason he's acting up all the time and you in particular need to be tougher on him,' bits of egg spattered out of his mouth when he spoke and Carol cringed. Everything he did lately annoyed her. It was like she had been blind to all his flaws, or had just ignored them for the sake of her own sanity, but now her eyes had been opened and there was no way back.

'Your Mum knows as much about bringing up Alfie as you know about the theory of relativity,' Carol said abruptly. Even she couldn't believe she'd just said that but she was reaching her limit with this buffoon and she wasn't going to be put down any more. Keith had spoken to her on the phone and apologised again for the other day. He also told her that he'd looked into Alfie's behaviour and believed that he was showing all the signs of Autism. She'd called Mrs Honeywell and had a lengthy conversation about what was best for him. Mrs Honeywell had been a breath of fresh air for Carol and it felt good to have some people on her side for once. This did a huge amount for her self-confidence and she'd, later that day, called the doctor and booked an appointment behind Gary's back. She would get Alfie the help he needed and screw Gary if he didn't want to be part of it.

'My Mum did a good job with me so she obviously knows how to bring up kids,' Gary cringed at his rash come-back, knowing he wasn't exactly the best man he could be. He had always struggled to communicate with those around him and often let his temper get the better of him.

'Whatever, Gary. I'm taking Alfie to the park today so if you could please make yourself useful and do the gardening that would be great. Those weeds are strangling the roses so unless you want a garden full of weeds, I suggest you start there,' her voice had a new tone of authority that made Gary nervous.

'Alright, I'll get it done,' he loved her with all his heart but was useless at showing it. Their marriage was on a knifes edge and he felt it. Alfie appeared at the doorway and whispered something to himself. He laughed and entered the room. 'What's so bloody funny?' Gary took his frustrations out on his son.

Alfie ignored him and sat in his usual seat opposite his dad. He stared blankly at the table until Carol spoke, 'would you like some cereal Alfie?' He nodded and smiled at her then looked back at the table, 'which one would you like baby?'

'Please may I have the sugary puffs in my bowl?' he didn't raise his head but at least he spoke.

'For Christ's sake Alfie, just look at your Mum! You're being rude,' Gary snapped, his fists banged down hard on the table which made Alfie flinch.

'Shut up Gary! Don't you realise he can't? he's not rude, he's ill,' Carol wished she could take it back but the words just spilt out of her like water from an overflowing sink.

Alfie jumped up and pushed his chair behind him, 'I'M NOT ILL, I'M DIFFERENT,' he ran out of the kitchen and up the stairs to his room, slamming the door behind him.

'See what you made me do,' she lambasted Gary who was staring blankly at her with the look of a deer in headlights. 'Just when I get him to take a step forward, you push him two steps back.'

'What do you mean he's ill? Is he sick or something? Is that what you're saying?'

'No, Gary, I mean he might have a disorder. He's doesn't act like the other kids no matter what your Mother says,' her voice was bitter when she mentioned his mother,

'I'm taking him to the doctor to find out what they think. To hell with you if you won't support me with this,' Carol was shaking all over, she hated losing control like this with him. She hated that he brought out the worst in her. She too felt their marriage crumbling, but right now it was about her little boy who needed her help, not about her useless husband and his failings as a father.

'I don't want to lose another son,' Gary mumbled, his forehead crumpled in frustration

'What?' Carol asked incredulously.

'If there is something wrong with him, I want to know, I can't lose another Son,' Gary looked at his wife, 'I know he needs help, I just hoped he would eventually get better, but your right we need to take him to the doctor.'

Carol couldn't believe it, was he actually showing an ounce of caring? 'Let me speak to him and I'll take him. He's calm around me lately so you just get on with the gardening and we'll talk later,' he nodded. 'Also, if you really want to help him, stop telling him off. It doesn't help him and all it does is make him hate you.'

'I know, I know. I just can't stop myself, he's so frustrating.'

'You need to sort that out yourself, I can't help both of you. He's just a little boy Gary, you're a grown man,' he nodded and she went after Alfie. Gary continued eating his breakfast and a little butterfly of hope snuggled in his stomach. Carol knocked on Alfie's door gently so as not to upset him further, 'I'm sorry baby, I didn't mean that you're not normal. You are normal, you just act a little differently sometimes that's all,' she touched the door with the palm of her hand.

Alfie opened the door, 'I'm not normal though, am I? All the kids at school think I'm weird but it's not my fault! I'm just smarter than them,' he sat on the floor and crossed his arms. Monty darted in and jumped on his bed. He walked around in a circle and did something with his paws that Alfie thought looked like he was making dough, before settling down on Alfie's pillow, his tail wrapped around him, his face content.

'You're definitely smarter than them Alfie, in fact, you're the smartest person I know. You know so many facts that most of the time I can't keep up, but I try my best and sometimes you teach me so much,' she sat down next to him.

'Did you know that big cats share less DNA with small domestic cats than we share with a gorilla?' Alfie asked, looking over at Monty.

'No, I didn't,' she smiled.

'Even though we know this to be a fact, some religious people still won't accept that we are apes, even though they have no problem accepting that a tiger and Monty are both felines,' he rolled his eyes like an impatient teacher.

'Why do you think that is?' she had become intrigued, but also understood that letting him talk at her was his way of self regulating.

'Brainwashing and a lack of interest in the truth, due to the fact that it shows their storybooks to be wrong on almost everything. It's called cognitive dissonance,' he stated confidently.

'How sad that they would rather live in a bubble of fantasy than accept the world for all its natural beauty and wonder,' she didn't necessarily believe this, but loved that they were bonding.

'That's what I always say to Ryan,' he stopped.

'It's okay to be sad Baby, we all miss him but I know you miss him the most,' she shuffled closer to him and held his hands in hers.

'He never saw the dragon I made for him, he was supposed to see it,' his eyes became red and welled up with tears.

'I know Baby, I'm sorry,' she wanted to tell him that it was her fault he went off that night but she couldn't face letting him down, not now they were finally bonding. What good would it do anyway?

'It's not your fault Mummy, sometimes bad things happen,' she couldn't believe how mature he could be. Such an adult head on this young child's shoulders, it broke her heart to think people treated him so badly.

'Will you come to the doctor with me so you can tell her some of your facts?' she asked gently still holding his hands.

'Okay Mummy, if you think it will help. I wonder if she knows about high oxytocin levels in dogs when they see their owners? Not a lot of people know about that,' he pulled away from her and began getting dressed.

'I think she'll love that fact Sweetheart. We're leaving in about an hour so when your dressed, come down and I'll make you your cereal. Is that ok?' she was really getting the hang of speaking with him but still felt anxious.

'Okay Mummy,' he continued to dress. Carol went back downstairs and began making Alfie's breakfast. She noticed, to her surprise and delight, that Gary was already in the garden and his plate had been washed up and put away. She felt a warm glow and hummed a happy tune to herself as she poured the cereal into the correct bowl. Maybe this was a sign things could get better? She could only hope.

Chapter 7

An hour and a half later Alfie was sitting in the doctor's
waiting room. It smelled musty and the walls were painted half
cream and half dark green. All the chairs were an identical deep
shade of crimson red except for one which was the same as the
others but had specks of paint on it. Alfie made sure to avoid this
one but couldn't shake off the feeling of how annoying the specks
were. He was reading an article in a magazine that was about
two years out of date. He had already read all the health
awareness posters on the walls and notice board and was sure
he was not suffering from lice or a sexually transmitted disease.
As he read, he wondered why they couldn't replace them
monthly. He concluded that not everyone cared about reading as
much as he did. This didn't surprise him but only made him feel
more alone in the world. As he read a piece about nuclear fusion
and its effect on the global economy his mummy sat next to him,
waiting anxiously.

'Isn't that a bit too grown-up for you?' remarked a woman
sitting opposite them. She was middle-aged and wearing a thick

blue coat with giant wooden buttons. Her handbag sat on her lap and she held it like it was her child.

'Intelligence isn't defined by age, it's defined by one's thirst for knowledge,' he replied without looking up.

'Well, aren't you the little professor,' she said it with a gentle tone but Carol could hear the hint of sarcasm.

'Thank you,' He said, oblivious to her rudeness. Carol was about to say something when the loudspeaker barked out Alfie's name.

'Alfie Fenix, Alfie Fenix to room five,' Alfie and Carol both stood at the same time and he held her hand as they walked to the room. Carol gave the women a dirty look before knocking on the door.

'Come in,' said a feminine voice that had a foreign tang to it. They entered together. 'Hello, I'm Doctor Fossil, you must be Alfie,' she looked directly at him and he turned his head to one side to avoid her stare.

'Yes, I like your name,' he said, 'my favourite fossil is an Ammonite, David Attenborough also loves them because it was the first fossil he ever found. I have never found one but I have one that Ryan bought me when I went to Charles Darwin's house. It is an English Heritage site near Kent and Ryan got a membership for us so we could go back. I have been there five times but they don't sell the Darwin evolved fish t-shirts because they don't want to upset Christians. Ryan doesn't care about that and he wore one last time we were there and I also wore one. Mine is red and Ryan's is green but he died so we can't wear them anymore.'

Unfazed by Alfie's monologue the doctor replied, 'I'm so sorry to hear that, he sounds like an amazing Brother. I have a Brother and I'll be honest with you Alfie he isn't half as good as Ryan sounds.'

'But he is alive, so that's better,' Alfie pointed out the obvious and thought the doctor wasn't very clever for not realising it.

'Perhaps, but that's for you to decide,' she had her work cut out for her but she was up for the challenge.

'This is my Mummy, her name is Carol,' Alfie introduced his mummy to the doctor because that's what polite people did.

'Hello,' Carol said.

'Hello Mrs Fenix, please take a seat and we can get started.'

'Please may I have this one Mummy? I don't like that one because it's brown.'

'Of course Baby, I'll sit on it and you sit on the green one,' Carol was beginning to understand the way his brain worked.

'Thank you, Mummy,' he sat down and stared at the picture of a boat in a storm behind Doctor Fossil. He started analysing what the Doctor had said about her brother. Then he started thinking about Ryan. His eyes started to sting and his stomach ached. He knew the Doctor had asked him something but couldn't concentrate on her words, his mind had slipped away from the conversation.

'Alfie,' Stubbs appeared on his shoulder.

'Hi Stubbs, where have you been?'

'Here, just very quiet,' he answered, 'can we go on an adventure?'

'Not now Stubbs. I need to speak to the Doctor so I can get better for Mummy.'

'But I love how you are; you're the best imaginer in the world, Alfie! Why would you want to change that?'

'Don't worry Stubbs I'll still go on adventures I just don't want to make Mummy sad, that's all.'

'It will make you feel better and we won't be long.' Alfie tried to stay focused but the pain in his stomach and the desperate need to escape at that moment was too much to ignore.

'Alfie, why are you whispering to yourself?' Doctor Fossil asked softly. Alfie stared blankly at the painting, wondering what was going to happen to the ship. It did look as though it was in a lot of trouble. 'May I ask you a few questions Alfie?' the doctor leaned forward, trying to catch his attention.

Carol had seen that look on Alfie's face before and she sighed, 'I don't think you'll get through to him Doctor. Sometimes he just drifts off if he gets distracted or upset,' she stroked his head but he kept staring at the painting.

'Not to worry, Mrs Fenix. We can chat for a bit and if Alfie feels that he wants to join in he can.'

The secret Captain

1

Alfie wiped the water from his face and as calmly as possible took in his surroundings. The ship was in real trouble, the mast was on its last legs and half the crew had been lost to the sea. The storm continued to smash into them with the ferociousness of a stampeding elephant, but still, Captain Alfie managed to hold onto the wheel.

'Captain! We can't take much more of this!' Stubbs shouted across the howling wind.

'We haven't got a choice, we just have to ride it out and hope that Poseidon doesn't take us!' he called back. Before he knew what had hit him, he found himself in the open sea. The waves crashed over him dragging him down under the water. He gasped for breath every time he resurfaced but was forced back down below over and over until he remembered no more.

He woke when a crab had decided to use him as shelter from the baking sun. It had tickled his nose as it brushed against it. He slowly raised his head which was caked in sand and spat out the granules from his mouth. The crab didn't take too kindly to being spat at and scuttled off as if in a bad mood, but really just fearing for its life. Alfie looked around from his flat position and saw he was on a huge beach that stretched both ways as far as he could see. In front of him was a forest or jungle, he couldn't tell from this angle, and behind him was the cruel sea which had taken him from his beloved ship The Curious Englishman. He had been the Captain of the exploration vessel for over two years and knew and respected every man that was under his command. He grieved inside for the loss he had suffered and cursed the sea God for taking them. He rolled over onto his back and was immediately blinded by the bright sun, forcing itself upon him through the cloudless sky. It was as if the storm had never happened; a beautiful day after such a terrible night. He didn't know what caused storms or how to avoid them, he just knew that if you're caught in one you batten down the hatches and ride it out as best you can. It's not like it was his first storm, but it was without a doubt the worst.

"Where the hell am I?" he thought to himself. His mouth was as dry as the sand he sat upon. He forced himself into an upright sitting position and looked out over the sea. The water was as calm as the sky but there was no sign of his ship or any other survivors. He got to his feet a little shakily but other than a headache probably from the heat, he was unharmed. He thanked whatever God was listening, if any even cared, and made his way towards the jungle. He could see it was a jungle now and wished it had been a forest. Jungles are denser and notoriously harder to navigate through, especially when you have no clue as to which direction you're supposed to be heading. He climbed over some huge roots and pushed aside leaves that were bigger than he was. He lost his footing regularly and swore every time he did. Eventually, he couldn't take the struggle any longer and was relieved to come to a clearing by a stream. He dropped to his knees and scooped his hands in the water, consuming gulp after gulp until his stomach felt like it was about to burst. He then fell back against the roots of an enormous tree.

'That's how you make yourself sick if you're not careful boy,' a brusque voice said behind him.

Alfie stood with a start and grabbed at his hip for the pistol that wasn't there, 'who are you and why are you sneaking up on me?'

'One question at a time boy. I'm Ryan Cook but my friends just call me Cookie. Who might you be?' he appeared from the dense bushes like a ghost through a wall. He was a slim built, but strong-looking man, who had the gait of a sailor and the face of weathered rock. Alfie guessed that he was in his late fifties.

'My name is Alfie,' he trembled, but only slightly, 'I was thrown overboard when the storm hit last night and I woke up on the beach,' he decided against telling this stranger that he was the Captain as it meant that he was wealthy and that could be a bad thing, especially with pirates possibly around.

'Well, that sounds like bad luck if I ever heard it. I work on a ship that's anchored not far from here. Follow me boy and I'll see you fed and looked after,' Cookie didn't wait for an answer he just disappeared into the jungle and Alfie momentarily hesitated, then his stomach rumbled at the thought of food and he darted after his new acquaintance. He dodged and weaved through the almost impenetrable mass of wood and leaves that blocked his way but never again lost sight of Cookie. He was determined to find his way off this island if that was what he was on. Eventually, he came to a clearing and noticed that Cookie had stopped dead in his tracks. He cautiously approached and peered over his left shoulder, 'what is it?' he asked.

Cookie didn't answer, he just pointed ahead then put a finger to his lips. Alfie looked more carefully and his body went cold. His fingers trembled and beads of sweat began to escape his brow. The two men stepped backwards very slowly making sure they made as little sound as possible. The huge black bear was busy eating something that evaded their gaze and they couldn't care less what it was as long as they weren't next. It just so happened that it was the first mate of The Curious Englishman, a man named Frances Higgs also known as Stubbs due to his missing hand. He had been Alfie's closest friend and confidant for many years and Alfie had been fortunate not to see how he'd met his end. They reached the edge of the jungle and slipped back inside. Once in cover, they peered out to confirm they hadn't been spotted. They had been lucky, they continued their journey this time avoiding the clearing and making a large detour around it. 'That was close,' Alfie said breathlessly.

116

'You don't say,' Cookie replied sarcastically. Alfie looked at him blankly but Cookie didn't notice as he was too busy trying to remember the way back to the ship, 'bloody bear, stupid thing got me all turned around and lost. What the hell am I going to do now? The Captain is going to tear me a new one if I ever get back...' his voice trailed off somewhat due to losing concentration but mainly because he disappeared off the edge of the cliff he had failed to notice. Alfie, having seen Cookie disappear, skidded to a halt and peered over the drop. It wasn't that far to the bottom but far enough to cause Cookie some discomfort as he bounced down the side knocking into rocks and shrubbery. When he did reach the bottom, he did it with a thud as his backside collided solidly with sand just inches away from some seriously jagged rocks, 'crap, that was too close!' he tried to stand but his leg was in a bad way.

'Are you okay?' called Alfie, carefully leaning over so he could see Cookie. As soon as he said it he knew it was a dumb question but he couldn't take it back. A tirade of abuse was hurled back at him with the occasional "boy" remark thrown in for good measure until the old sailor had tired himself out. By this time, Alfie had begun to vigilantly climb down using various branches and rocks, the same that bashed the body of Cookie, to aid his steady descent. He reached the bottom slightly less dramatic than his new companion and approached the moaning man.

'Took your bloody time didn't you,' Alfie didn't understand the statement. He decided to ignore it and just help Cookie to his feet. Alfie wasn't a small man by any means and most people would describe him as a "strapping young man". He had heard people say, "you wouldn't want to mess with him down a dark alley" which was strange to Alfie because he wondered why being in a dark alley would be different from being in a light alley, but he decided to ignore this whenever it was said. 'My ship isn't far. Will you be able to carry me?' Alfie nodded and the two of them headed off.

2

'There be something coming down the beach Cap'n. It looks like two men, one carryin' the other,' Wiggin snarled and rubbed his sore leg.

Captain "Ginger Beard" Savage picked up the telescope that his dying father had given to him before he left Scotland and peered through it. He was quite shocked to see his first mate being carried over the shoulder of a large, young man both looking the worse for wear, 'damn it you lazy dogs,' he shouted at some men that were unlucky enough to be within listening distance, 'get down there and help them or do you all want to be swimming with Davey Jones tonight?' they did not want to be swimming with anyone that night so all four of them disembarked into a small boat and rowed towards Alfie and Cookie.

The "isn't far" part of Cookie's statement had been a gross understatement and it turned out to be a little more than two miles that Alfie had to carry him. He was so relieved when he saw the ship in the distance and the men rowing to presumably help. He lay Cookie down and fell to his knees gasping for breath and dying for some water. 'There's a beautiful sight if I ever did see one, eh boy?' Alfie nodded guessing that he meant the ship. She wasn't the biggest he had seen but it was certainly intimidating. Her wood was dark brown oak and the sails were as black as the night is dark. The rails had spikes sporadically placed on them around her edge and the figurehead at her bow was a strange creature with the body of an octopus and the head of a lion. Its tentacles clung to the sides of the ship as though it was going to drag her to the depths of the ocean. 'Come on boys I haven't got all day,' he called out to the men, who had reached the sand and were now galloping towards them. Alfie noted that he also called these men boys so was suddenly less offended by the terminology. The men reached them simultaneously and three of them picked up Cookie and the other helped Alfie to his feet. No words were spoken as they made their way along the stretch of beach to the rowboat but silent respect hung in the air between the pirates and Alfie, the secret captain of a lost ship.

They climbed in and Alfie sat next to Cookie who was beginning to look very pale, 'you look awful,' he pointed out.

'Why thank you, boy, you look like warmed up seaweed,' Cookie chuckled but grimaced as his ribs were surely broken.

'You're probably right, but at least I never decided to go cliff diving without a rope,' Alfie smiled.

'Stop it ya begger, you'll make me laugh again,' the other pirates looked incredulously at each other. They'd never heard Cookie joke around before, not even with the captain and they were inseparable. They kept their heads down and rowed. They didn't want to annoy Cookie, they knew what he was like when he was angry and none of them wanted to experience that again. Even in his wounded state, they believed he could kill them without even breaking a sweat. Blissfully unaware of the danger he was putting himself in, Alfie smiled. Mainly because he was alive, which was lucky enough but also as he was about to be rescued and all in the space of one afternoon. He couldn't believe his fortune. Nevertheless, fortunes change and this one was about to do just that. As the rowboat pulled up to the ship, Alfie could see her in all her glory. She looked as though she had seen been in quite a few battles, with war-torn wood and sails that had patches sewn to them to cover what Alfie guest were canon ball holes. But despite these things, She was immaculately kept. Alfie thought how disciplined and organised the crew must be to keep her in such good shape.

Captain Savage greeted them as they climbed aboard the ship. He eyed Alfie suspiciously before embracing his friend with a quick hug and a tap on the shoulder, 'good to see you Cookie. You had me worried for a bit.'

'Get lost ya, washerwoman,' Cookie growled, 'I was only gone for a day, no need for soppy stuff.'

'You disappeared from the landing party. We searched for hours and couldn't find you. Where were you? What happened?' the captain frowned as Cookie was being blasé.

'I got lost following a small bird through the trees. I thought if I could capture it, it'd be worth a pretty penny. But alas it escaped my grasp and when I turned around to look for ye, ye were all gone,' he looked over to Alfie, 'I was wandering around for hours until I found my way again and that's when I met young Alfie here and I'm damn glad I did. I fell a fair height on the way back to the ship and this one carried me the rest of the way,' he put his left arm around Alfie's shoulders and shook him gently.

'Nice to meet you, Alfie. I am Captain Savage. Thank you for dragging my first mate back to me,' he extended his hand. Alfie shook it. He looked the captain up and down. He was a tall, slim built man with classically handsome features and was, Alfie thought, an extremely preened man for a sailor. Most sailors he had met were as rough as the sea when the winds were at their worst. He had a neatly trimmed ginger beard and the ends of his moustache curled ever so slightly. His eyes were piercing green and his teeth were unusually white. He dressed in a navy-blue coat with gold oversized buttons. Underneath he had a white shirt with modest frills on the collar and cuffs. His trousers and boots were black and his hat was large and almost comically over the top. He almost looked like a storybook version of a captain.

'It is I that must thank Cookie. If he hadn't come along when he did, who knows where I'd be now,' Alfie said.

'Stuck on the bloody island still, that's where you'd be,' Cookie laughed, then Alfie joined in. The captain stared at the two of them while smiling, but secretly inside he burned with jealous rage.

'Come now lads, it's getting late and no doubt you built up quite an appetite,' the captain turned and solemnly headed towards his cabin, 'will you please join me and Cookie for dinner Alfie?' he said through gritted teeth.

'I'd love to,' Alfie replied, still blissfully unaware of the type of ship he was on and the type of people with whom he was now conversing.

'I'd eat all the tentacles of a giant squid and still be hungry for its babies,' Cookie claimed.

'So, you're hungry then?' Joked Alfie.

'Like a bear before winter,' Cookie answered and winked. The captain was getting more and more enraged as the two of them joked and laughed. Cookie was his closest friend and he could never get him to joke around. It was as if this stranger had put some sort of a spell on his first mate and he was not going to rest until he found out all there was to know about this so-called Alfie. He opened his cabin door and stepped inside. The two men followed and closed it behind them. The moment the lock clicked, the ship erupted with chatter. All the men were speaking amongst themselves about who this man was and why he was on the island in the first place. However, the strangest of things they wondered was why Cookie had suddenly changed so much around him. What had happened in the jungle and what would the captain think of this new friendship? Some believed that the stranger was a spirit and he was here to lay judgement upon them for their pirating sins, whilst others believed Alfie was a merman who had grown legs and was trying to pass himself off as human. Other nonsensical theories were suggested, all as ludicrous as the one before, but all had one thing in common, that Cookie was under a spell and Alfie wasn't who he said he was.

Inside, the captain's mess was cramped but rather eloquently decorated. It was nicer than his own captain's mess and Alfie wondered who this Captain Savage was and why did he present himself so finely? His movements were flamboyant and out of character with his crew and he had an odd gate when he walked which was almost feminine. They all sat down, the captain at the head of the table, Alfie and Cookie on either side. The food was laid out before them by the hunch back cook, who kept his head down and never looked any of them in the eye. Alfie had never seen such a feast. Even as a captain himself he'd never been treated to such rare delicacies such as dodo bird and shark fin soup. He had to admit that they weren't any tastier than chicken and beef soup, but he kept his mouth shut and just enjoyed the fact that he was being treated with such honour.

'So how did you end up on the island?' the Captain enquired as he poured some more wine into Alfie's cup, 'Or did you just sprout out of the ground?'

'He was thrown overboard during the storm last night. We were lucky to be on the other side of the island and only got tickled by it,' Cookie butted in.

'It was hardly a tickle Cookie,' the captain argued, 'we very nearly became grounded on the sharp rocks out near the cliffs. Two of our men died when they were tossed from the mast trying to keep the sails from flying away.'

'And I'm eternally grateful to the scum, but the rest of us are still here so no need for whining,' Cookie scowled and downed his wine. This was a tough beast who wasn't easily moved, thought Alfie. Even he was surprised that a man this heartless and grim could act so differently to him. He had noticed the strange looks from the crew and, even more worryingly, the evil stares from Captain Savage. He wished that Cookie would stop being so friendly, but he certainly wasn't going to tell him.

'You didn't answer my question,' the captain rested his wine glass on the table and calmly, but intensely, stared at Alfie.

'As Cookie said, I fell overboard during the storm,' Alfie avoided eye contact and looked down at his plate.

'What sort of ship was it?' The captain continued his enquiry as he cut deep into a slice of the dodo. His huge knife, not usually meant for a sophisticated dinner, scraped on the plate and sent a chill down Alfie's spine.

'An exploration vessel. Our task was to carry out scientific discoveries of new animal species to broaden our knowledge of all God's creatures,' Alfie looked the captain straight in the eyes this time, to show he was not going to be intimidated, 'I am a collector you see. My passion is butterflies, but I'm partial to the odd beetle or mollusc.'

'Fascinating,' the Captain replied seemingly satisfied with Alfie's answer, at least for the time being. 'So, you are the only survivor,' it was a statement rather than a question. He used his thumb and forefingers to fiddle with the ends of his moustache, thoughtfully rolling the hair between them, curling it even more.

'I don't hold out much hope for the others, but if we could possibly look tomorrow, I would forever be in your debt.'

'We went all over that island and never saw another person, if we had, they would be here with us. I'm sorry but it would be a waste of our time.' Alfie looked at him confusedly. Why would he not even try and look? Just because they didn't find anyone, doesn't mean there is no one. There was tension building in the air and all three of them could feel it.

'So, your job is collecting bugs?' Cookie asked to help move the conversation along and break the tension. He poured more wine for himself and Alfie.

'In a sense, yes,' Alfie could see what Cookie was doing and decided to go with it.

'I collect birds. Live if possible but dead ones are good too. The brighter the better if you ask me. Some are worth good money to the right people, but most I keep for meself,' Cookie was visibly excited and Alfie could see a childlike quality in him, that was otherwise deeply suppressed.

'Why do you think God made all those animals?' the captain growled under his breath.

'Pardon,' Alfie gawped and almost spilt the wine he was about to drink.

Cookie burst into laughter, 'Don't mind him, he doesn't believe in no god but the god of the sea and, even then, he's as sceptical as a man buying booze from a drunk.'

'If there's a God above, he's not a friendly one,' Captain Savage smiled without humour and gave him a dead-eye stare. He was hoping Alfie would argue with him. Angry men find it harder to lie.

'Opinions are like mouths,' Alfie said, 'everyone's got one and not everyone knows how to use it,' this had Cookie and the captain laughing out loud this time and Alfie breathed a sigh of relief that this was the reaction and not a knife to the throat. The mood was lighter after that and even the captain, who was also interested in birds, became more relaxed around the stranger they called Alfie. He never let his guard down and would occasionally try to catch Alfie out, but the young man was sharp

of mind and never let himself be tricked despite the copious
amount of wine they consumed.

3

Alfie opened his eyes and blinked profusely. The sun was blinding him and his mouth was dry. He could hear the sound of water lapping against the wood and feel the ground he lay on move from side to side. The sky also moved from side to side and this combination had only one outcome; Alfie stood up unsteadily, then wobbled over to the side of the ship. He looked down at the steady waves brushing the base of the ship, then vomited into the crystal-clearwater.

'Better out than in,' Cookie slapped him on the back.

'Better to not be hungover in the first place,' Alfie grumbled as he wiped his mouth on his sleeve.

'Come on you big baby. You hardly drank anything.'

'Two bottles of wine each is hardly nothing,' Alfie couldn't believe Cookie wasn't even looking slightly worse for wear, then again, this was one tough begger.

'We're on our way to the next island, hopefully, this one will have some reward for our hard work.

'What sort of reward. You mean some specimens?'

'More like some treasure, me boy,' he smiled and looked up. Alfie followed his gaze and almost choked when he saw the flag flying from the mast. It was black with a white skull and two sabre swords crossed behind it. It was the unmistakable symbol of a pirate ship and Alfie couldn't believe this was the first time he was seeing it.

'You're pirates!?' he blurted out.

'To be sure, to be sure,' Cookie croaked and grinned from ear to ear. Alfie took in his surroundings with a fresh perspective and saw things very differently. He noticed that all the crew carried swords tucked into their belts and not one of them wore a uniform or looked as though they'd washed for some time. Some had eye patches, some had wooden legs and some had both. One particularly hefty fellow even had a hook instead of a hand. Apart from their outward appearance they carried out their duties like any ordinary ship's crew; professional and very well organised.

'Does that bother you?' Captain Savage walked menacingly down the steps from the ship's wheel. He was still dressed in black, tight-fitting boots and trousers but had changed into a black baggy shirt under a knee-length grass-green coat that flapped at his sides in the wind. His head was bare and his long ginger hair was tied onto a ponytail.

'Not at all,' Alfie lied confidently. He felt so dirty compared to this perfectly kept man and wished he could wash and change immediately.

'Good, I would hate to have to make you walk the plank,' it sounded like a joke but his face was deadly serious.

'Give over,' Cookie interrupted, 'we don't even have a plank and if we did what would be the point of it. If we wanted someone off the ship we would just chuck 'em over the side.'

'Fair point, but it's always fun to play up to the stereotype, wouldn't you say?' the captain looked him straight in the eye. Alfie smiled nervously but wasn't really afraid. He knew Cookie had taken a shine to him and if they were going to hurt him they would have done it by now. At least he hoped that was the case.

'LAND, I SEE LAND,' came the call from the crow's nest. The ship came to life with the men busying themselves in preparation for the potential pillaging. Some disappeared into the ship and reappeared with guns and more swords while others prepared the rowing boats for the trip to the shore. Captain Savage went to the front of the ship followed closely by Cookie and Alfie. He produced a golden telescope from the inside pocket of his coat. He extended it and put it to his right eye.

'What can you see Captain?' asked Cookie excitedly.

'It's a big one this time and it looks as though we aren't the first ones here. Another ship is anchored on the east side, a fancy looking vessel if I don't say so myself.'

Alfie's stomach turned. He knew what pirates did to other ships and unless it was military they would no doubt be planning on killing everyone on board and taking whatever they fancied. He had heard tales of some pirates taking people for slaves, but this was rare as it was a burden to have extra mouths to feed as well as never knowing when they could offload them. They would always leave a few alive to spread the word of the pirates' infamy, as this was as important to a pirate captain as his loot and booze. Before leaving on his voyage he had researched these sea scum and felt as if he knew them before he even left port. But this bunch of criminals were nothing like the evil devils that were portrayed in the books. He even liked one of them and now his mind was awash with confusion. 'Ready the men for the attack. We'll board them before they even know what's hit them,' Captain Savage ordered. He closed the telescope and put it back inside his coat.

Without thinking what he was saying Alfie blurted out what was in his head, 'don't kill them!,' as he said it he knew it was stupid, but there it was hanging in the air like a bad odour. Cookie rolled his eyes and rubbed his head. He liked this boy and would stand up for him even if it meant angering his best friend. He had planned, when he first met him, on using him to get to his ship then slitting his throat. However, after Alfie had helped him by carrying him back to his ship, his heart had been touched and he had felt a brotherly kinship for the first time. Secretly he hated his fellow crewmates and hated himself even more. The things he had done in the name of piracy haunted him, but this young man was his possible redemption. If he could help him and protect him, it might begin to make up for his crimes.

'We'll try our best young man but if they don't co-operate then death is the only option,' said the captain bluntly and without even a hint of solace. For him, it was a business and if people decided to get in the way of his livelihood, however distasteful it might be, then he would end them by blade or bullet. He was prepared to ignore Alfie's outburst out of respect for his friend, his friend who he loved, more than he had loved any man. He suppressed these feelings of attraction to the same sex and buried his urges deep down inside. This often made him angry and he took it out on his crew. Alfie didn't reply, instead, he looked ahead at the ship and hoped beyond all hope that they would see a recognisable flag. Just then, he heard a flapping noise, he turned and saw the flag being taken down and replaced with a white flag with a yellow circle in the centre. He had never seen this flag before, but he guessed that it was to trick the other ship into thinking they were friendly. He was filled with dread but there was nothing he could do, at least not for now. The closer they got the more dread swept over Alfie and beads of sweat dripped from his brow like a slow running waterfall, splashing to the deck below.

Cookie had been watching Alfie intently and he too was getting nervous. His eyes darted between the two men who were natural enemies but had been almost forced together by his bad judgement. "Stupid idiot," he thought, "why did you have to rescue this poor boy and bring him into this terrible world". He wished he could turn back the clock and have never followed that stupid bird, but life moves forward and he had to think of a way to protect Alfie from Savage. The old captain was seemingly calm from his outward appearance but inside he knew his friend was planning on killing Alfie the first chance he got. His best friend could be unreasonably jealous, which was often the case, but he didn't understand why. Not to mention the fact that the boy was mouthing off against the pirate way and that just wasn't done without severe consequences. The other ship put up no defence as they approached to pull up alongside it and there was even a group of men and women waiting eagerly along the side. The flag that had been raised was that of a merchant ship called the White Sun and was relatively well-known in these parts for having rare and exotic merchandise. Of course, what these unsuspecting fools didn't know was that Captain Savage and his crew had pillaged and sunk the White Sun and killed everyone on board. That's where they got the food and wine that Alfie had enjoyed so much the night before.

'Hello there,' called an elderly man with a bushy grey beard, 'what treasures do you have for us today?' The looks on their faces changed very quickly when the two ships came side by side and giant boards were placed between them. Twenty heavily armed pirates rushed aboard and ten of the younger men, who foolishly tried to put up a fight, were ruthlessly cut down. The others cowered in a corner by some barrels and were subsequently tied up and gagged. It was a scary sight to witness as this ragged bunch of sea slime were as efficient as a highly-trained army. The captain stood proudly and watched as his men took control of the ship. They disappeared below and in no time at all, they had rounded up the entire crew and its passengers and brought them to the deck. Some were bleeding, others were crying and some even looked as though they might be dead. Alfie strained his eyes and was shocked to see that there were even a few children amongst the captives.

'Captain, please tell your men not to hurt them. You can see they're beaten, there's no need for further violence,' Alfie stood tall and firm showing no signs of weakness.

The captain turned and punched him hard in his stomach. Alfie fell to his knees unable to breathe, 'If I were you, mister Alfie, I'd keep my trap shut unless you want to join them,' he turned back around and continued to watch the horror show unfold in his honour.

'Get up, you stupid boy and don't say another word or I'll gut you meself. What do you think this is? A democracy?!' Cookie helped Alfie up, then pulled his sword from his belt and walked over to one of the boards. He looked back at Alfie with sorrow in his eyes and hoped that the young man would not hate him after he did his duty. He steadily, considering he was still quite badly hurt, crossed the board and jumped down onto the other ship. He winced from the pain but continued, undeterred. 'Ok scum that's enough. He pushed through a crowd of pirates and found that they'd surrounded a pretty girl who couldn't have been older than twenty. She had long black hair that draped like silk across her back. Her eyes were brown with a hint of green and her face was as fresh and beautiful as a summer morning. She was bleeding from her upper arm and held her hand over it. Cookie knew that if Alfie saw her he would more than likely try to rescue her and get himself killed doing it. There was no way he would let that happen. He knelt beside her, checking that Alfie could not see from the ship, 'I'm sorry dear but you pose too much of a risk and if I didn't do this then the lads here would do so much worse,' her eyes looked at him with watery pools in their corners and like a swift wind, Cookie sliced her throat and held her in his arms.

'Aagh come on Cookie we could have had fun with that one. Why did ya do that?' a dirty pirate with several missing teeth asked.

'Cos she looked at me funny. Now do you want some or are we gonna get what we came for?' The others knew better than to argue and they continued, taking as much loot as they could carry. The other pirates had followed Cookie and were now helping bring their ill-gotten gains back to their ship. It seemed that this was a transport ship that had been taking passengers from England to Spain but had stopped off at the small group of islands for some sightseeing. The majority were rich men and women and in some cases, their children had also joined them. The pirates, much to Cookie's relief, left the children alone except occasionally scaring them so their parents would cooperate more easily. No one else was killed but the elderly man that had greeted them collapsed from what was probably a heart attack and perished where he lay as no one was brave enough to help him. Alfie inwardly wept at what he'd just witnessed and even though he hadn't seen the girl being killed he couldn't help thinking ill of Cookie for taking part in this evil act at all. He had to bring an end to this but what could one man do against so many? He was trained in combat but was as green as a winter-surviving pine tree. He had to be smart and bide his time and that's when a plan formulated in his mind.

4

'Alfie sweetheart, Mummy asked you a question,' Carol was staring deep into her son's eyes trying to see signs of recognition, but none were present, at least as far as she could tell.

'I'm afraid that his Brother's death has triggered something within him that means the signs of autism have become far more prevalent, Mrs Fenix,' said Dr Fossil.

'But what does that mean? how does he have autism? I thought that's for weird kids that don't talk. Alfie talks, sometimes even too much,' she cracked a brave smile. 'My friend thought Alfie has autism, but I'm so confused as to how.

There isn't just one size fits all, it's a spectrum, Mrs Fenix,' Doctor Fossil explained.

'Please, call me Carol,' she leaned forward in her chair.

'Ok, Carol. Autism is, what we call, a spectrum condition. It varies greatly from each individual to the next, but what is always common is that they find it hard to find the appropriate way to communicate with us, the neurotypicals to be precise. This is as much our fault as it is the conditions. Alfie, more than likely, has a form of autism known as Asperger's which is a term not used any more due to complicated reasons. This means he can communicate and participate in everyday society but most will find him odd or like you said, weird,' Carol looked away in embarrassment. 'But the problem at the moment seems to be that Alfie has regressed into a more impaired autistic state and his mind is shutting out the outside world to protect itself from the overwhelming hurt that it has been subjected to,' she looked down at her notes and pushed the askew papers together neatly.

'I knew he wasn't bad,' she mumbled to herself frowning slightly.

'No Carol he's not bad, he's just very different and, in some cases, take Einstein for example, different can be very good. The best thing you can do for Alfie is to try and understand him. I have some leaflets and a web address that will help you get started, but I would also recommend reading some books on the subject and I've heard there are some good videos on YouTube as well. Perhaps start with Joe James Neurodiversity Awareness. He is an autistic adult who talks about being Autistic and how his brain works. But as I said, everyone on the spectrum is different, so get to know his strengths and weaknesses and then work from there.'

'Thank you so much doctor, you don't know what this means to me and what it will mean for Alfie,' Carol took her hand and shook it wildly.

'I will need to refer you to the local mental health team who work with people on the spectrum and they'll be able to get you an official diagnosis. I can only recommend him for this but I have no doubt that he'll be accepted and you can start getting him the help he needs. They'll even be able to recommend a school where Alfie can flourish.'

'Did you hear that Alfie? You can go to a different school. No more stupid bullies for my baby boy,' she searched for a reaction but came up short again. Her heart ached for his attention but she knew she had to be patient and let him play out whatever was going through his mind.

5

'I don't trust him, Cookie,' Captain Savage sat hunched forward lighting the pipe in his mouth with a match. The flame lit his face and the dark shadows below his eyes gave him a sinister and almost demonic look.

'You don't trust anyone, Captain,' Cookie replied grinning broadly and slamming his booted feet up on the captain's table.

The captain shook out the flame and leant back in his chair. He sucked on the pipe and inhaled deeply, the smoke drew into his lungs and he released it into the air. It swirled around him like a dancing cloud and drifted up towards the ceiling, 'I trust you,' he said in a low voice almost as if he were embarrassed to admit this.

'And I'm eternally grateful,' Cookie nodded low as if to bow.

'You stupid old git,' Captain Savage shook his head, 'but seriously Cookie how can you be sure this boy won't betray us?'

'I can't, but I also can't be sure that any of these dirty sea scum won't betray us.'

'Well that's reassuring,' the captain took another hit from his pipe and scratched his bearded chin, 'don't think I won't be watching him old friend. The moment he steps out of line your little wannabe friendship is over, do you understand?

'I'll kill 'im meself Captain,' he didn't take his eyes off the captain to reassure him his seriousness.

'I hope you're right, Cookie, I really do.'

6

Two weeks passed and Alfie had blended in like a chameleon on a leaf. He had pierced his ear and wore a black bandana that Cookie had given him as a gift. They had attacked another ship, but this time Alfie was forced to join in. He had reluctantly obeyed as he knew his life was in danger if he didn't. He threatened and abused, beat and terrified all the while hating himself. He had played the part but failed to kill a young man similar in age to himself when the captain had ordered it. His hand had shaken uncontrollably and Cookie had shot the man between the eyes to save Alfie from having to do it. The captain remained suspicious of him but Cookie felt that it was just a matter of time before Alfie would be accepted and he and Captain Savage would be good friends. A few days after that he had helped the crew carry the loot to an island that he had not been allowed to know the whereabouts of and they buried it in a cave. Day by day he was becoming more and more like one of them.

'You know the rules scum,' Cookie shouted to the huddle of pirates anxiously leaning towards the side of the ship, greatly anticipating their shore leave and the touch of a woman. They'd set anchor at a Spanish port so the boys could have some downtime. 'Don't steal, don't rape and above all don't murder. We don't want any unnecessary attention while we're here and any begger than brings it will face my blade,' he drew his sword and showed them exactly what he meant. They shuffled nervously looking accusingly at one another as if someone had already broken a rule. Alfie stared at them and couldn't help wondering how many of them would give up their own mothers to avoid Cookie's wrath. He suspected it was most of them and pushed the thought away from his mind. He hated the filth but he had to admit, for all their evil, he was oddly having a good time. They still didn't trust him but they had warmed to him when they realised that he was just a lost sailor and not a demon or sea monster. Cookie had taken him under his wing and the two of them were fast becoming great friends and almost like brothers. His mind was awash with conflict and at times he would find himself making excuses for Cookie being a pirate trying desperately to come to terms with his vicious behaviour. The man was a paradox, he was equally good as he was bad and Alfie was torn between the two. He was however looking forward to having some time away from the ship and maybe even escaping if the opportunity arose. He planned to kill them all but in fleeting moments of weakness, he just wanted to go home and forget any of this ever happened. But he thought, "if I don't do something how many more will die by their hands and does that mean the blood will be on mine?" He rubbed his eyes and cleared his dry throat.

'You ok?' Cookie turned and looked at him with genuine concern etched on his face.

'I'm fine, Cookie. Just a little tired that's all,' he forced his lips to rise on either side of his mouth, 'are we going to get drunk or are we standing around all day chatting?'

'The former I thinks,' he turned and faced the men, 'now get lost and we'll be seeing ya in two days. Anyone not here when the sun goes down will be considered dead and left behind,' they roared in delight and disappeared within minutes, pushing and shoving as they bundled over the side.

'Shall we?' Alfie said.

'We shall,' Cookie climbed down and Alfie followed. Together they made their way to the nearest tavern to begin their night of frivolity. A lone figure stood on the ship, covered in shadow, watching them walk away down the cobbled road, he lit a match and sucked on his pipe, his eyes narrowed, his brow furrowed.

7

Alfie looked up at the ceiling and, for a full ten seconds, had no idea where he was. His vision was blurred and his throat was desert-dry. He could hear his heartbeat in his ears pounding like a marching band drum. He was hungover, laying on a bed he didn't recognise, next to a woman he didn't know.

'Good morning, Captain Fenix,' a deeply calm voice murmured from an unseen area of the room, 'I hope you slept well. You have a busy day ahead of you.'

Alfie pushed himself up straight and searched the room for the source of the voice. A middle-aged man, rounded in the stomach and balding on the head, sat on a chair in the corner. His arms were rested on his lap and his hands were closed together as if he were praying. He wore what looked like some sort of uniform that Alfie didn't recognise but it looked as though this man was very important from the amount of over embellishments that covered it. 'Good morning,' Alfie said, his voice was like gravel under a boot.

'Can I get you a glass of water?' the stranger asked, 'we don't want you uncomfortable now do we,' he smiled.

'I'm fine, thank you,' Alfie lied, 'who are you and why are you in my room?' At least he assumed it was his room.

'I am General Phillipe Honduras and I am here to help you, Captain Fenix,' he stood and looked over at the girl sleeping deeply on the bed next to Alfie. Once he was satisfied that she was asleep and not pretending to be he continued, 'you have found yourself in a very fortunate position Captain.'

'Really, how do you figure that?' he tensed his jaw with annoyance.

'You have been accepted as a friend by the pirate known as Ryan Cook. One of the most notorious and evil men to have ever sailed the seas,' he approached the bed and sat down next to Alfie. He leant in close, 'and we want you to kill him along with the rest of the crew,' he drew his face back and studied Alfie's reaction to this revelation.

'I was planning to,' he replied coldly. Even though deep inside he wondered if he could actually go through with it.

'Wonderful, we would hate to have to hang the son of an English Earl for piracy,' he stood up and stood back.

'How do you know who I am?'

'Young man, your ship went missing weeks ago, do you really think your father would have just forgotten about you? No, no, no Captain, he has sent messengers to every port searching for information about what happened. His love for you, dear boy, is to be envied by us all.'

Alfie pondered this information for a moment then replied, 'you surprise me, Sir, my father was not so kind to me before I left.'

'The loss of a man's only child can stir something inside of him that nothing, not even God, can explain,' the General smiled again. 'Now back to the matter at hand. Please, tell me everything,' he shifted his stance.

'My ship went down, God knows where, and I believe I was the only survivor,' he paused as he remembered his crew, 'I awoke on an island and was rescued by Cookie,' the General raised his eyebrows in confusion, 'sorry, I mean Ryan Cook,' he continued, 'at the time it was my only option and I didn't even realise it was a pirate ship until we had already set sail. I watched them commit horrific crimes and could do nothing but grin and bear it or be killed myself.'

'I'm sorry Captain, that sounds genuinely terrible,' the General sounded sincere.

'I've been planning how to kill them for nearly two weeks, but I haven't had the opportunity or the guts to do it,' he hung his head ashamed of his cowardice.

'You have nothing to be ashamed of young man. That filth is the worst of the worst and no man I know would want to be where you are at this moment in time.'

'But you still want me to go back I'm guessing,' the General nodded slowly. 'I already have a plan but I'll need time. Captain Savage doesn't trust me. He hasn't taken his eyes off me since I got on board his ship.

'I can give you a week to take them down from the inside,' the General stepped forward, 'then we're coming after them with everything we've got.'

'Why not just arrest them now. Take the ship, it's down at the docks,' Alfie pointed in its rough direction.

'Which one?' the General asked inquisitively.

'Its flag has a white sun on a yellow background. They stole it from a merchant ship and use it to fool other ships before… well you know what they do.'

The General nodded his eyes dropped, 'we could but I'm afraid Captain it's not that simple. It's, how do you say? complicated,' the General looked over to the window.

'What do you mean? Oh, I know what you mean,' Alfie frowned, 'you want to know where their treasure is before I kill them, don't you?

'Very good Captain. You are as intelligent as you are brave. We would be more than happy to share it with you as a reward,' he sounded more desperate like a child caught with his hand in the biscuit tin just before dinner.

'I don't want the treasure, I just don't want them to kill anyone else,' he was getting agitated, and his voice was raised. The girl next to him stirred but didn't wake.

'Please keep your voice down,' the General whispered firmly, 'you don't have a choice. If you won't help us we will assume you have been turned and you will be hanged as a pirate,' his voice was calm and measured.

This was no empty threat and Alfie knew it. He was stuck between a rock and a bigger rock so he would choose the rock. Better a ship full of pirates than the entire Spanish navy. 'Fine,' he said bluntly, 'what now?'

'Now you will return from your shore-leave unhindered. I suggest you make the most of it and stay close to Ryan Cook. We will arrest a few of the crew tomorrow at the break of dawn and fake an attempt at arresting Mr Cook. You will rescue him, then get him and the rest of the crew back to the ship safely, hopefully gaining the full trust of the Captain and lulling him into a false sense of security,' the General turned on his heels.

'Sounds like a plan,' Alfie was impressed. This could actually work. 'How will I contact you when and if I'm done?'

'We won't be far away Captain; you can trust me on that. When you're done, we will know,' he walked over to the door, opened it and left. Alfie lay back down and stared again at the ceiling. What the hell happened last night that resulted in a General of the Spanish navy sitting in the corner of his room? He racked his brain but came up empty-handed. The booze from the night before had washed his memory clean and there was no way of his getting it back any time soon. Whatever had happened it was irrelevant now. He had no choice but to follow through with this plan, the only problem was, he now only had a week to do it. He knew, if he didn't, the navy would steam in and he would no doubt die in the crossfire. As much as they wanted that treasure they wouldn't risk leaving the most dangerous pirates in the known world free to continue.

8

The plan went down exactly as the General had described. Alfie had met up with Cookie that morning, finding him unconscious on the bar of the inn they'd been drinking in. The landlord had been too scared to disturb him. They'd wandered the streets looking for somewhere to eat and eventually found a tavern that served breakfast. Later that day they'd met up with the rest of the crew and had all settled in the same tavern for another night of drinking. Alfie has been more conservative with his consumption as he wanted a clear head. That morning, as they all lay on the cold, wooden floor, the door had burst open and Spanish soldiers barged in and began arresting the semi-conscious men. As predicted many escaped and most importantly Cookie and Alfie escaped together. One of the guards almost caught Cookie but, as planned, Alfie intervened (probably saving the guards life more than Cookie's) and punched the guard, knocking him clean out. The others had seen this and rushed to his side and together they all made their way to the docks and onto the ship. The captain hadn't expected them back so early and was furious to see at least ten of his men hadn't returned with the others. They set sail just as the soldiers reached the docks and swiftly disappeared over the horizon, blissfully unaware of the four Spanish warships that followed them from a distance.

9

The sea was calm and the waves broke weakly against the sides of the ship. The sun had just disappeared behind the horizon leaving a streak of orange light along its brim. 'He saved my life and ye still don't trust him?' Cookie was directly in the captain's face; his jaw was clenched and his fists were tight. A vein appeared on his forehead and throbbed, 'I swear if ye don't let that boy be, it'll be the worst decision you'll ever make.' The boat creaked, the noise was as common place to these men as a horse hoof clopping on a road is for a carriage driver.

'Get out of my face and sit the hell down First Mate,' he dragged the words out, 'I think you forget who you're talking to. I am Captain Savage and this is MY SHIP,' he screamed the last two words so they were almost incoherent but Cookie got the message.

'Sorry Captain, but I won't be sitting anywhere,' he looked at him with his penetrating stare searching into the soul of his once best friend then stormed out pushing past the captain.

'Cookie,' the captain's voice was once again calm but it was too late and he flinched when the door slammed shut.

Out on the deck, the remainder of the crew quickly busied themselves when Cookie appeared and they avoided eye contact at all costs. All, of course, except Alfie who approached him cautiously, 'is everything alright?' he had to keep Cookie on his side even if the captain was playing hard to get.

'That stubborn begger still thinks it was you who tipped the soldiers off, but why the hell would you do that then help us escape. He's lost his mind through jealousy,' the sails flapped as the wind suddenly picked up and the night sky drew over them. Alfie had suspected for some time that Captain Savage had wanted more than just friendship, but was yet to make his move, 'you can't exactly help who you fall in love with,' he said quietly so only the two of them could hear. There was a long pause, he thought maybe he had misread the signs and in half a second he would be looking down at Cookie's sword buried deep in his abdomen.

'How did you know?' Cookie asked incredulously as he searched around them for any prying ears. He himself had suspected for a while now, but this confirmed it for him. He trusted Alfie completely.

'I just do. Do you feel the same?' this was his opening and he wasn't going to blow it.

'Of course not, what sort of a man would I be?' Cookie spat.

'Exactly,' Alfie lied, as he had no issue with any type of love. But he knew if he could drive a wedge between the two, it would benefit him immensely.

'What should I do about it?' asked the pirate.

'Just don't trust anything he says. He is trying to trick you into loving him,' he hated himself for this deceitful act.

'I wouldn't trust him if he was my own Mother,' Cookie folded his arms and the two smiled at the odd saying. Alfie had him where he wanted him, but remained sad because he had to betray his friend.

10

It had now been five days since they left the port and time was running out for Alfie. He hadn't dared ask about the treasure's location for fear of arousing suspicion, but the captain didn't need a reason to be on his guard, his hatred for Alfie was enough. The time was now or never and his nerve was wavering because of his fondness of the old pirate. The general had been very clear, that it was them and him or them by him, either way, someone was going to die that day. 'You cheated!' a hefty oaf of a pirate bellowed and pushed over the small table sending playing cards flying across the cabin. They spread far and wide covering the floor and some even landed on the beds.

'I guess that means the game is over?' Alfie joked and most of the men laughed. A few tapped him on the back and they all made their way to their bunks. An hour later, all was quiet and every man, except one, dreamed of treasure and booze. Alfie sat up and looked around in the darkness. The only source of light came from a few port windows and the moonlight beaming through them. He placed his feet silently on the floor and stood up. The floorboards creaked but no man stirred. He made it to the door and slowly opened it. It groaned as it always did, but in the dead silence, the noise was heart-stopping. He turned around fully expecting someone to have woken, luckily all remained in slumber, "it must be my lucky night" he thought. He glided out of the door and continued along the corridor. He stopped beside a barrel and carefully removed the lid. He placed it on the ground and looked inside. It was full of straw, exactly as he had left it, and he felt around inside until his fingers felt the cold steel of the sword he had hidden when no one was looking. He pulled it free and tucked it into his belt. He took as much straw as he could and stuffed it into his shirt, then he walked to the end of the corridor and stopped by Cookie's private quarters. He put his left ear against the door and listened carefully.

'He's up to something,' he heard the captain say angrily, once again trying to convince Cookie that Alfie was dangerous. He had to admit, the captain was a remarkably intuitive man.

'You're paranoid and jealous,' Cookie snapped back, his voice was slurred from the alcohol that rushed around his veins. Alfie was glad to hear both men were together. At least that meant he didn't have to deal with the captain separately.

'Rubbish! You're just so blinded by his friendship you can't see the nose in front of your face,' the captain raged on, 'from day one I knew he was trouble and there's no changing my mind no matter what that empty space between your ears thinks.'

'What does he have to do to gain your trust?' Cookie swigged more wine from a bottle in his hand.

'Kill someone, rob someone, rape someone, do something that proves he's one of us,' Alfie shuddered at the thought.

'Why do you have to ruin him? Why does everything you touch turn to scum?' Cookie sounded defeated like he had reached the end of his tether. Alfie backed away and laid the straw at the foot of the door. He used the sword to jam the door closed and took a match from his pocket. He jumped back as something smashed into the door which caused it to wane at its hinges. 'I'LL KILL YOU,' Cookie screamed and a gunshot echoed down the corridor. Alfie ran. He climbed the stairs leading to the deck and walked swiftly over to the base of the mast. Without making a sound he climbed to the top and using a knife that he had hidden in his shirt he cut the throat of Scragger while he slept in the crow's nest. He wondered how it would feel taking a man's life for the first time and was scared to find that he felt nothing. He slid down and walked over to the barrels of rum that were stored on deck for late-night drinking. He systematically carried them to the edge of the below deck opening until there were seven of them surrounding it. He then took the match from his pocket and looked up to the sky. This was it. He was about to end all their lives and possibly be stranded in the middle of the ocean for good. He had to do it when they were far from land for fear someone might have seen the blaze and tried to help. He struck the match on its box and threw it down the hole. It spun through the air almost hypnotically and landed in the straw. The fire caught immediately and Alfie swiftly pushed the barrels down the hole blocking the exit and adding to the impending blaze with seventy percent proof alcohol. He could hear a man banging on a door and shouting, but he didn't wait to hear what he was saying. He ran over to the side of the ship and jumped into a rowing boat. He lowered himself down but just as he was about to reach the water something stopped the rope dead.

Cookie leaned over the side, his face black and burnt, his hair still singeing and his sword raised, 'you cowardly begger!. You couldn't face me yourself, you run away like a dog! Everything I did for you, I trusted you and this is what I get,' he hurled himself overboard and landed heavily in the boat next to Alfie. He swung his blade missing Alfie by millimetres. Alfie reacted by lunging forward with his knife cutting the arm of his assailant.

'You killed innocent people, what was I supposed to do? I couldn't let you continue,' Alfie cried out as the flames of the burning ship licked the sides of his boat.

'I loved you like a Brother. I trusted you. I never wanted this life but I had no choice. If I hadn't done what I did then they would have turned on me,' he slumped back onto the seat, 'you don't understand.

It was getting hotter and Alfie's skin was starting to tighten, 'why didn't you tell me?'

'I thought you were becoming like them. You sure had us fooled,' Cookie looked up at Alfie and still felt a kinship.

'Come with me,' Alfie begged, 'we can we can hide away and change our identities,' screw the general, friendship was more important.

'You tried to kill me!' Cookie screamed over the ever-growing noise of the flames that licked the ropes that held them suspended in the air.

'Can you blame me? It's not as if you would have helped me and I couldn't risk telling you.

'No, I suppose not. But do you know what that means boy?'

Alfie shrugged, 'No'.

'We'll never trust each other fully again and that means one of us must die so the other may live or we'll be looking over each other's backs for the rest of our days and I, for one, don't have the energy for that,' he stood up, his knuckles whitened as they tightened on his sword handle. Alfie readied himself for the attack. The old sea dog who had fallen for the lies of a secret captain, with a passion for collecting bugs, lifted his blade to his throat, 'Sandy Mountain Island,' he said and pulled across it. Blood poured from the gape and with a last glance at this man he called brother, he fell backwards into the dark water, never to be seen again.

Alfie barely had time to protest when the fire forced the ropes to snap and the boat concluded its journey into the sea. Alfie was knocked down and for a second or two barely had the strength to stand. "Why had he killed himself?" he thought. They could have got through this; it didn't have to end like this. He heard the crackling of wood above him and saw the mast engulfed in red and orange sway in the wind. He quickly grabbed the oars and rowed as fast as he could. The mast snapped and came plummeting down towards him, he stepped up a gear and blistered his hands while he rowed harder. The crow's nest missed his boat by a couple of feet and Alfie breathed a sigh of relief. He continued to row to a safe distance and watched as the vessel, which had brought death and sorrow wherever it went, was sent to the bottom of the ocean where it belonged, along with its crew of murderers and thieves.

Alfie waited in his boat for a day and a half until the Spanish fleet finally came to rescue him. He was taken back to Spain and given a hero's welcome. His father had been told about his reappearance and was waiting for him at the docks. He embraced his only son as he had never done before. 'Hello Father,' Alfie said as tears welled up in his eyes.

'My Son. Thank God you have returned to me. I searched for you every day. I never gave up hope,' he hugged him tighter.

'I never stopped trying to get back to you, but I had to stop them. I had to end their reign of terror,' Alfie pulled away and stood straight and tall.

The general pushed past several people in the crowd and addressed Alfie, 'did you find out where the treasure is?' he said breathlessly.

'No,' Said Alfie, 'I nearly died trying to but the captain never let me in. He died mistrusting me.'

'Clever fellow,' his father said smiling nervously.

The general's face contorted with anger, 'we had a deal,' he growled.

'Leave my Son alone General, or the King will hear about your abuse of power and how you risked the life of an Earl's Son for your country's financial gain,' he stood in front of his son, though he was at least half a foot shorter, the gesture was still well-meant. The general was about to say something, then decided better of it. He turned on his heels and stormed off back through the crowd. 'You know where it is don't you?' his father faced him and smiled wryly.

He thought of Cookie's last words. 'Maybe,' he said and smiled back.

Ryan had died again, even when Alfie had tried his best to save him. But every time he had to see his brother perish, he came to terms with his loss a little more.

'How are you feeling?' asked Stubbs.

'Sad, but better, I just wish I had listened to the doctor, but I couldn't help drifting away,' Alfie looked out of the car window at the fields rushing by. He wondered how many cows were in all the fields in England and he decided he would search for the answer when he got home.

'Hello Alfie,' Carol had noticed him looking around, 'are you back with us then?'

'Hello, Mummy. I met some pirates and one was a homosexual,' he continued to look out of the window.

'Oh,' replied Carol a little startled that he even knew that word, 'how did you know he was a homosexual?'

'He loved Ryan who was a pirate, but Ryan didn't love him back. Then Cookie killed himself to protect me.' Carol was a little confused as usual, but overall she was delighted. He'd never before shared his internal adventures with her and she perceived this as progress. She decided not to push it and sat happily for the rest of the drive. She finally had her answer to the question that had plagued her for years and she was seeing the world in a whole new light. She was going to look after her baby and no one was going to get in her way. She pulled up to the drive but stopped at the pavement due to another car blocking her parking spot. She hadn't ever seen this car before and wondered who it could belong to.

She went over to Alfie's door and let him out. He ran towards the house twitching his head from side to side, 'Alfie, slow down,' Carol called suddenly becoming a little overprotective. The door opened and Carol went cold.

'There's my handsome boy, come and give Mummy a hug,' said a woman standing in her hallway.

Chapter 8

They stood in the kitchen opposite each other. Gary leant against the worktop with a mug of tea in his hand. Carol stood with her arms crossed, jaw clenched and feet apart just inside the open doorway. 'Why is she here, Gary?' Carol held back the anger boiling in the pit of her stomach. She'd made so much progress with Alfie and this bloody, estranged woman had come waltzing back into the picture and could now seriously turn her son's world upside down.

'I don't know, perhaps because her Son died?' he sarcastically retorted putting the mug on the surface, spilling some tea over the side, 'so what's wrong with him?' he asked his eyes a little softer.

'Like you care!'

'Of course, I care. He's my Son for christ's sake.'

'When it suits you and when you're sober,' she'd reached the end of her tether and now there was no holding her back. Seeing Tiffany was the straw that broke the camel's back.

149

'Nice, Carol, very nice. You know damn well why I've been drinking. It's the only way to stop hurting,' his face was weary with regret.

'I know but that's no excuse to ignore or lambast your remaining Son. He needs a father figure now more than ever and you are all he's got,' her tone had dropped and she was almost pleading with him. 'The doctor seems pretty certain he has Autism. We'll know for sure once we get him officially diagnosed, but all the signs are there so it should be open and shut,' she dropped her arms to her side and walked across the room. She took his hands in hers,' we will get through this. You will get through this. You just have to try harder that's all, for me, for Alfie, for Ryan.'

'Ok,' he said softly, 'I'll try,' he took her by the waist, drew her close and they hugged.

Alfie sat with his estranged mum in the living room playing with his Lego. He didn't really know who the lady was at first, and he certainly didn't appreciate it when she tried to hug him. He had struggled away and even kicked her in her shins which had made Carol laugh so he did it again. He liked to make his mummy happy and was glad to see her smiling. He always noticed what shape her lips were as he preferred looking at them rather than her eyes. The new lady didn't get mad though, instead, she knelt beside him and said she was sorry. She asked him if he recognised her, which he didn't reply to and she told him she was his mum and that she'd come back from a faraway land to be with him. Alfie wasn't daft, even if others thought he was, and he backed away and hid behind Carol. The two of them had a heated discussion about what Alfie had been told about this lady and Carol had asked why she thought she had any right to "just waltz in and out of his life, willy nilly" was the exact wording that she'd used. Alfie was very confused by all of this, but he remembered that Ryan had always thought lovingly of this new lady and that meant he would at least give her a chance. Gary had come out, made them calm down and they all went inside. He then told Alfie to get his Lego and Tiffany sat in the living room on the floor eagerly waiting to play with her son. 'If you separate all the pieces at the start then it makes it easier to build something that you haven't built before,' Alfie explained, 'first we can build the base of the starship, then we can start adding all the complicated machinery that makes it work.'

'And do you like doing this often, Alfie?' Tiffany asked in a tender tone of voice.

'Oh yes, it's my favourite. I usually play on my own though as most of the time I don't want people touching my things. You can help me if you like, but we are building a starship so you have to do that,' his head twitched surreptitiously.

'Can I make my own thing please, Alfie?' she asked reaching for one of the pieces.

'No,' Alfie raised his voice, 'you can't take the pieces, I need them for the starship,' he snatched the piece she was about to pick up and looked at her heatedly.

'Well that's not very nice, Alfie,' her voice was not so tender this time. Alfie ignored this pointless accusation as he was under no obligation to be nice to this lady and especially when she wasn't listening to him. He felt he was very clear about the rules of playing with Lego and he had no time for people who couldn't grasp simple instructions. He looked down at his piles and began sticking the pieces together, making the image in his mind become a reality. 'Alfie, I'm speaking to you. Don't ignore Mummy.'

'You're not my Mummy!. You're a stranger with a stupid accent and I don't want to play with you anymore,' he turned to one side, so he was facing away from her and continued to build.

Tiffany was losing patience. Her ankle was still throbbing from where he had kicked her. She had been warned by Gary that he behaviour problems and she tried her best to ignore his rudeness, but everyone has a breaking point 'Listen to me young man...' she didn't get a chance to finish as Carol rushed in and interrupted.

'Tiffany, can I see you in the kitchen, please? We need to talk,' she smiled at Alfie, but he was lost in his own world again. She sighed and disappeared out of the door.

Tiffany stood up and followed her, 'what's his problem? What's wrong with him? I can see you haven't taught him any manners,' she pointed an accusing finger in Carol's direction.

'Keep your bloody voice down Tiff,' Gary snarled quietly so Alfie couldn't hear, 'Carol took him to the doctor today and it turns out that he's not quite right in the head.'

'Thank you, Gary, for that ridiculous description of our Son's condition,' she rolled her eyes.

'So, what is it then?' Tiffany asked, staring at Carol as though she'd caused it.

'He has ASC which stands for Autistic Spectrum Condition,' said Carol expertly as though she had been rehearsing the line in her head, which in fact she had.

'How did he get that? Was he in an accident?' Tiffany once again looked accusingly at Carol.

'No, he was born with it,' Carol replied restraining herself.

'Oh, so now it's my fault, is it? I suppose you told him that did you?' she sat down, crossed her arms and narrowed her eyes.

'Of course not Tiff,' Gary came to Carol's side defensively, 'the important thing is we know why he is like he is and how we can help him,' Gary was like a different man.

'So, my little Boy has autism,' she said to herself and closed her eyes so she could process the information. 'So, my firstborn is killed and then the other is mentally challenged,' she continued to reflect inwardly sighing at the injustice of it all, as though she was the one with the problem.

'Whatever you want to call it, we know Alfie better than anyone and there's no way you can define him completely by labelling him "challenged". He's unbelievably smart and the sweetest most loving child you are ever likely to meet. He has an amazing imagination and the structures he can build out of Lego using only his mind are phenomenal,' Carol argued with pride stamped on her face.

'But he can be a bloody nightmare at times, Carol,' Gary pointed out, 'I'm not being out of order, I'm just stating the truth. You yourself said you couldn't handle him most of the time, that's why we always left it to Ryan. 'Carol cringed but couldn't say anything as she knew Gary was telling the truth. She hated herself for it but at least felt mildly vindicated that she'd always defended Alfie when others said he was naughty or perhaps she was just defending herself.

'Is that right?' Tiffany sneered, 'I guess I'm not the only crappy Mother around here.'

'Shut up, Tiff. How dare you come into my house after eight bleeding years and have the audacity to tell Carol what sort of mother she is,' Gary realised he'd opened a can of worms and desperately tried to claw his way back into Carol's favour, 'where were you when all the temper tantrums in the middle of shops and parties went down? Where were you every time the school rang us and told us Alfie was in trouble yet again? Where were you when our beautiful firstborn Son was dying in his flipping car?' he began to weep and leaned against the kitchen side for support.

'It's ok, Gary,' Carol hugged him and he squeezed back, feeling so much relief that he could finally share his sadness with her. Tiffany just sat there unable to speak. She'd beaten herself up over the loss of Ryan and pined over the fact that she wasn't there for him. It'd been Gary's mum who'd rung and told her of her son's death; she'd recently split with her husband and was living alone in a flat in Sydney. She'd settled her affairs and decided to restart her life back in England and the first thing she'd do is reconnect with her remaining son. She just wanted a chance to make up for her mistakes but her temper, as usual, kept getting the better of her.

'I finished my starship,' Alfie stood in the doorway with the Lego model in his hands.

Tiffany looked at him but he wouldn't look up. She was overwhelmed and began to feel dizzy and sick. She got up a little too quickly and stumbled towards Alfie. She knocked into him and the model slipped from his grasp. It fell on the kitchen tiles and broke into several pieces. He started to scream. Rather than try and comfort him she panicked, 'I can't deal with this right now,' she rushed out the front door, grabbing her handbag as she left.

'Baby don't cry, it's ok we can rebuild it?' Carol approached him carefully and knelt beside him making sure she wasn't to close. Alfie stopped. It was as if someone had pressed a button on the back of his head and he went silent and sat on the floor.

'There he goes again,' sighed Gary, 'do we just leave him or shall I try and take him upstairs?'

'Take him to bed,' she said, 'it's been a long day. I'll take the Lego,' she began collecting the pieces.

Gary lifted Alfie very carefully into his arms and to his delight he held him tightly, 'wow, two hugs in one day. It's like winning the lottery,' Alfie stayed silent but Gary didn't care. He wasn't going to ever let his son down again, he had promised Keith. After Carol had mentioned that she'd spoken to him, he'd rang his best mate to ask why he was sticking his nose in other people's business. Keith had soon set him straight and told him that he was a lucky git to have such an amazing, patient woman and that if he had half a brain he would realise that his son needed help and not discipline. Gary, who respected his friend's opinion, had calmed down and confessed that he was scared all the time that Carol would leave him and he wouldn't be good enough to bring up Alfie on his own. He'd foolishly listened to his mum and others around him, rather than seeing that Ryan and Carol were always there. He swore that he'd be a better man and Keith, though secretly in love with his wife, had said he'd help him in any way possible. He'd then heard the doorbell ring and when he opened it, he'd almost had a heart attack.

Alfie lay in his bed looking up at his glow-in-the-dark star stickers while his parents watched from the door, 'where do you think he's gone this time?' asked Carol.

'To the moon and back probably,' Gary laughed, but he wasn't far off.

The Jargons

1

The dark plethora of space is a never-ending vacuum of particles smashing into one another and occasionally forming an object. What we believe to be a universe full of galaxies, stars and planets is a void of emptiness, ubiquitous dark matter with the very rare appearance of matter. A collection of this matter flew through the void on a mission of great importance.

'Lieutenant Fenix, do you read me?' a deep voice said over the intercom.

'Loud and clear Admiral,' he replied leaning over and touching the comms screen.

'I just wanted to say, good luck son. We all believe in you,' the admiral's voice shook slightly.

'Thank you, Sir, I won't let you down,' a huge flash covered his screen in bright blue light and the space around him warped as if bent by a mirror. When he could finally see again, after a few seconds, the wormhole had opened up in front of him and he prepared for cross-galactic travel. He slowed down to a steady three hundred miles an hour and cruised like a neutrino passing through a cloud into the swirling whirlpool, 'I love this bit,' he said to Ryan his BRO (Bodyguard Robotic Organism).

'Whatever gets you going, Sir,' the android joked.

'Kind of regretting installing that humour chip now, Ryan,' Alfie smirked.

'Me to Sir,' the Android was programmed to protect Alfie, but also hugely admired him. They had been together for a long time and it was as close to friendship as an Android was able to understand. The ship rapidly picked up speed as the wormhole took hold of them and their life was now in its hands. It shook them wildly like an earthquake, throwing them around in their seats. Alfie gripped the armrest of his chair and dug his fingers into its sides. He couldn't help being reminded of the old television show Star Trek. 'Shields are holding at ninety-five percent, Sir,' the ship settled and the cockpit went silent and still. A blue light flashed on the wall behind him indicating that all was well.

'Good, we don't want them going below seventy, that's when we start to panic,' Alfie swiped his wrist comm and a holographic screen appeared just above it. He searched through the data using his free hand and went over the mission one last time. He liked to be prepared. Earth was under threat from a distant galactic force known as the Jargons. Their only purpose was to wipe out every sentient life form in their galaxy, according to the Inter Galactic Council who was the governing body in the known universe. Earth had received a message from the Milky Way Council to send one representative to an emergency meeting in sector seven, otherwise known as the Andromeda Galaxy NGC 224. They were to rendezvous with Bagarth Klamindo, an Inter-Galactic Council representative, who would then take them to the secret meeting planet for further briefing. Lieutenant Alfie Fenix had been handpicked by the admiral as Earth's best representative and no one could disagree. He was held in such high esteem for his heroics when Earth was attacked by the Alpha Centauri Alliance five years ago. He'd bravely led a team of Dark Soldiers, as they were known, on a covert mission to the home planet of the Alliance's leader, where they captured his son, who'd been training troops for the attacks, and held him ransom. The leader surrendered and handed himself into the Milky Way Council and was sentenced to hyberspacenation a permanent state of hibernation in space. The Alliance tried to fight on, but without their illustrious leader, the infrastructure fell apart and they were easily defeated with a little help from Pluto. On a side note, many astrophysicists had to eat humble pie after finding out that Pluto was a huge planet and that it had a protective Holo shield around it that made it appear smaller so no one would attack it. 'I'm going to try and get some sleep. Wake me if anything changes,' Alfie made his way out of the cockpit. The doors hissed as they slid open automatically.

'No, I'll just quietly watch while everything goes wrong around me and wish really hard that you will come and save us,' Ryan replied, his eyes didn't blink.

Alfie ignored him and made a mental note to remove the humour chip as soon as he got a chance. He made his way down the corridor and came to a stop outside his cabin, 'Lieutenant Fenix code 162,' he said clearly.

'Recognised,' a soft female voice announced and the doors slid open. He stepped over the threshold and the doors slid shut behind him. He walked over to the bed and sat with his feet over the edge resting on the floor. He removed his boots and kicked them across the room. One landed next to the door, the other five feet away against a wall. He rubbed his chin feeling the two days of stubble and thought about shaving. He decided it could wait as his eyes would barely stay open. No sooner had he put his head on the pillow he was dead to the world.

2

'Why you? That's all I'm saying Alfie, why you?' Sandy finished packing the dishwasher and closed the door.

'Because they asked,' he said defiantly, 'I can't exactly say no. It's my job,' he held her by the waist and turned her around to face him. She looked so tired. She'd barely slept all night after he'd told her the news. He thought, foolishly, that she would be excited, he'd expected her to jump for joy when hearing the news that, of all the people on Earth, he had been chosen for this mission.

'It's always your job. Why can't it be someone else's job this time that's all I'm saying,' she perched on her tiptoes and kissed him.

'You know why,' he said softly and stroked the back of her head.

Her eyes dropped and she looked down at nothing in particular, 'I know, it's just not fair that's all,' her bottom lip stuck out like a toddler and he always found this adorable.

'I'll be back before you know it,' he gently lifted her head and he looked deep into her eyes, 'I promise,' they kissed again.

3

Alfie woke to see a shiny metal head peering over him with a toothless grin, 'for flip's sake Ryan,' he cried out, 'what the vlar do you think you're playing at you junk head? Do you have a screw loose, literally?

'Sorry Sir, but we've arrived at the coordinates and I'm afraid the news isn't good,' the android stepped back and waited for a reply.

'How "not good" are we talking?'

'Well the ship we were supposed to meet is here.'

'Good, that's a start,' Alfie said hoping there wasn't anything coming after but knowing there would be.

'But it's in about one thousand tiny pieces,' Ryan made his face look glum to fit the sombre mood that the situation called for.

'Bloody hell,' Alfie punched down on his mattress.

'Sir, there is some good news,' Ryan smiled oddly.

'What?'

'The ship's black box was still intact and I used the tractor beam to retrieve it. Would you like to listen to the recording, Sir?' he looked blankly at Alfie.

'Of course, play it,' Alfie said impatiently.

Ryan closed his eyes and an unnerving noise came out of his gaping mouth, 'this is Bagarth klamindo of the Inter Galactic Council and I'm under attack,' a panicked voice blurted out. Explosions could be heard in the background and an alarm was almost drowning out Bagarth's voice, 'it's the Jargons, they've found me. If anyone can hear this, listen carefully,' there was a pause and a voice could be heard faintly warning that the shields

159

were down to twenty percent. 'The Inter-Galactic Council is no more,' he continued, 'the Jargons have destroyed nearly all the ships that came to help and the others have fled for their lives, not that it will do them much good. I came here to warn the Milky Way's representative to prepare your planets for an attack, but it looks as though they were following me. There's no chance of unity now, the Jargons have seen to that. Perhaps you can still help, but it's more than likely that we are all on our own and..' the recording ended.

Alfie held his hands to his face and rubbed his eyes. He stood up, went over to the small mirror in the corner of his quarters and looked intensely at the face he saw. He was weathered but it suited him. He had stubble and a shaven head with wings tattooed on his neck. The scar, he picked up in the battle for the moon against a group of religious zealots called the Sun People that thought it was an evil god that needed destroying, stretched from the right corner of his lip to a centimetre below his eye. His build was large, but he was as nimble as a lightweight boxer and his shoulders were broad. Then again, they would have to be, they carried a lot on them (metaphorically speaking that is). His eyes had the intensity of a man who had seen too much but knew that they weren't done seeing. He thought about what Bagarth said just before his ship was presumably destroyed. "Perhaps you can still help". That was crazy, he was just one man in a class M infantry ship. It wasn't large but it did have the firepower to spare, so that was something. He had Ryan with him, but that hardly made an army. Perhaps he should go home and regroup with the Dark Soldiers? He wished they'd come but why would they when this was only supposed to be a briefing mission.

'What are we going to do now, Sir?' the android broke the silence.

He made the decision that would cement his destiny. 'I'm not going back, there's no point. If they're on their way to Earth I'm not going to catch them and if they aren't they will go there eventually so the plan remains the same.

'What plan, Sir?'

'To kill them all before there's nothing left to fight for,' he blinked and turned to face his BRO.

'But Sir, how will you do that?' the android was confused. It had worked out every possible aggressive response scenario and had concluded that there was only one in a one hundred million chance that an assault would be successful.

'I'll hit them where it hurts,' Alfie said calmly with an unmistakably gritty huskiness to his voice, 'same as we did with the leader of the Alliance.'

Ryan quickly calculated the odds for this new strategy and the numbers were somewhat better than before, but still heavily not in their favour, 'I'm sorry Sir, but I must advise against this course of action, as it will inevitably result in your demise and that would be against my protocols. I am after all your Bodyguard Robotic Organism.'

'Noted, but what your calculations don't take into account is the fact that there is no other choice. Unless you're a coward, that is,' he opened his locker and pulled out his grey bomber jacket and a fresh plain black t-shirt.

'Sir, I beg you to reconsider or at least think it over. Perhaps the Jargons don't know about Earth, it is a very small planet mainly inhabited by a barely developed species of ape that have been at war with each other since they gained any sort of self-awareness. I doubt that, even if they came upon it, they would even notice that it was a threat.'

Alfie smiled at Ryan's analysis of the human race, how accurate it was and how he'd never really thought of it like that before. Perhaps when you are part of something you don't often take stock of exactly what it is you are part of. You just go along for the ride and do your best to avoid the bumps in the road. He preferred to fix the bumps and that's why he stood out, 'I hope that's the case, but I just can't take the chance,' he said grimly.

'Okay, Sir, what is our destination?'

'Is there any way of tracing the black box to its point of origin?' Alfie thought out loud as he pushed his arms through the sleeves of his jacket.

'I can trace it as far back as a week, but it will take about ten minutes,' the android almost sounded embarrassed by this statement.

'Great, do it. In the meantime, I'm going to fly us to a safer place. We don't want the Jargons to come back for any reason and find us sitting here with our fingers in our mouths.' Ryan looked at him confusedly and walked away, 'I miss my unit,' Alfie said to himself. His mind flitted to thoughts of Sandy, but he pushed them back for now. He had to concentrate on what to do next and not dwell on what might be happening back at home. He finished dressing, put his shoes on, after retrieving them from where they fell and made his way to the cockpit.

Ten minutes later Ryan entered the cockpit and sat down beside Alfie, 'I have the coordinates of the last place Bagarth's ship was.'

'Put them into the computer and see where it is on the map,' Ryan did as he was ordered and the holo map lit up in front of them. It showed their position amongst a plethora of stars as a green flashing dot and the destination entered as a blue flashing dot. Alfie touched the blue flashing dot and the map zoomed in on the planet, 'Info,' he said loudly in the most monotone voice he could muster as the computer was occasionally hard of hearing like an elderly person who wanted to be left alone.

'Calculating,' it replied in its intellectual female voice. 'Destination no longer available,' it said.

'What?'

'The destination selected is no longer available. Please enter a new destination.'

Before he asked how this was possible, he sorrowfully realised what had happened. 'The evil scum have destroyed it!'

'That is not a recognisable destination, please enter a valid destination,' the computer reiterated.

'Information on the previously selected destination,' he tapped his fingers on the control impatiently trying to stay calm.

'Obiquetitas was a class S planet with a population of five billion humanoids known as Obiquetons. It was also home to seventy thousand other more primitive life forms and one hundred thousand species of flora. It was approximately three billion years old and was home to the Inter galactic Council.'

'All those lives wiped out like they were crap being scraped off a shoe,' he growled.

'Not the nicest obituary, Sir, but I get your point'.

'Not now, you metal fool,' he looked back at the map and wondered, 'computer is there any information in the system about where the Jargon's planet of origin is?'

'Yes,' it answered.

Alfie sighed, 'OK, where is it?'

'The exact location is not known but there was a coded message built into the retrieved black box that suggests the Jargons planet is near the Regina Star at the northern edge of the Andromeda Galaxy.'

'That's what the briefing must have been about. They must have found out where the Jargons were and wanted to form a plan of attack.'

'I concur, Sir. It seems that Bagarth's last act was to pass this information on to us. Perhaps we are the last hope,' said Ryan.

Alfie nodded, 'set a course for the Regina Star and set engines to maximum power. Divert it from the shield, if you have to, just get us there as soon as possible,' he closed the map and sat back in his seat. He arched his back, which clicked several times, then relaxed.

'Destination arrival in approximately five hours,' the computer relayed.

'Sir, what are you going to do when, and if, we find it? The mission to capture the Alliance leader's son was done with your entire unit. Surely it would be more sensible to go back to Earth and get reinforcements,' Ryan tried to reason with Alfie again.

'I know you mean well Ryan and you might even be right, but every minute we waste not taking the fight to them the better chance they have of wiping out many more planets until there are none left!' his gaze was set on the screen in front of him.

'Yes Sir, I understand,' he wanted to say more. He wanted to try and convince his lieutenant that his life was just as important as all the others but that was what he was built to do. The chip in his head was having a bigger effect on him than it was supposed to, perhaps it had malfunctioned or he just had a bad one. Whatever the reason it was making him not just need to protect Alfie as he was pre-programmed to do, but wanting to protect him because he cared. This was a foreign feeling to him and he did his best to ignore it as the danger was close and he didn't have time for self-reflection.

Alfie re-opened the map and searched the surrounding area of the Regina Star for likely planets in the Goldilocks zone (the zone not too hot and not too cold, but just right for life to evolve) he found seven planets that could have life on them and, judging by the Jargon's predilection to extinguish any sentient life they came upon, he surmised that only one of them would now actually have life on it and that would be the Jargon's planet. He would scan the planets for life when they arrived using the ships probe droid. Then something caught his eye that made him blink to make sure he wasn't seeing things. Not far from the Regina Solar System was a dark mass with several stars and planets hovering around it like scouts around an invisible campfire, 'computer,' he said, 'what are the probabilities that this is a black hole?' he pointed at the gathering spot with his index finger and waved it around in a circular motion to emphasise his point.

'Calculating...' she replied, 'according to the Hawking black hole parameters there is a ninety-five percent chance that this is a black hole.'

'Holy Vlar,' he said almost getting excited but remembering that the position he was in was perilous and being excited was not quite the reaction to have, 'I know what to do.'

4

Carol and Gary lay in bed both red-faced and exhausted. They hadn't been intimate for quite some time so both were a little relieved when it finally happened. 'Are you okay?' asked Gary his head was turned to one side on his pillow to face her.

'I think so,' she replied, a little confused by the question, but appreciating the sentiment, 'it's just I can't stop worrying about Tiff and what she's up to,' she shuffled into a more comfortable position.

'Don't worry about that cow, she wasn't interested in Alfie when she thought he was normal, I doubt she's gonna be interested knowing that he's... well you know,' he put his finger to his head and circled it around his temple.

Carol thumped him on his upper arm and he stopped, 'don't be such a git Gary. That's your bloody Son for crying out loud,' she turned her back on him to signify her discontent.

'Sorry sweetheart, I didn't mean to be nasty, it's just I don't really know what to think of all this. I trust the doctor, but to me, he's just Alfie and I know he can't help it but he drives me up the wall. I promise to try harder,' he pulled her back over to face him and made a stupid puppy face with his bottom lip protruding.

'The sooner we get the official diagnosis, the sooner we can start applying for a place in a special school,' she said.

'I hate that word,' he snorted.

'What, "special"?' she asked.

'Yeah, it sounds so stupid. What's so special about being retarded?'

Carol thumped him again this time harder and turned back over to face away from him, 'you're going to need to change that attitude quickly Gary Fenix or your bigotry will lose you everything,' the threat was cold and very real. Her voice contained no hint of sarcasm, just a definitive tone that left him thinking all night long.

5

Alfie smiled to himself as he formulated the details of his master plan and conferred with Ryan deep into the five-hour journey. Just before they came into range, to release the probe to scan the first planet, they admired the grandeur of the Blue Giant called Regina. It's pure and utter colossal size was incredible enough, but added to that was the enormous glow that surrounded it. The blue light engulfed the ship and everything else it touched. They were a fair distance away from it and had to use the ships computer screen to view it safely. 'I've never seen one this close before,' Alfie stared at the screen in wonder.

'It is beautiful, Sir,' Ryan admired.

'How would you know?' Alfie asked, 'you're a machine.'

'I don't know Sir, but I think this chip is having a strange effect on me.'

'Do you want me to take it out?' he asked kindly.

'No thank you, Sir. I think I like it,' liking something was also a new experience for Ryan and he liked, liking things.

'Alright, we'll leave it in for now but if it becomes a problem I'm ripping it out like it or not,' he didn't wait for a reply as he felt he didn't require one and continued, 'computer launch probe, destination planet Seven Four Bravo.'

'Launching probe,' said the computer, 'probe launched,' it confirmed.

'How long until the first readings are completed?' he said anxiously.

'Probe has arrived at the destination. Commencing scanning,' she paused for two seconds, 'planet scanned, there are no signs of life.'

'One down, six to go. Computer scan planet Six Four Bravo,' he leaned forward in his chair inadvertently.

'Probe has arrived at the destination. Commencing scanning,' she paused again for two seconds, 'planet scanned, there are no signs of life.'

'Computer scan planet Five Four...' he stopped. A huge shape almost covered their view of the sun like a cloud passing over their heads. 'Computer what was that?' he knew the answer but wanted confirmation.

'Scanning,' a pause, then, 'according to the most up to date information it matches the vague description of the Jargon warship.'

'Where did it come from?' asked Ryan unable to contain himself.

'The Regina Sun,' the computer replied.

'How is that possible?' Alfie shouted.

'It is not,' the computer replied.

'What the Vlar is going on? What are these things?' Alfie sat back in his chair shaking his head from side to side in disbelief.

'Sir,' said Ryan, 'their shields may be so powerful that they can withstand the heat of the sun.'

'Or,' Alfie rubbed his chin, 'that isn't a sun at all. Computer scan the Regina Sun.'

'Of course, it's a Sun, we can feel the heat,' Ryan argued uncharacteristically.

'Scanning,' said the computer, 'Holo shield detected. Type fifteen planet scanned. The planet contains life.'

'Clever gits,' he laughed, 'lucky for us we have the tech to scan for it after the Pluto alliance was signed.'

'Hiding Pluto was one thing, making your planet look like a sun is a whole other ball game,' Ryan couldn't believe the nonsense he was spouting but it was oddly euphoric to sound so human.

'Indeed,' said Alfie, 'computer where is the actual Regina Sun?'

'Scanning... Regina Star found. Location ten light-minutes north of type fifteen planet.'

'They hid the sun as well. These guys have been busy. Talk about paranoid. I wonder what made them this way. They can't have just woken up one morning and thought "hey I know what would be fun let's hide our planet inside a fake sun, hide the real one and destroy all sentient life in our galaxy."

'Perhaps that's exactly how it went down?' joked Ryan.

'Perhaps,' Alfie was getting used to the android sounding more human, he was even starting to like it. He liked the idea of having a companion and not just a glorified robot bodyguard.

'Computer, scan the planet for possible landing sites,' he pressed a few buttons on the panel in front of him.

'LZ found, commencing cloaking,' Ryan looked at Alfie stunned, Alfie smiled broadly, 'cloaking complete. Stealth mode active.'

'I had the Plutons add a little something before we left. I never thought I'd need it but thank Jupiter I did.'

'Why didn't you inform me?' Ryan asked, he felt hurt which he didn't like.

'No offence Ryan but you're an android and I'm pretty sure I don't have to inform you of any upgrades on my ship.'

'You're right Sir, I apologise. I won't let my insubordination effect the mission again'.

'Alright, alright calm down. From now on just trust me and know that I always have a plan,' he looked at the screen in front of him and guided the ship towards the LZ.

'Yes, Sir,' Ryan was genuine in his sincerity.

6

The planet below wasn't big, it was about as big as Earth and Mars combined and basked in a bright blue glow from the shield above it. The grass was yellow, and the majority of the plants were the same. Water, just like on Earth, was abundant and teemed with life of the most fantastic variety. The water itself reflected the brilliant blue colour of the sky which made it look like the seas of Alfie's home. The landmass wasn't split, like on Earth, instead, it was one giant island that covered about a third of the planet's surface with a few very small islands surrounding it like its children.

They landed to the north of the largest city in a yellow woodland within an even more yellow field. There was no way that they could have been seen, as the ship was not only invisible but completely silent. A quondonapher, which was a six-legged giant beetle that was used by the Jargons like humans use cattle, was startled when a door opened above it and out stepped a strange-looking creature followed by another strange creature. It galloped off towards the trees and disappeared, 'that was a big beetle,' Alfie exclaimed.

'No kidding, do you think they have tiny elephants?' Ryan asked.

'Let's just concentrate on the mission and leave the biology exploration for another time,' Alfie stepped down onto the grass and checked his helmet's oxygen levels. He saw that he had twenty hours of oxygen and an extra five in backup reserve. That should be plenty he thought. He opened his comms channel and spoke, 'computer do you read me?'

'Loud and clear Lieutenant Fenix,' the PC answered.

'Has the drone finished scanning the surface?'

'Scanning complete, I'm sending the map to your HUD.'

'I knew I could count on you.'

'The main power station that probably controls the shield is about two Earth miles south,' Ryan pointed out.

'You mean the building below the huge blue beam shooting up into the sky?' Alfie rolled his eyes.

'Yes, Sir.'

Alfie checked his weapons. Photon rifle, plasma shotgun, carbon pistol and atom collapsing grenades. All were fully loaded and ready to cause serious damage. He hadn't ever used the atom grenades in the field but was very impressed with them during training. They disintegrated everything within a ten-metre radius and left a hole where anything made of atoms once was. He scanned the immediate surroundings for any signs of life, however, apart from a few bizarre-looking woodland creatures the coast was clear. 'Ryan.'

'Yes, Sir.'

'I have one more surprise for you,' he activated the camo and disappeared.

'Sir?' Ryan panicked.

'Over here,' he reappeared on the opposite side of Ryan.

'Personal Holo shields. That is brilliant Sir,' he was very impressed.

'Another gift from the Plutons,' he said with a satisfied burr. 'Be aware though, they can only last for one minute at a time when you're moving or until your suit takes any damage. They only take ten seconds to recharge but try not to be seen at that time. Stand still and they last as long as you need them because our movement is erratic the Holo shield can't keep a lock on us like it can a planet or a ship. But still pretty awesome.'

'Very awesome,' replied Ryan. The two of them moved swiftly through the forest and out into the open fields. They never used their camo as they surprisingly never saw a single Jargon. There was the occasional freaky looking creature, that they

171

hoped was friendly and turned out to be, but not one residential humanoid alien. They got to within a stone's throw of the power station and marvelled at the huge blue beam streaming out of a large funnel.

'Ok, that's the target,' Alfie scanned the area and pinpointed the east side entrance as the best incursion point.

'How do you want to play this Sir?'

'You're the lookout, I'm the assault. I'll sneak in and take them by surprise, then I'll contact you and you can assist with setting up the link,' he readied himself but was still suspicious as to why there were no signs of intelligent life to be seen.

'Yes Sir, good luck,' he awkwardly tapped Alfie on the back.

'Don't need it,' Alfie said cockily as usual before going into dangerous situations. He crouched low and hustled down a bank then up to the building, all while keeping his rifle shoulder-high ready to fire. There was no obvious security and he assumed this was because they never imagined that anyone would ever find them, let alone land on their planet undetected and attack their main power station. It was annoyingly easy but he probably shouldn't complain about that especially as it wasn't going to be easy for long. He reached the door and found to his surprise that it was unlocked.

'They aren't expecting this,' said Ryan into his comms still aware that he had to keep an eye out as there were Jargons on the planet they just hadn't met one yet.

'No, but let's not assume they're stupid either.'

'Yes Sir,' the android agreed. Alfie opened the door and entered cautiously. He found himself in a large almost empty room. Its walls were a brilliant white and the floor was jet black. The contrast hurt his eyes. The only thing it contained was a white desk and matching chair that sat smack-bang in its centre. On the desk was what looked like a Personal Computer from the nineties (the one with the coloured back) and on the chair sat a very small man. Alfie activated his camo as soon as he spotted him and a sixty-second clock appeared in the corner of his HUD.

He edged closer, gun ready. He knew this would activate the timer and the seconds began to count down. He made it to within five feet of the man when he suddenly, and very alarmingly, swivelled around on his chair and faced Alfie. He looked right at him as if he could see him but the timer said Alfie still had thirty seconds of camo left. He didn't know what to do and his hand hovered over the trigger of his rifle which he was now aiming at the man. Wait, no it wasn't a man, it was a young boy. He couldn't have been much older than twelve. His face had a similar setup to a human's, except the skin was a light hazy purple and his eyes were completely orange and as big as cricket balls. His nose was petite and his mouth was a small slit below it, barely big enough to fit a straw in. His head was bereft of hair and there were no eyebrows or eyelashes either. Last, but not least, he had no ears just dents in the side of his shiny purple head. Alfie didn't know what to expect. He had seen many aliens in his time with the Dark Soldiers but for some reason this one had him rattled. Twenty seconds remaining on the countdown and still the boy stared straight at him.

'Hello,' the boy said. His voice was soothing and sounded more like it floated over to Alfie than shot through the air as a sound wave. Alfie didn't move, the clock said eighteen seconds. 'I said, hello,' its eyes turned a brighter orange and Alfie gave up believing he was invisible to him.

'Hello,' Alfie replied.

'Why are you here?' the boy asked and his head tilted slightly to one side.

'To stop you,' Alfie said defiantly. The clock ran out and the suit became visible again.

'There you are Mr shadow man, I can see you properly now,' his head moved over to the opposite side.

'How did you know I was here?' Alfie could think of nothing else to ask for some reason.

'I saw you like you were a shadow. My eyes can see all things that move as they are hypersensitive to light.' Here we go again with the biology research Alfie thought. 'Why do you want to stop me?' the boy asked innocently, 'I have done nothing wrong to you.'

'What do you mean nothing wrong? Your warship has destroyed planets, has killed billions of beings and plans to wipe out all sentient life in the galaxy,' Alfie let in a mouthful of air.

'That's how you get hiccups,' the boy pointed out.

'Hiccups,' yelled Alfie, 'who gives a damn about hiccups when your species has killed billions and plans to kill billions more.'

'It is self-defence,' the boy looked at him but Alfie couldn't read his expressions as he had none.

'What have we ever done to you?' he asked his finger was still on the trigger.

'Several years ago this planet had a population of three billion Jargons. We were peaceful science enthusiasts and wanted nothing more than to explore the stars and meet new, fascinating creatures like yourself. If my father had met you ten years ago he would have fallen over backwards with excitement,' the boy's eyes changed shape to look like a sideways oblong and Alfie didn't know whether it meant he was happy or sad.

'So why destroy us?' Alfie growled.

'Because you started it,' the boy's eyes turned dark orange and narrowed. 'Just after the launch of our first mission to reach out to other worlds, we received a message from a planet ten light-years away called Origy. We were so overjoyed at the prospect of extra-terrestrial relations it never crossed our mind's they might be dangerous.' Alfie's heart sank when he realised what the boy was about to tell him but he had to remain strong and stay focused on completing his mission. The boy continued, 'they took control of our vessel and forced the crew to take them back to its planet of origin. They resisted as best they could but they were subjected to torture that no creature could endure. I know this because my Father was the captain of the exploration ship and he told me before he died what they had done to him,' his eyes went sad again, the oblong shape was unquestionably sad. 'It turned out that this race of aliens thought that we were primitive fools. They wanted us to be indoctrinated into their belief system and make us work for them as slaves, to repent for our sinful unbelieving of their lunatic deity Slarwendal. They killed so many of my people and those that survived were taken as currency to be traded on distant worlds. When they had ravaged our home, of everything they wanted, they left and only a small group of children that had been hidden away by our parents remained. That was two years ago now and at that time we found a damaged Origy ship they left behind. Using our scientific brains, we harnessed their destructive technology and within six months we had repaired it and improved it. We invented the ability to hide our planet from any other invaders and trick them into thinking we were our own sun. We programmed the ship so we could control it from here and set about taking our revenge. Within a few weeks, our superior warship had found and destroyed Origy but we had to make sure we were safe.'

'That doesn't mean you had to kill every living thing,' Alfie interrupted.

'That's not what we wanted. We sent a message out into the universe as far as our transmitter could reach and explained that we would destroy all sentient life that posed a threat to us or any other peaceful planet. We were met with violence and an army of ships came to meet our vessel. They stood little chance and we defended ourselves justly.'

'But you weren't even onboard, so why did you kill them?'

'I told you, they posed a threat. They were not interested in peace, they wanted our warship for themselves. They saw what it did to the much-feared Origies and they thought that they could take it from us. They were wrong,' these last three words he said very slowly and with a menace that Alfie had never heard the likes of before.

'So, you were just standing up to the bully,' Alfie could relate to that. He had been bullied chronically as a child which is why he beefed himself up and joined the Space Navy.

'Precisely,' his eyes went a friendlier colour, 'after that the Inter Galactic Council declared us enemies of the Universe and we have been hunted ever since. We searched almost a year for the home planet of the Council to put an end to the corruption they spread and the more we searched the more we found out about their evil ways. The Origy were just a small group that worked for the Council. They forced entire races and species to believe in deities that don't exist, to keep them under control so the Council could rule unchallenged throughout the Universe. They would either take over and desolate entire planets that posed no threat or trick the stronger ones into working with them.'

Alfie felt used, 'damn scum!'

'Indeed,' a beeping noise like an alarm clock sounded from the computer and the boy swivelled in his chair to face it. He pressed a few buttons on its screen, swivelled back around then stood up, 'It looks as though you were followed.'

'By whom?' Alfie asked incredulously.

'By the Council of course.'

'You destroyed the Council or at least their home planet,' he said standoffishly.

'No, we did not,' the boy's eyes narrowed.

A sudden wave of sickness rushed over Alfie as he realized that he'd just been played. The Council must have known the humans had the holo technology from the Plutons, that's why they requested a ship was sent to meet them. They must have faked the black box and destroyed the ship hoping Alfie would act as humans do, irrationally. The computer must have been blocked from finding the Councils home world so he would assume it had been destroyed, thereby driving him into a further state of anger. They must have been watching from a distance tracking his every move. That's why they gave his ship's computer the so-called coded information on the possible whereabouts of the Jargon's home planet in the black box. Only a human ship could and would be stupid enough to sneak close enough to the sun without being detected and show the Council exactly where the hidden planet was. After that, he had just acted as a distraction. A door opened in the far west corner of the room and out stepped twenty other children of various ages, but none older than fourteen, one at a time.

'This is all that's left of your species?' he asked subdued by sadness.

'Yes,' the boy answered in an equally sad way.

Alfie sighed, 'Okay then,' the children shuffled shyly over to them and they all stared at Alfie with their huge orange eyes. He felt their pain and a wave of new anger and determination surged through him, 'I know what to do,' they gathered around him and he explained the plan.

Ryan heard all this over the comms and his emotions were at a new and uncontrollable peak. He felt sadness for the children and hatred for the Council. He felt love for his friend and loyalty that far surpassed any programming. He looked to the sky when he heard a loud engine noise coming from above. Five drop ships were landing right on top of him and he dashed for the building while activating his camo. He burst through the door into the room much to the children and Alfie's surprise. 'Damn it Ryan what are you doing?' Alfie yelled in surprise.

'They're here, Sir. The Council drop ships are landing outside. Five of them to be precise,' he closed the door behind him.

'Computer are you still there?' Alfie asked through his comms.

'Receiving Lieutenant, how may I be of service?' she asked still in a smooth tone which Alfie only now realised was to help the user keep calm.

'Scan the dropships and give me some numbers,' he turned to face the children who were huddled together like scared kittens, 'where's your warship?'

'It's cloaked and hiding behind the fifth planet from our sun,' the boy answered.

'You know what to do; you know it's the only way. I promise you, I won't let any harm come to you as long as I'm alive,' the boy nodded, 'one last thing,' he said, 'what's your name?'

'My name is Stubz.'

177

'Okay Stubz, I'm Lieutenant Alfie Fenix and you're not dying today,' he checked his weapons and ran to the door.

'There are five drop ships each containing ten Arch Angel warriors and five Pawns,' the computer stated.

'Crap, that's a lot. But I've handled worse,' Alfie decided not to mention that he had had his entire squad of fifteen men to help him.

'Where do you want me?' Ryan asked.

Alfie handed him his pistol, 'if anything comes through that door, that isn't me, shoot it. Do you understand?' he looked him straight in the eye.

'I understand, Sir,' and he hugged him.

'Thanks,' he activated his camo and ran out the door.

7

The ships were just landing as he climbed a ladder to the top of the building. With his camo still active, he covertly set himself up on the roof and attached a sniper scope to his photon rifle. He peered down it and saw the troops pile out of the ships and set themselves in an orderly formation at the top of the bank. He looked for the biggest, baddest looking git he could find, took aim and fired. Fogorow, leader of the Arch Angel warriors was a proud and distinguished veteran of fifty years in the Inter Galactic Council Navy. He was known as the Origy that would get the job done and this job was going to be the sweetest one ever. At last, he would have his revenge against the cowardly scum that had wiped out most of his species from existence. How dare they stand against the awesome might of the Council, 'the human is somewhere on the planet. Hopefully, he hasn't finished the Jargons off for us,' his men mumbled between themselves. 'Remember that he is now a threat that also must be eliminated. We cannot allow him to leave,' there was a crack in the air like the end of a whip smacking a naked back. The Arch Angels shuffled nervously and looked to their leader. His head was missing and all that remained was a swaying body that subsequently fell to the ground with a thump.

'That's one,' Alfie said out loud to himself, 'now for two, three and four,' three more Arch Angel warriors' headless bodies dropped to the ground before the others realised what was going on and began to react.

'How's it going, Sir?' Ryan asked excitedly.

'Not now Ryan, I'm kind of busy,' Alfie took another shot but it missed just to the left of a diving Pawn. The rest of the troops produced their light shields rendering the photon rifle useless. Alfie decided to test his atom grenade and pressed the button on the side of the little orb. He launched it as far as he could and it landed next to a group of about five Pawns. It didn't even make a noise, there was a flash which turned the darkening sky pink, then there was a hole where the vicious ten-foot-tall aliens had just been. A split second later, the remaining twenty Pawns had jumped on the roof and were franticly searching for their attacker. They were like wild monkeys scrambling up using their huge claws for grip. They bared dozens of sharp fangs and grey drool dripped down their chins. Alfie lay on the ground facing up, his Shotgun at the ready and his camo on. The clock didn't move and neither did he. The Pawns clicked and squawked in a disturbing assault on the ears and one almost tripped over him but narrowly missed his feet. He waited until they were sufficiently spread out and chucked another grenade at the only ones left in a small group of about seven. He rolled away and the clock began to count down on his HUD. Another flash, but this one was followed by plasma blasts and Pawn body parts flying through the air. He dived to his left and fired, a Pawn exploded in front of him and he dove through the haze of blood left in its wake. He smashed into another and it fell over backwards, he jumped on top of it, pulled the trigger and its head and shoulders were removed.

There were three left when he'd run out of rounds and camo charge so he hid behind a small metal box waiting for his suit to recharge. The remaining Pawns screamed and sent shivers down the spines of even the Arch Angel warriors. Eight seconds till charge, they hunted him. Six seconds till charge, they were close. Three seconds till charge, they found him. One second till charge, he had reloaded and shot one in its armoured chest. Charge complete, he disappeared and left a present for the other two in the open chest wound of the injured Pawn. They looked down at the flashing orb peering out of their friend and the sky went pink. Alfie dived off the roof and landed heavily on his side, luckily for him it was on grass.

The Arch Angel warriors hadn't wasted the time that Alfie had been distracted. They'd been attacking the building and trying to break through the door. Ryan was on the other side of it and held it shut as there was no lock. His immense robotic strength was holding firm but it couldn't hold forever. They'd set up a plasma cannon and were preparing to blow the door apart. Alfie, who was still in camo mode, sprinted towards the cannon.

He touched his belt expecting to find his last grenade but was appalled to find it had come loose when he'd landed and there was no time to go back for it. He noticed the two who were setting up the cannon no longer had their shields active and he whipped out his rifle, knelt on one knee aimed carefully (there was no point in rushing it and missing) and fired. With one well-aimed shot, two Arch Angel warriors hit the ground. The others spread out but still couldn't see him. There were thirty seconds of camo left and he had to use it wisely. The warrior's shields were raised so the rifle was no good, for now, he was out of grenades and his pistol was with Ryan. They were too far away for the shotgun to be useful and he couldn't reach them before his camo ran out and he was shot to pieces. He racked his brain.

The ship's computer was no ordinary bit of kit. She'd been designed by the finest minds known to the Universe in a lab as secret as the knowledge of life itself. She'd been gifted to the humans by the master species, the Plutons. Their technology was sought after throughout the cosmos and the humans had been lucky enough to live practically next door. They took some time before they even managed to travel to Pluto whereas the Plutons had been travelling to Earth for millions of years. They'd seen this funny little race of aliens grow from something as small a mouse to an ape building spaceships. They'd helped a little by ridding them of a nasty predatory reptile species that had accidentally evolved quicker than they had. The Plutons had given them a fair chance to evolve but to no avail. They hadn't moved past eating one another for one hundred and seventy-five million years and it was about time someone else had a go. A redirected asteroid later and it was the mammal's turn. The Plutons felt as though they had to look after the humans as they had championed their ascension to the most powerful species on Earth. So, from a distance, they kept them safe. Of course, they didn't realise that the humans would, for the most part, try and kill each other and be wrongly led by made up beliefs in various gods. This they long suspected was the doing of the ever-growing Inter-Galactic Council. They'd been faking religious history and indoctrinating species for as long as the Plutons could remember but they'd never been approached as they were hidden in plain sight, disguised as an insignificant dwarf planet. They weren't happy when the Milky Way Council had ordered the humans to send a representative and had prepared Alfie as best they could for his journey. They never trusted the IGC, but the Earthlings had ignored their warnings, thinking they knew better. They didn't blame Lieutenant Alfie and made sure that every step of his mission was reported back to them by the ship's computer. Alfie's time had run out and he stood exposed in the middle of the battlefield with an onslaught of guns pointed in his direction, 'I'm sorry Ryan, I've blown it,' do your best but if you can, get the kids out another way.'

'Yes, Sir,' the android held back waterless tears.

The Arch Angel warriors took aim and a barrage of light fire was released through the air. Alfie closed his eyes and Sandy's face appeared. She blew him a kiss and he ached for her touch. He had failed to keep his word and he mouthed the words I'm sorry. A few seconds later and he was still alive. He opened his eyes to the most wonderful sight he had ever seen, in all his years. The Plutons had landed, camouflaged and unnoticed by the IGC ships and fifty strong they were attacking the warriors. Alfie watched on as the warriors fell and a large battalion appeared in their place. The barrage of light fire had come from them. 'Good to see you're still alive Lieutenant!' shouted the battalion commander.

He recognised the voice but it couldn't be, 'Dash, is that you?'

Dash walked over to his dearest friend, grabbed and shook his hand, 'damn glad to see you Fenix.'

'Where the hell did you come from?' he was more than a little confused.

'Typical human,' the Pluton laughed, 'always the last to know what's going on. I'll explain later but right now we have the largest assembled fleet the Universe has ever seen looking for that warship.'

'Don't worry about them,' Alfie said confidently.

'Are you mad!?' his friend retorted.

'Now who's the last to know?' he smiled and let his friend in on their little secret.

8

While the battle raged just outside the door, Stubz had taken control of the warship and was covertly flying it to the edge of the Regina solar system. About the same time as Alfie was blowing holes in the Pawns, the ship became visible and within seconds had been detected by every IGC ship. While Alfie had been recharging his shield the warship had destroyed about thirty ships, however, there were hundreds remaining. As Alfie was diving off the roof the warship had, at full speed, headed towards the group of planets that were sitting around an invisible campfire. The other ships including the mothership containing the entire council chased after it convinced they had it within their grasp. As Alfie was pulling off the greatest snipe shot he had ever done the ships reached the edge of the black hole. They hadn't seen it because, as Alfie had guessed, they weren't looking for it. They only cared about one thing and that was the warship, which was now inside the black hole and as time has no meaning in this vast abyss it looked as though it was still within reach. Whilst Alfie was waiting to die, the IGC had passed the point of no return on the horizon and were being sucked into nothingness.

Stubz appeared in the opening of the doorway and Ryan stood behind him with his pistol pointing out into the night air. 'Stand down Ryan, it's all clear,' ordered Alfie.

'Yes, Sir,' but I do believe I need to apologise.

'What for my friend?' Alfie asked incredulously.

Ryan liked the term friend, but it only made it harder to tell Alfie the problem, 'I'm afraid an Arch Angel warrior managed to sneak through a vent and took us by surprise,' he stepped out from behind Stubz and Alfie saw the gaping hole in his stomach. All his wires were showing and some were torn apart. He was leaking fluid and small sparks lit up his insides.

'He saved us, he used himself as a shield and killed the intruder,' Stubz stated with admiration.

'Oh Ryan no,' Alfie grabbed him as he collapsed. 'It's gonna be okay, you know I can't do this without you.'

'Of course, you can Sir, you are Alfie the greatest hero the galaxy has ever known,' Ryan shuddered, and his head twitched.

'You were more than just my Bodyguard...' Alfie began to say, but the light had gone from the eyes of his android and he knew he was gone. He finished his sentence anyway, 'you were my Bro'.

'I'm so sorry Lieutenant,' Dash comforted his friend.

Alfie remained silent. He knew the Plutons could fix his BRO, but his personality and memories would be gone and that is what made Ryan more than just an android. Dash began ushering the children out into the open and the Plutons outside surrounded them.

'Hey! Wait for a second,' Alfie protested, snapping out of his pondering.

'Don't worry, we're not here to hurt them, we're here to help them, the same as you,' Dash put his hand on Alfie's arm, 'we've been listening to your comms this whole time. We know exactly what these kids have been through. We'll look after them, I promise' Alfie waved at Stubz and he waved back. They were safe now and the most dangerous force, as well as the deadliest ship, had been destroyed in one fell swoop. The universe was a better place and that was not a bad day at the office, thought Alfie.

After saying his goodbyes, he boarded his ship. He carried the body of his BRO in his arms and laid him in his bed out of respect for his fallen comrade. The journey home was long and lonely, but the homecoming he received was glorious. He was an intergalactic hero, who had freed the galaxy from it's greatest threat. He was given the highest honours and Ryan was also remembered for his invaluable contribution. Alfie retired after that and lived peacefully with Sandy for the rest of his days.

'That was a good one,' Stubbs smiled at Alfie.

'Ryan keeps dying, but it's okay because he died a hero,' Alfie wiped away a stray tear.

'How are you feeling?' asked Stubbs.

'Much better thank you,' and he really was.

'Morning Baby,' said Carol cheerfully, as Gary had apologised profusely half a dozen times already this morning and she was feeling in control and full of confidence. She couldn't wait to start understanding her son and helping him understand her, 'how are you feeling this morning? Did you have a good night's sleep?' she opened the curtains, but not fully as he didn't like that and looked down at Alfie. He had a huge grin on his face like a cat that had all the cream. 'Nice to see you too, Baby,' she smiled back thinking his grin was for her, but Alfie knew that he had saved the universe and, even better, Ryan had helped him. That was definitely worth showing some teeth over.

'Morning, Son,' Gary leaned around the door and did his best to smile. He wasn't much of a smiler but knew how to lift the corners of his lips to make the right shape. Alfie stared at him blankly wondering why he was doing that weird thing with his mouth, and that perhaps he was ill. 'So, what are you going to build today?' Gary asked straining the smile now so it looked out of place on his bearded face. Alfie continued to stare unable to take his eyes off his father's mouth. 'You know, out of Lego,' his eyes widened as if hinting for his son to respond, but still, Alfie said nothing.

Carol could see her husband was getting upset and decided to intervene before he did something he would later regret, 'up you get Alfie, it's time for breakfast,' she kneeled beside his bed and caught his gaze.

'I had an adventure with Ryan,' he said excitedly then jumped out of bed. Carol looked over at Gary who looked back at her. They both had the same expression of confusion and sadness written on their faces. Alfie ran around the room with his arms out making whooshing noises and pow pow sounds like a laser gun. He rolled on the ground and stared up at the ceiling as if he was seeing something that only he could see.

'What I wouldn't give for five minutes in your head, Alfie,' Carol laughed when she realised her boy seemed happy.

'Probably make you mad as he is,' Gary snorted and went off to start breakfast.

Carol threw daggers after him with her eyes and let out a long whistling breath of pure frustration. She fretted over whether this stupid, stubborn man would ever accept his son. She wondered if it was even in his remit of skills to let go of so much bitterness and resentment towards a child. She looked at Alfie lying on the floor, so innocent of the hatred towards him, or perhaps he wasn't and instead he just chose to ignore it. How hard it must be she thought, to be misunderstood by so many people, and then the one person who really knew you was no longer around. All because of her. She dismissed the memory of that night so as not to well up with tears in front of Alfie. He had enough to deal with without her stressing him out as well.

She'd been up until the early hours of the morning after her disagreement with her husband researching autism on her notebook PC. She'd read all about the variety of symptoms, or traits as they were known, and had linked so many with her little boy. She was almost angry that no one had picked up on it beforehand, especially the school. Well, there was Alfie's teacher who she'd spoken to, but Gary had said not to listen to her. Gary. His name made her teeth clench. The stupid oaf who refused to acknowledge his own son's difficulties all so he could go on pretending that everything was fine and living in his little fantasy bubble. While she'd been reading, she'd also noticed that a lot of the traits mentioned could describe Gary's behaviour sometimes as well, and autism had been linked to genes. She decided against bringing this up with him, considering his up and down attitude, and just hoped he could connect with his son. After that, she might mention it. She then had remembered the YouTube channel that Doctor Fossil had mentioned and decided to take a look. She was prepared to see an odd looking man with an obvious condition clumsily try and explain autism to her, even though she believed she already understood it because of what she had already been told and also just read. She couldn't have been more wrong. Instead, what she saw when she clicked on the page of Joe James Neurodiversity Awareness was a photo of a young, handsome (if she did say so herself) man, next to a stunning blonde that was apparently his wife. It turned out he was married with two autistic children and a very good job. He also took stunning photos and accredited this to him being Autistic (she had discovered that most Autistic people prefer identity first language as they felt Autism was an integral part of them and not a condition they had). She began binge watching all the videos and was astounded how much she learnt and how wrong so much of what she had learned from the "experts" was. It turned out that the best way to understand her Son was by listening to him and also Autistic adults. By the time she was finished with the videos Gary was already mulling around and trying to apologise, so she decided to watch more later.

'Please may I have toast and chocolate spread, Mummy?' Alfie was still lying on the floor.

'Only if you get up and dressed right away,' she had learned it was good to set boundaries and lay out specific instructions as clearly as possible.

'Yes, Mummy,' he stood up and went over to his dresser drawer and began dressing.

'I'll be downstairs, so come down as soon as you've dressed,' she left, almost tripping over Monty who gracefully dodged to one side and into the room.

'That was so much fun,' said Stubbs sitting on Alfie's left shoulder. He jumped off onto the bed when Alfie pulled off his t-shirt, then dived onto the floor when Monty jumped up.

'Mummy seemed happy this morning, but Daddy was very confusing.'

'I think he was happy as well, but he didn't sound it. His mouth was, but maybe he wasn't?' Stubbs leapt back onto Alfie's shoulder now he was dressed.

'I wish he was always nice to me. I keep getting my hopes up when he is. Then he does or says something that ruins it and makes me hurt inside.'

'I know little Dude, let's hope this time he can stay nice.'

Alfie did hope, but he wasn't going to hold his breath, 'at least I have you and Mummy,' he said cheerfully.

'Always,' Stubbs patted him on the shoulder and the two of them headed off for breakfast.

Chapter 9

Over the next week, Alfie and Carol were inseparable, except when Alfie had to have his downtime due to being overloaded with what neurotypical people call "life", but Alfie considered an "overexposure to a confusing mess of a world". She'd made such an effort to understand him and make sure he was happy, but always remembered to set boundaries when they were needed. She'd rung the school to explain why he wasn't coming back for a while, although she was hoping to find a better school for him as soon as possible. She'd continued to learn as much as she could and had already read two books, watched countless online videos and a documentary on TV. She also joined online groups run by actually autistic people and was well and truly making an effort. Alfie had responded to this by making more eye contact and hugging her occasionally. She never forced him to do anything and let him guide her every step of the way. She loved every minute they spent together and even when he had a meltdown in the supermarket which used to be her biggest nightmare, she didn't care what the other people were thinking or saying. She'd calmly coaxed him back to a calm state by singing him his favourite song and took him for ice cream afterwards to show that he'd done nothing wrong. She knew the world was a scary place sometimes for any child or adult, but especially for those who were Autistic. Like Ryan, she was starting to see the loving little boy more and more, just by being patient. She wished she could say the same for Gary but that would be a lie and as Alfie kept saying "lying was wrong because it was false and being false was bad". He'd tried to communicate with Alfie but never really gave it more than a few minutes at a time and that wasn't nearly long enough to get his attention. Every time he would get frustrated and storm off muttering something rude and nasty under his breath, then she'd have to speak to him later to convince him not to give up. It was like having two children at times and Alfie was more grown up. Tiffany had been sniffing around and had turned up at the house a couple of days later, except Gary had told her to back off for a while. She'd said she only came around because she wanted to say sorry for breaking Alfie's toy. Carol had said it was ok, but Alfie didn't want to see her. They agreed that she would try again in a week or so and they hadn't heard from her since. Carol hoped she'd scarpered back to Australia, but she knew deep down Tiffany would be back.

Today the two of them were at the zoo and Alfie was in his element. His "special interest" as they are known as, apart from his Lego, was animals. He wanted to be a television zoologist like his hero David Attenborough one day and tell people thousands of facts on TV. That way he didn't need to meet them or interact with others, but he would still be able to teach them about the things he loved. 'Mummy did you know that there are lionesses in Africa that look like male lions?' he joyfully explained as he stared at the huge lion through the glass.

'Really, how do they do that?' she asked legitimately interested.

'It is most likely a mutated gene that seems to be beneficial in some way, therefore becoming more widespread among the species. At the moment only a handful are known to us but it's more than likely that there are more or there will be more. The benefit is thought to be that, in the pride, they are more secure from other lions if it looks as if there are more males. So, it possibly acts as a defence disguise against attacks from other prides,' he peered closer to the glass as the lion walked by and glanced fleetingly in his direction, 'Mummy he looked at me.'

'Maybe he's hungry?' she chuckled.

'No Mummy, it said on the poster that their feeding time was at two o'clock and now it is,' he looked down at his watch, 'three forty-seven, so they wouldn't be hungry again so quickly.'

She rolled her eyes behind her sunglasses and gently touched his head. He shook his head and she let go, 'sorry Baby I forgot you don't like that.'

'It's okay Mummy, I forgive you,' he stepped away from the glass and pulled the map out of his pocket. He focused on it for a few seconds, 'Now we can go and see the Tigers, they're my favourite,' he began to walk away but was so busy looking at his map he didn't notice the toddler next to him and bumped into her. She fell on her backside and began to cry.

'You stupid pratt,' a large woman wearing black tracksuit trousers and a pink tracksuit jacket ran over from the opposite enclosure that housed the lynx, 'watch where you're going!' she grabbed her daughter and scooped her up into her arms.

'Sorry,' Alfie didn't look up from his map. He was too afraid to look at the woman and felt as though she was going to attack him at any moment.

'What the hell is wrong with you?' Carol jumped to his rescue, 'don't blame him for your kid being in the way. Where were you?' she visibly tightened.

'I'm not the one with the retard kid who can't see where he's going,' she snapped back stepping towards Carol, her heavy frame wobbled uncontrollably.

'Sharon, just leave it,' a sorrowful sounding noise came from her skinny boyfriend who wore a similar outfit to hers but a green jacket and a red cap which he wore backwards.

'Shut it, Damien, this cow thinks she's better than us,' she put her daughter down and squared up to Carol nodding her head from side to side.

'He's not retarded, he's flipping autistic,' she slapped the woman across the mouth as hard as she could, and her lip split open. The woman was so startled she couldn't even move. She just stood shaking with a blank look on her round face and a handprint on her cheek. 'Come on Alfie, let's go,' she held out her hand and he grabbed it as if it were a life preserver and he was drowning in a sea of judgment and hatred. They walked off and the boyfriend moved out of their way and went to comfort his girlfriend. She screamed something unrepeatable, but Alfie didn't listen. He was with his mummy now and she would keep him safe. Perhaps he thought that instead of shutting down this time he would just take relief from her and the world seemed a less scary and confusing place with her in it. 'Here we go Alfie, look there's a Tiger, just there on that treehouse thingy,' she pointed so he could see where she was looking. She was shaking all over, the adrenaline rushed through her veins. She'd never hit anyone in her life before, but it felt so good, it felt so powerful. She hated to admit it, but she had never felt so alive. Her dopamine levels soared to new heights. She knew it was wrong, but that woman had deserved it.

'That is a male Amur Tiger. They are the largest Tigers in the world, and they can weigh up to six hundred and sixty pounds,' he narrated. His brain monologued while he nodded his head involuntarily.

'How did you know that?' she asked half expecting that he'd read it from a sign put up by the zoo to provide interesting information about the animal you were looking at.

'It was in my brain,' he said steadily as if he was telling her the time.

She looked around and saw the sign, but it was nowhere near them and there was no way he could have read it from where they stood. She shook her head ever so slightly in as much acceptance of his brilliant mind as disbelief that he could be related to Gary, 'my little professor,' she said and this time when she accidentally touched his head he didn't recoil or shake her off but instead moved closer to her and they watched the magnificent cat yawn and stretch with joy in their hearts.

When they arrived home, Carol found an envelope on the floor underneath the letterbox flap. She leaned over and picked it up. It was on top of several other letters, bills probably she thought, but this one was different. She picked up the pile and took it into the kitchen. Alfie followed her and they found Gary sitting at the kitchen table with his head in his hands and an open beer can in front of him.

He looked up, 'where the hell have you been?' his voice was slurred.

'We went to the zoo. I told you this yesterday,' she looked at him pityingly.

'I don't remember,' he took a sip from his can.

'I thought you'd stopped all this,' she stared directly at him and he looked away embarrassed.

'Did you have a nice time?' he asked ignoring her accusation, trying to change the subject.

'Yes, thank you, we had a great time.'

'What, with that weirdo?' jealousy writhed up like bile in his throat. He tried to hold it back but failed miserably. Alfie stormed upstairs again, which, deep down, was exactly what Gary had wanted. The less he saw of him the less he was reminded that his son would never be "normal".

'You just had to ruin it didn't you?' Carol seethed, her eyes widened with anger. She stared at him with a deadly look and said, 'get out.' The command was cold, and he shivered as she said it.

'I'm not going anywhere. This is my house and, if you don't like it, you can leave,' he sat back in his chair but wasn't close to being as comfortable as he was trying to make out.

'Get out,' she repeated not taking her eyes away from his.

He looked away, too cowardly to stare her down. He stood up and walked over to her, 'make me.'

'I won't make you Gary, I'll ring Keith and Keith will make you,' she pulled her phone from her pocket.

'I knew you were sleeping with him,' he viciously spat.

'Don't be stupid. He's a friend,' she unlocked the screen.

'He's MY bloody friend, or at least I thought he was,' he was face to face with her now and they were almost touching, 'you dirty town bike, I bet everyone's had a ride on you!'

She tried to hit him, but he grabbed her arm and punched her in the face. It wasn't hard and he didn't mean to do it, but he had and now it was too late to take it back.

'GET OUT!' She screamed as tears welled up in her eyes then poured down her cheeks.

He couldn't say anything; he was as shocked as she was. He stepped back with a look of horror on his face, turned around and left via the back door. Carol stood, short of breath, her heart pumped so furiously she felt faint and decided to sit down before she did. She stayed there for a long time before she was able to calm herself. She looked down at the envelope still gripped tightly in her hands and opened it. With shaking hands, she read the letter. It stated that Alfie Fenix had been approved for an appointment with the community mental health team and the time and date of his appointment was written at the bottom. As happy as this made her, her heart was breaking. This should have been a wonderful moment that they could have all rejoiced in, but instead, her husband had assaulted her and stormed off and her son was upstairs, probably lost in another world somewhere. She decided to check on Alfie so she could at least share the news with him. When she looked in his room, she found him curled up in a ball under his covers and she recognised the look on his face. She kissed him tenderly on his head and left him to his fantasies.

The Dentist

1

It had been raining that night and the tarmac on the road glistened under the streetlamps that lined up along the path. Puddles had formed in every crevice and dent, but the rain was a distant memory, gone but not forgotten. Two eyes watched from a distance as Susan and her friends Bonny and Piper wandered along the street, laughing and joking about their night out. 'That guy was checking you out Susan, I'm telling you, he definitely fancied you,' Piper said her voice was slurred and her gate unsteady.

'No way,' Bonny interrupted, 'he was checking me out. He was giving me the eyes,' she made her eyes bigger with her fingers and wobbled her head.

'You wish, he was way too hot for you,' Piper retorted and shoved her gently.

'Shut up the pair of you. I don't care who he was looking at. He was fit, but there's no way I was ditching my girls just for some man meat,' Susan stated before all three burst out laughing in unison. They carried on walking for about half an hour, their mood never dropped, their friendship unbreakable and all the time the eyes were watching. They narrowed with concentration as if the watcher was attempting to listen in.

'Are you sure you're ok walking the rest of the way on your own?' Bonny asked when they reached the door to her and Piper's flat.

'I'll be fine,' Susan replied, 'it's only around the corner and there's plenty of light around' she could see the concern on Bonny's face, 'seriously Babe I'll be okay.'

'Alright, but text me when you get in, so we know you're fine.'

'Yes Mum,' Susan said sarcastically, and Piper laughed but didn't know exactly why, as she was drunker than the others.

'Are you going to the gym tomorrow?' Bonny asked as she brushed her long brown hair behind her left ear more out of habit than necessity. 'I'll meet you there at about nine,' she paused remembering they'd been drinking, 'actually, better make it ten.'

'Perfect,' Bonny pulled her keys from her handbag and grabbed Piper under the arm with her spare hand, 'come on you, let's get you into bed before you fall asleep out here and the postman gets a nasty shock in the morning.'

'See ya,' Piper waved stupidly.

'See ya,' Susan blew them a kiss then headed home. From a hidden place, eyes watched them. Then the eyes widened and followed Susan. Susan looked around nervously as a cold feeling ran through her spine, almost making her pee a little. Her steps quickened and the echo of her high heels bounced off the brick walls lining the side of the road. She breathed a sigh of relief when she saw her front door, still unable to explain why she was feeling so scared. She blamed Bonny for making her nervous but knew her friend was just being caring. She pushed all thoughts of danger from her mind, however, she still felt something wasn't quite right. A motorbike boomed past her, the rider not giving two damns about the speed limit. She jumped and her heart nearly came to blows with her oesophagus. She bent over with her hands on her knees and vomited. She wiped her mouth, then spat a few times before unsteadily walking the last few steps to her front door, all the time inwardly cursing the idiot biker. The eyes began to move towards her. They bobbed up and down getting closer to her by the second, with a look of intensity that would rival the world's best poker players. She fumbled in her coat pocket for her keys, still nervous and still unable to understand why. The eyes were almost on top of her now. The keys slipped from her hand. The noise as they hit the ground was louder than she'd expected in the quiet of the night. She cursed, knelt and scooped them up. It was too late, the eyes were next to her and she'd run out of time.

'Flipping hell Jacob! What are you doing sneaking up on Mummy like that?' she stroked the top of his head. Jacob stared up at his owner and purred. He licked his paw and brushed himself up against her leg. 'Silly cat, you scared the life out of me,' she selected the correct key and let herself in. She removed her coat and hung it on the peg that was supposed to be for keys. Not realising the door hadn't fully closed, she stuffed her keys in the coat pocket cursing herself from the future as she knew she'd forget she did it and spend about half an hour the next day searching for them. She slowly made her way to the kitchen to grab a drink of water before heading off to bed. Jacob ran up the stairs uninterested in her activities. She entered the kitchen and reached for the light switch but paused when she felt someone behind her. She knew it wasn't Jacob this time, she knew there was something wrong and she held her breath, unable to move. The stranger grabbed her before she could even open her mouth to scream.

2

His phone buzzed as it vibrated on the table next to him. Alfie looked down at it and grunted when he saw Ryan's face looking back at him. He didn't remember taking the picture and definitely didn't recall putting it on his phone but guessed his partner must have done it without him knowing. He made a mental note to put a password on it and picked it up, 'Fenix here,' he grumbled into the tiny black rectangle.

'It's Ryan, there's been another one,' Alfie could hear sirens in the background as Ryan spoke, 'it's the same as the others. Blonde, pretty, young and living alone.'

'Did they leave anything?' he asked gravely before taking a sip of his morning coffee.

'Nothing, but her teeth are missing,' Ryan explained, 'don't touch that, that's evidence you pratt,' Ryan told off a Bobby who was just about to pick up a discarded piece of hair. The hapless man just stood, frozen in action as his colleague sniggered. 'Sorry boss, sometimes I think they get these guys from the local dog track and stuff them in a uniform before sending them to fudge up my crime scene.'

The phone was silent for a second as Alfie contemplated his answer, then he replied ignoring Ryan's rant about the rookie officer, 'third one this month, the bastard's getting greedy.'

'I'm going to interview the neighbours and see if they saw anything.'

'They won't have, but do it anyway,' his voice was as deep as a Chicago blues singer, but with a south London accent. It had become softer over time, making it sound more like he came from Surrey; that was until he got angry, then there was no hiding the cockney twang.

'Okay boss, I'll see you when you get here,' Ryan hung up the phone.

Alfie put the phone back in on the table and took another sip of his coffee, 'I've got to go,' he said trying to sound friendly but swinging and missing. He was having breakfast with his girlfriend who was frying him some eggs and singing to herself. She was by far the most beautiful girl who had ever given him the time of day and he was head over heels in love. She was what kept the nightmares at bay and her sunny disposition brightened even the darkest of moments. He'd been alone for so long before she came along and he was beginning to give up hope that he'd ever meet anyone after Jane passed away. Then, like a shot of adrenaline to his heart, Samantha turned up to rescue his sorry backside.

She shook the eggs on to a plate and walked over, 'you aren't going anywhere until you eat something and that's not up for negotiation.'

He knew better than to argue with her, so instead just tucked into the food, 'fine,' he said with his mouth full.

'Lovely,' she remarked.

'Sorry,' he downed his coffee and wiped his mouth on his shirt sleeve leaving a faint discoloured watermark behind.

'Give me a kiss then,' she said puckering her lips. He pecked her cheek and left, grabbing his long black Crombie coat on his way out. The morning was fresh from the rainfall the night before and a steamy haze drifted just above the grass in the front garden. He unlocked his black VW Golf and sat behind the wheel. It wasn't a fancy car, he didn't need fancy, he bought it because it was practical just like him. He turned the key in the ignition and the engine gunned into life. He switched on the radio and drove. At that time of the morning, he expected to find the roads packed with cars, but for once his journey was mostly unhindered. This put him in a slightly better mood but as usual, it wouldn't last, but that was all part of the job he supposed.

Ryan was just finishing interviewing Mrs Bushell, a very talkative lady who seemed more interested in the welfare of the victim's cat than the victim herself. As it happened the cat was fine, her brother had found it sitting next to the girl licking her hand. He'd come over to give his sister her birthday present and take her out for breakfast. She hadn't answered the door, so he let himself in using a spare key and found her in the kitchen, lying face down on the pale blue tiles. At first, he thought she might have been sleeping off the previous night's alcohol, but when she didn't wake from his calling, he tried shaking her and when this didn't work, he turned her over and was confronted with the pale stunned face of his lifeless sibling. 'Yes, Mrs Bushell I'll mention to her Brother that you're happy to take the cat. I just think that right now isn't the best time,' Ryan was losing his patience.

'But what will it eat today if no one feeds it?' she grabbed his arm preventing him from leaving.

'Fine, Mrs Bushell I'll make it my priority to look after the cat. I'm sure the murderer who was lurking around your street last night can wait,' he inwardly scolded himself for losing his cool, but she was getting under his skin.

She let go of his arm and huffed, 'I was only trying to help Detective, there's no need to be rude,' she turned and stormed off muttering something no doubt unpleasant, under her breath. Ryan used his thumb and forefinger to pinch his eyes and the bridge of his nose. He was so tired lately. The other murders similar, if not identical to this one, had him pulling serious overtime, but he never complained and never let it affect his police work. He heard a car approaching and looked up. A black VW Golf was trundling towards him and he recognised his partner's car immediately.

Alfie pulled up next to the curb and soaked in his surroundings. The street was a nice one, the kind of street you would see in a movie about suburban housewives. The houses were all relatively similar and looked almost new. Evergreen trees lined up neatly along the thin grass verge that ran alongside the path and most of the neighbours were either in their gardens staring or peering from the safety of their windows. He felt uneasy with all those eyes watching him and he hesitated momentarily before exiting his car. He stepped onto the grass and almost into some dog mess, not so perfect after all he thought and frowned at the red dog bin, not three feet from where he stood, 'bloody typical,' he growled like he was gargling grit.

'What is?' Ryan asked as he approached him.

'Doesn't matter,' he lied as it mattered a great deal to him and he didn't even know why. With all the horrors he had seen over the years, something like that shouldn't have bothered him, but beyond all reason and sense, it did.

'I interviewed most of the neighbours with the help of some uniforms and as you said, they didn't see anything,' Ryan waggled his notebook.

'Sometimes I hate being right,' Alfie shook his head. He felt in his pocket for his cigarettes, a habit he'd done for years when he heard bad news but forgot he gave up for Samantha a month ago. Instead, he pulled out a vape and puffed on it. It made a bubbling noise as he inhaled the spit from its previous use, then exhaled. A candyfloss smoke cloud rose and disappeared into the air.

Ryan scrunched his nose, he hated the overly sweet smell. 'Her Brother said she was out with friends last night. He was the one that found her. He'd come over to see her on her birthday. I interviewed him first, made sure his memory was fresh just like you said to do. He wasn't happy but I explained why it was so important and he told me everything. As far as the friends are concerned, I was waiting for you so we could go and speak to them together.'

'Let me see the girl first then we'll head over there,' he wrapped the coat tight to his chest and followed Ryan up to the house. He stopped just before the front door and hovered a while.

'What're you doing boss?' Ryan asked impatiently.

'Thinking, now shut up,' the grizzly detective looked around searching for signs of a break-in. He pulled out some latex gloves from his inside jacket pocket and slid them onto his hands.

'If you're looking for any signs of a break-in, I already checked and there are none,' Ryan explained confidently. This statement had no visible impact on Alfie, and he carried on looking. He ran his fingers up and down the inside of the door frame feeling for anything that might seem out of place. So far, when investigating the previous two crime scenes involving young, blonde, pretty women he hadn't found anything, but he had a routine and he liked sticking to it. This time though his fingers stopped as they reached the hole of the locking mechanism and they carefully grasped at what seemed like thin air. 'You got something boss?'

'A hair,' he said so quietly it was as if he was speaking to himself, 'small one, but it's a hair.'

'Christ, I can't believe I missed it,' Ryan blurted out.

'I can,' Detective Fenix had no sarcasm or humour in his voice, he just said what he was thinking. This would occasionally get him into trouble with his superiors and fellow coppers, but he was a results man and the result was normally that he caught the killer and justice was served, so for the most part they left him alone. Ryan was the only DC that would work with him and had gotten used to his sharp tongue. He wanted to learn from this veteran and if that meant having to put up with his rudeness from time to time that was fine by him.

The hair was placed in an evidence bag. It was virtually invisible unless you knew what you were looking for. They continued inside to the kitchen. The body hadn't been moved since the brother had found her and Alfie knelt by her side. He could see straight away the bruising around her throat indicating strangulation but suspected that, like the others, this wasn't what'd killed her. He opened her mouth and confirmed that her teeth had been removed, taken no doubt for a trophy. The killer risked being caught just to have their memento of the occasion. Then he found what he was looking for, the blood in her ear coming from the puncture wound to her brain. They probably used a long screwdriver or something similar but in the other cases they were unable to find any trace of the weapon, so he knew the killer was clean. They knew how to sterilise stuff and Alfie thought there might be a clue in that somewhere. He stood up groaning a little, his knees weren't what they used to be, then pulled off the gloves, 'let's go', he said.

Ryan nodded, 'poor girl probably didn't even see it coming.'

'They never do,' he glanced at her lifeless body, so young and once full of potential and his heart ached. He always felt their suffering but never showed his pain. He was stone-faced and serious just like his father had taught him to be.

They walked out of the house and Ryan spoke to the uniform officers who were mulling around in the front garden looking like lost children, 'don't touch anything until forensics say its ok,' they all nodded, then carried on chatting.

One particularly dense officer decided it would be a great idea to take a selfie and pulled his phone from his pocket. He held it up to his face and smiled. Just as he was about to press the screen a hand swooped in, snatched his phone and threw it over the garden hedge, 'if I see anyone trying anything like that again at one of my crime scenes, I'll beat seven bells of crap out of them and shove the phone where the sun don't shine,' Alfie glared at the shocked officer who was going redder than a fried tomato, 'do I make myself clear?' no one said a word, instead, they shuffled their feet nervously and looked anywhere but in his direction.

'C'mon you old bulldog,' Ryan gently encouraged Alfie away by firmly putting his hand on his partner's shoulder, 'let's go see the friends and get to the bottom of this before some other poor girl loses her life,' these words were enough to get the senior detective moving and the two men walked in silence around the corner to Bonny and Piper's flat. Alfie's mind was like a huge clock with its cogs turning slowly but steadily, never stopping. He tried to connect what little information they had but came up blank each time. They reached the door to the building and Ryan pressed the intercom buzzer for flat number two.

'Hello,' a croaky voice answered.

'Hello, this is Detective March and I'm with my colleague Detective Fenix, please may we come inside as we have some news concerning a friend of yours, Susan Morris?'

'I know Susan, is she alright? Nothing's happened to her, has it?'

'Best we talk inside Miss,' Ryan said, and the door buzzed then clicked. The two men went inside, and Alfie knocked on the door of flat two.

A curvy girl with short jet black hair answered in her nighty and Alfie didn't know where to look, 'come in, sorry about the mess. We had a bit of a session last night, then decided to make something to eat.' Alfie stayed silent and followed her with Ryan just behind. They walked to the end of a corridor and slipped past a bike that was leant up against the wall. They entered the living room and the three of them sat down. The men on the three-seater and the woman on a chair. 'Would you like a cup of tea?' she asked nervously.

'No, thank you,' Ryan replied, and Alfie just shook his head.

'Is it just you here? We were told you have a flatmate,' Alfie asked.

'Oh, you mean Bonny. She went to the gym to meet Susan. Did something happen to her?'

Ryan leaned forward, 'I'm afraid last night Susan was killed at her home. I'm so very sorry.'

'What? What? You're kidding, please say you're kidding!'

'Why would we kid about that?' Alfie asked but Piper ignored him. She was too upset to even hear him, let alone respond to his straight talk.

'Are you sure it was Susan?' she asked. Alfie had seen it so many times before, when a friend or a family member received bad news, they always asked the same sort of questions. He used to get frustrated when they seemed to be asking whether he had done his job correctly, but he accepted that they weren't questioning his ability and instead were suffering in disbelief.

'I'm afraid so,' Ryan answered for him, 'her Brother found her this morning.'

'Oh God, poor Jason, is he ok?' her hands were shaking, and her face went pale.

'He's understandably shaken up, but physically he's fine.'

'Do you remember anything about last night?' Alfie said pulling his notebook with a pencil attached to it by a rubber band out of his pocket.

'What?' she replied a little shocked at his insensitive tone.

'Last night? You'd all been drinking, so I was wondering how much of the night you remember?' he pulled the rubber band off and flipped the notebook open.

'I remember everything,' she said slowly, the frustration was evident in her voice.

'Good, was there anyone you can recall that stood out? Anyone who might have approached you or that you approached?' his pencil was poised above the paper.

Her eyes looked up as she tried to recall, 'there was this one man who was chatting Susan up. She gave him her number just before we left the pub.'

'Was that the last place you went? Were there other people around?' he was blunt, but it was important. 'I'm just trying to gather as much information as I can so I can find whoever it was that killed her, so they don't do it again.'

'Sorry,' she said and threw up on the floor.

3

Back at the station, Alfie sat at his desk going over his notes. After Ryan had help clean up the girl's vomit, she'd told them that the aforementioned man was the only person she could recall Susan fancying. When they'd met him, they were in the Star pub on North Street. The detectives visited the pub on their way back and asked the landlord if he remembered the women. It turned out that he had due to them being so loud, but he didn't remember any man with them. They had asked for the CCTV footage and the landlord was more than happy to help and now Ryan was scanning through the digital files, something Alfie didn't know much about. He would still have an old Nokia 2110 with the great game of snake on it if it was up to him. That's when phones were phones and not these confusing contraptions that needed someone with an IT degree to operate. Samantha had bought him his latest rectangle and he used it to keep her happy and to not look like a fuddy-duddy. He was only forty-three after all.

'Got him,' Ryan called out from the glass conference room. Alfie walked over to him and leaned over his shoulder to view the computer screen. 'There,' Ryan pointed at the screen.

Alfie looked closer and could see the man's face and Susan standing next to him, 'show this to the landlord and see if he knows the guy. In the meantime, I'm going to talk to the coroner and see if she's found anything new.'

'Ok Boss,' Ryan pressed print and Alfie walked away.

4

'Do you know him?' Ryan asked the landlord of the Star pub. It was lunchtime and the place was hectic.

'I'd love to help out, but I don't know him. We aren't that sort of a pub. You know, with regulars.'

'Mind if I ask your staff?'

'Go ahead but try and be quick. I do have a business to run,' the landlord said curtly.
Ryan had something in his head he wanted to say about three women being dead and this guy being a pratt, but he didn't have it in him to be like Alfie and wished his boss was here to say it for him.

He went around to each member of staff and asked them the same question he had asked the landlord, but no one recognised the man. He was about to leave when one of the waitresses came running after him, 'Detective! Wait!' she called.

'Yes?' he spun on his heels to face her.

'Can I see the picture again?' she held out her hand expectantly. He handed it to her and she quizzically looked it up and down, 'I thought that was him. I didn't recognise him at first because you asked if I knew him from the pub and I had my hands full with a drinks order, but then I remembered his face. Not from here, but from the dentists. That's Doctor Stubbs, my dentist,' she poked the picture where the man's face was like she'd won a competition.

'Where's his office?' he asked almost as excitedly.

5

Alfie knocked on the window and Doctor Salmon waved for him to enter her office. He liked her as she was no-nonsense too and that way there was no need for pointless chit chat. 'I've just finished up with your woman. Same as the others, she was killed by a sharp object entering her brain and the strangulation was probably used to subdue her. No other wounds present and no skin under the fingernails. Nothing we didn't know from the previous two,' she opened a packet of crisps, took one out and popped it in her mouth.

'What about the hair?' he asked.

She swallowed the crisp, 'I've sent it to the lab, and we will have results as soon as they process it.'

'Time of death?' he asked.

'Approximately between 11 pm and 1 am.'

'She got home about midnight so the killer might have followed her in without her noticing. Seems likely they surprised her in the kitchen,' he rubbed his chin thoughtfully.

'I haven't got a clue Detective, that's your department, not mine,' she crunched down on another crisp.

'Have a nice lunch,' he said with the sincerity of a footballer wishing the opposition team good luck, then left. As he walked up the stairs, he avoided taking the lift because he needed the exercise. His phone rang and vibrated at the same time in his pocket. He hated this feature, but it was useful if they were in a crowded place and he couldn't hear it, 'Fenix,' he answered.

'Boss, we've had a result. Turns out this guy's name is Doctor Stubbs. He's a dentist and has a place over on Garret Avenue. One of the waitresses recognised him and...'

'I'll meet you there,' Alfie interrupted and hung up. He put the phone back in his pocket and quickened his pace.

6

Twenty minutes later the two men were walking into the waiting room of Doctor Stubbs' dentistry. A robust woman with short curly hair sat behind the reception desk glaring at them as they approached, 'can I help you?' she asked in a nasal voice that sounded like it came from a train tannoy.

'I'm Detective Fenix and this is Detective March. We would like to have a word with Doctor Stubbs.'

'He's with a patient. Take a seat and I'll let him know you're here,' she nodded towards the chairs.

'This is a police matter Miss…' he read the little badge on her white uniform, 'Jemima,' he hated the friendliness of name tags. He would prefer it if they had their last name on it.

'He's busy,' she stared him down.

'Either you go and get him now or we will. What do you think would look better to his client?' he leaned over; the palms of his hands rested on her desk.

'Patient,' she barked.

'What,' he barked back.

'They're not clients, they're patients,' she rolled her eyes melodramatically.

Alfie's blood boiled, then he said through gritted teeth, 'fine, what do you think would look better to his patient?' he dragged the word out.

'Do what you like; I'm not going to bother him. It's more than my job's worth,' she didn't budge. She wasn't intimidated by Alfie, she'd met worse in her life and he could see it in her eyes.

'Fine,' he stood up straight and marched over to the closed office door in the corner of the small room with Ryan in tow. He didn't bother knocking, his mood was as foul as sewer air.

The door swung open and the nurse dropped the little metal tray she was carrying. It crashed loudly on the floor making the dentist jump and very nearly hurt the man he was working on. He looked up from his patient's mouth then pulled down his mask, 'what the hell do you think you're doing?' his tone was throttled with anger.

'This is Detective March and I'm...'

'I don't give a damn who you are, get the hell out of my room,' he pointed to the door with his dentist drill. Alfie looked at it carefully and thought that it would be a good description of the murder weapon. It certainly would fit the profile.

Alfie wasn't having any of it, he felt this guy either was who they were looking for or he could help them find who they were looking for and he'd be damned if he was going to be patient, 'we're here about the girl you met last night at the Star pub,' he dropped the pitch of his words, then said with utter sincerity, 'she's been killed and we need to talk.'

'What? She's dead? No. Wait a minute you think that...'

Ryan interrupted, 'no one thinks anything yet Doctor Stubbs, we just want to talk, and we believe you're in a good position to help us with our enquiries.'

'Rubbish, you wouldn't be barging in on me working if all you wanted was a statement and a friendly conversation. You could have rung for that,' the drill shook in his hand, an involuntary movement that hadn't gone unnoticed by Alfie.

'We're sorry for intruding like this but your receptionist wasn't exactly the most helpful,' Ryan attempted to calm him.

'I'm not surprised if this is how you conduct your police business. Now get out and wait for me to finish up. I'll be out shortly,' he turned back to the man in the chair who was looking as nervous as a rabbit being hung over a boiling pot and continued drilling. Alfie looked around the room for a possible exit and was satisfied that the dentist wasn't going anywhere; the nurse began clearing up the mess on the floor. The two men left and sat down in the waiting room.

The receptionist smiled, her double chin wrinkled enough to make a third, 'went well, did it?' she sneered. They ignored her and waited with their arms crossed and egos wounded.

Ten minutes later the door opened and the nervous man stepped out and hurried past as quickly as he could. Alfie was reading an article about deep-sea diving and Ryan was playing on his phone.

'Ok gentlemen, let's talk,' Doctor Stubbs was much calmer, but there was still a hint of frustration in his voice. The two detectives followed him into his office and he shut the door behind them, 'sorry there aren't more chairs but you're more than welcome to sit in the reclining one in the middle,' he grinned uneasily at his poor attempt at humour.

'Standing will be fine,' grunted Alfie and he pulled his notebook from his pocket. He looked the man up and down trying to decide if he was naturally anxious because he was being visited by the police or if it was something else.

'You said that Susan's been killed, can I ask how it happened?' the dentist asked.

'She was strangled,' he didn't give away the real cause of death, he was keeping that to himself. He stared deep into his eyes. He could tell a lot from the eyes, they couldn't hide anything. They were an open book and he was a scholar when it came to reading them.

'Strangled? That's horrific,' his eyes widened with shock and gave no indication he was lying.

'You met her last night at the Star pub and exchanged numbers, is that correct? Ryan asked.

'Yes, but that's the last I saw of her all night, I swear. She left with her friends and I stayed. I met my Cousin, and we went

213

on to another pub called the Duck's Bill where we drank until about eleven, eleven-thirty, something like that. After that I went home,' he shifted his weight from one foot to another which wasn't suspicious for someone standing, but Alfie missed nothing.

'We'll be checking that out and if you could provide us with your Cousin's details that would help a lot,' said Ryan.

'Of course, anything I can do. I'm more than happy to help but, as I said, I met her very briefly.'

'What did you say to each other?' Alfie enquired, his voice almost sinister in its seriousness.

'I asked her if she would like a drink. You know, the usual chat-up line. She said no thanks as she had one and she was leaving soon. I told her she was gorgeous and she liked my suit. We spoke about how rubbish the weather was as it'd been raining all day and that's about it.'

'Nothing else?' There was always something else Alfie thought.

'Not really. Her friends were hassling her to get going and she wrote down her number on an old receipt she found in her handbag and gave it to me. She asked me to call her and we could finish our conversation without being interrupted,' he looked down at his feet, 'and now you're telling me she's dead. You think I did it? I didn't do it, why would I? She gave me her number, I thought it might have gone somewhere, I hoped it would go somewhere,' his voice trailed off as if he was thinking about something else entirely.

'We don't think you did it, Doctor Stubbs. In fact, I know you didn't do it,' Alfie said calmly. Ryan shot him a glance that said "what are you doing" but he ignored it and carried on regardless. 'Did you notice anyone else watching her or maybe follow her and her friends after they left? Any small bit of information might seem unimportant but could turn out to be invaluable,' his pencil touched the paper in anticipation.

'I'm sorry, no,' he looked annoyed at himself for not remembering anything helpful rather than being annoyed at Alfie for the continuous questioning.

'If you recall anything, call me. Night or day,' Alfie gave him his card and nodded to Ryan that it was time to go.

'Goodbye Doctor Stubbs,' Ryan said as he followed Alfie out the door. The dentist sort of smiled out of politeness but his face told a different story. Something else was bothering him but Alfie couldn't think what. There was some information buried deep in his subconscious and Alfie knew it. It was pointless pushing him as he'd most likely retrieve it on his own. The man was not a murderer and even less likely a serial killer but he was connected, Alfie just didn't know how yet.

7

They'd argued in the car on their way back to the station. In fact, it was Ryan who'd argued and Alfie had for the most part ignored him. Ryan was mad because his boss wasn't letting him in on his thoughts. He wanted to know why Alfie hadn't pushed the guy harder and why he'd left without letting Ryan have a go. Alfie just told him that "the guy didn't do it. Trust me I know a killer and he's not a killer. He'll call though, he'll remember something". The younger detective was losing his patience but held on to his tongue after that and the rest of the journey had been in silence. More as a protest from Ryan that had completely gone over Alfie's head as he was too busy going over the case in his mind.

Alfie returned to his desk and sat heavily down on his chair, the springs creaked as if in pain. He furrowed his brow and pulled his notebook from his pocket. Around him, the hustle and bustle of the office blurred into one. He couldn't see individuals, only images and only then was he able to concentrate. He rolled the pages over until he reached the interviews from the first case and his eyes darted from side to side as he read them. The woman's name was Anna. She was twenty-seven years old. She, like Susan, was blonde and pretty. She had also been out drinking but with her work colleagues. They were celebrating her promotion to team leader. A taxi had dropped her off at her house and when she hadn't turned up for work the following day, they called her at home but got no answer. A neighbour, curious why she hadn't put her bins out, had knocked on her door but when no one came she looked through the kitchen window. It was the same scene as with Susan, she was lying on the floor, face down with her teeth missing and had been killed by something sharp entering her brain. Face down he pondered that and stored it in his hippocampus. They'd interviewed all her colleagues and found that she was chatting-up some guy during the night, but also that she'd been chatted-up by her boss. She'd given him the brush off quite publicly and he became the focus of their investigation until the second girl was discovered with the same injuries and missing teeth. They'd checked out the fancy wine bar but the CCTV showed very little as it was grainy and the place was crowded. They also checked the video from the town CCTV but saw nothing suspicious. He looked up and saw Ryan eating a sandwich, this made him hungry as he'd forgotten to eat but that wasn't important right now and he could do with skipping a meal anyway. 'Can you look over the CCTV from the Anna Lipton case and see if you spot the dentist, then do the same with the footage from the Gemma Harding case? Remember she'd gone for a drink with her mum the night she was murdered and I refuse to believe that that isn't connected somehow.'

Ryan nodded but his mouth was full. He swallowed and said, 'no probs. Sounds like you might be on to something. I'll do it right now,' he went into the conference room, as it had the best computer, and took his sandwich with him.

'Thanks,' Alfie made an effort. He flipped back more pages until he reached what he was looking for and looked over his notes from the Gemma case, scrutinising every detail. Then he saw the most obvious connection that had him kicking himself. How did he forget that she'd also given a guy her number? He was tired, mostly because of the stupid diet he was on. The lack of carbohydrates was affecting his thinking. He looked at the description her mum had given them which was vague but unmistakable if you'd met the man. It read: White male, mousy blonde hair, approx. 6 feet tall, stubble but not a beard and very handsome. They'd just come from his office and Alfie's stomach turned. Had he been wrong? He was sure the guy was a straight shooter. He picked up the phone and called the number of the cousin Doctor Stubbs had given them.

'Hello,' a man said in a squeaky pitched voice.

'Is this Alan?' Alfie asked.

'Yes, how may I help?'

'My name is Detective Fenix and I'm calling regarding your whereabouts last night,' he was authoritative in his manner which made it easier to get what he wanted.

'I was out with my cousin,' he answered.

'Is that a Doctor Stubbs?' he asked.

'Well, I call him James but yes that's him. Why are you asking?'

'He's been helping us with some inquiries and he gave us your name as an alibi for last night.'

'Sounds as if he's suspected of something more than helping you,' Allan retorted.

'By eliminating him from our suspicions he is thereby helping us so we can then look elsewhere,' Alfie explained.

'Makes sense, he was with me all night, first at the Star pub, then we went on to the Duck Bill where we stayed the rest of the evening until going home just after eleven. Does that help?'

'Do you remember him getting a woman's number?' Alfie scribbled in his notebook.

'He told me that just before I turned up he got a hot girl's number, but I didn't see her. He gets a lot of attention from the ladies, so it never surprises me,' he chuckled.

'Do you remember if he got a number from a woman named Gemma?'

'I think so, that was about a month back, she was with her mum and she couldn't take her eyes off of him all night,' he was smiling, Alfie could tell by his voice.

'That's right. What did you do after that?'

He carried on with what he was saying, brushing Alfie's question aside as he reminisced, 'the looks that girl gave him had me in stitches. Sorry, what did you say?'

'I said what did you do after?' Alfie was trying to hold his temper.

'We all went on to a night club, Cinderella, in the centre of town.'

'Did the woman and her mother go with you?' she hadn't mentioned this when they spoke. He went to check over his notes again.

'No, we invited them but the mum had a meeting in the morning and Gemma wouldn't leave her behind. So it was me, James, the two nurses that work with him Steph and Jemima and a mate from my gym, Stuart.'

'Do you recall seeing anyone last night that was there that night?' Alfie was thorough.

'I saw Steph at the bar ordering drinks but that's it. Now, if that's everything, I need to get going because my train's getting in soon and I've still gotta get a ticket.'

'Thank you,' he hung up. He had written it all down in his book and packed it away in his pocket. So, it was the dentist who Gemma's mum had seen her talking to, but why would he kill her? Psychos don't need motive, they just kill, but the dentist didn't strike him as cold and empty. He still believed that he wasn't the killer, he knew that the dentist knew more than he was letting on and now he had proof.

'Boss!' Ryan called.

Alfie walked over to the conference room and stood in the corridor, 'yes?'

'It's grainy as a snowstorm at night but look at this, it's from the night Anna was killed.' Alfie walked over and looked, 'tell me that isn't the dentist,' Ryan stated.

He couldn't see much but in the haze was a tall man with mousy blonde hair and a suit, 'could be,' he grunted.

'Ok, now look at this,' he pressed on his mouse and another image popped up onto the screen, this one was much clearer and it was of the outside of the pub from a camera across the road.

He didn't wait for Ryan, he saw what he was looking at, 'that's him,' Doctor Stubbs was outside sitting at the pub picnic table chatting with some women. You couldn't see their faces but one was stocky and thick with short hair and the other was skinny and had long ginger hair. 'They're the dental nurses,' Alfie pointed at them.

'Oh yeah, I was so busy looking at him I didn't notice them.'

'When was this?' he asked the young detective.

'Just before Anna leaves, keep watching,' the video rolled on and Alfie could clearly see Anna come out of the front door. Doctor Stubbs seemed to say something and she turned around. She walked over to his table and stood with her back to the camera, then handed him something. He took it and she walked away.

'Does he follow her?'

'No. But Jemima, the super friendly nurse leaves not long after and then the ginger one slightly later. Then he goes back inside and appears a couple of hours later.'

'So, there's no way he followed her home then,' Alfie pointed out.

'Not unless she told him where she lived or he's a psychic.'

'No. Something else is going on here. Maybe someone's setting him up; we need to talk to him again.'

'I'll ring his office,' Ryan picked up his phone and asked Google the number for the dentist's office. It appeared on his five-inch screen and he pressed it, then held the phone to his ear, 'hello this is Detective March, can I speak to Doctor Stubbs please?' he paused as he got a response, 'Ok, do you know where he went?' he paused, 'great, thank you.' Alfie looked at him impatiently, 'he left just after we did and told the ginger nurse he was going for a drink, she thinks he might have gone to the Duck Bill as it's his local.'

'Let's go,' Alfie was already halfway out the door.

'Do you have anything?' asked Detective Inspector Dell as he stood in Alfie's way. He looked up at DS Fenix and stuck out his chest.

'We have a suspect and we're on our way to bring him in,' Alfie brushed past him.

'We'll fill you in as soon as we get back Sir,' said Ryan as he pulled his arms into his coat.

'Very good DC March, just watch he doesn't blow it. You know what he's like,' his eyes followed Alfie out of the room.

'Yes Sir, I know he's a great detective and he's about to solve yet another murder,' Ryan spoke out of turn and he knew it. He was going to regret defending his partner but in the heat of the moment, he lost his cool.

'That's not what I meant DC March...' but before he could continue Ryan had followed Alfie out of the office. The small-statured man shook his head then shouted, 'BACK TO WORK YOU LOT, CRIMES DON'T SOLVE THEMSELVES,' the rest of the office had gone silent and were watching the confrontation. In unison, they all got back to work and the ones who weren't working pretended to.

Doctor James Stubbs sat at the bar, His head was down as he solemnly stared into his almost empty glass. A small amount of cloudy liquid sat in between two pieces of ice and he rocked it from side to side. The liquid, once dark and strong tasting, swished in unison with the ice cubes like a storm swaying two little glass boats. "Why?" He thought. "Why would someone kill that poor woman?" She was so kind and sweet and this time he thought she'd answer if he called. The other women that had given him their numbers recently never picked up. He didn't continuously bother them but had tried a few times before giving up. He never seemed to have much luck with women and this latest lot of setbacks had him doubting he ever would. He wasn't exactly a confident man but he knew women liked the way he looked. Perhaps they didn't like him? Perhaps he was too keen or boring? He thought they'd just changed their minds or given him a false number, either way, he never would have guessed that they'd all been killed shortly after paying him some interest. He wasn't aware of the other two, but he dwelt on Susan.

A familiar face watched him from the corner of the pub. They watched him mope and waited for just the right time to approach. They had been watching him a lot lately and had yearned for him ever since they had first seen him. They had hated it when women talked to him but loathed it when they gave him their numbers. They wanted him for themself, he belonged to them. As long as the harlots never answered when he rang he would think they didn't want him, then at his lowest moment, they would pounce like a lioness on a sickly wildebeest. They stood up but dropped down when the two detectives burst through the door.

'Doctor Stubbs,' Ryan called out.

He slowly looked over his shoulder not recognising the voice, also because he was quite drunk, 'ah Detective Marsh and Detective Fenik it is nice to see you, would ya like a drink?' he started to fall backwards off of his stool and luckily caught the bar with his free hand, but he still managed to spill the rest of his drink.

'Watch it,' Alfie pushed him back upright.

'Thanks mate,' he slurred.

'You need to come back to the station with us, we need to ask you some more questions and get you some coffee by the looks of things,' Alfie took the glass out of his hand and gave it to the barman.

'Come on mate, let me help you up,' Ryan gently put a hand under his arm to guide him off of the barstool.

'Get off!' he pulled away and fell across the bar knocking over a beer glass he had emptied just before he ordered the whisky.

'Get up, you idiot,' Alfie was losing his cool and he grabbed him roughly by the shoulders and almost lifted him off the stool.

'Come on then, you want a fight,' he threw a punch in Alfie's direction but missed by a country mile and fell flat, planting his face hard on the wooden floor. Something caught Alfie's attention in the corner of the room, a figure had visibly stood halfway up, then thought better of it and sat back down. It barely registered as a movement but Alfie saw it and it set off alarm bells in his head. He stared at the figure completely forgetting about the man by his feet who Ryan was seeing to. He stepped over the dentist, his gaze fixed on the corner and the figure shuffled in its seat uneasily. He knocked into a woman sitting at a table and removed his stare for just a few seconds to apologise, but when he looked back the figure had gone. He darted his eyes searching the pub and saw the back of the figure leave through a fire exit. The alarm went off and the barman swore. Alfie ran for the door and disappeared through it before Ryan even knew what was happening.

'Boss,' he called, but Alfie didn't slow. He exploded out into a side alley and searched up and down. He saw the huge blue bins and the black bags filled with who knows what, sitting next to them. He saw the stain against the brick wall opposite him where someone had relieved themselves recently and he saw the figure at the north end of the alley with its short stocky frame lumping up and down as it ran, 'STOP!' he called out in vain. He didn't want to run, he hated it. He never understood why people would do it voluntarily. It seemed mad to him, especially the ones that did it indoors like hamsters on a wheel. The figure was gone and he stepped on his right toes and sprinted off after it. Ryan flew out of the fire exit after him and within a couple of seconds had caught up with the older man. He was one of the runners that Alfie hated and he'd told Ryan this on many occasions. He knew his boss would have to eat his words later but for now, he just ran.

'Stocky guy,' Alfie panted. He pointed in the direction of the suspect, 'that way, stop him.' Ryan went up a level of speed and left Alfie struggling for breath. He had the guy in his sight and was catching up fast. The figure darted in and out of people walking along the path with ease and ran into a building. Ryan wasn't as nimble and knocked into countless people as he pursued. He didn't notice the figure waiting inside the door to the bank and ran straight past. The figure, who hadn't noticed Ryan take over from Alfie, thought that it was the same guy who'd begun the chase and left the bank confident they had lost him. They walked back up the street the way they'd come, smiling to themself.

'Damn,' Ryan cried out, 'damn it, the boss is going to go mental,' he looked one last time but couldn't find the figure, so he started heading back towards Alfie. Alfie had given up running and was now walking unsteadily catching his breath, but still heading in what he hoped was the right direction. The pavement was busy and he hated having so many people around him at one time. His world began to spin a little so he concentrated hard and stared dead ahead. He saw a face he recognised which made him feel a little better and his hippocampus knocked on his cerebrum. All of a sudden, his mind was transported to previous images he'd seen throughout the day. The grainy video of the wine bar, the CCTV of the meeting outside it, the conversation with the dentist's cousin and how he'd thought it was funny that some girl had watched him all night long. Then he remembered the video of the Star pub. The face he saw standing behind Doctor Stubbs and the dentist's reception that had rudely greeted them as they entered where this same face.

Their eyes locked and Jemima turned to run, 'no you don't,' he wanted to get her but he was just out of reach. She started to move but stopped as Ryan grabbed her. She struggled and screamed, passers-by stopped with concerned looks on their faces, 'don't let her go she's the one, she killed those women,' Alfie called out, much to the dismay of the people around him. Ryan could barely contain her; she was strong and fought him like a small bear. He was about to let go when Alfie grabbed her by both arms, twisted them behind her back and slapped his handcuffs across her wrists, 'you're under arrest, you do not have to say anything, but it may harm your defence if you do not mention, when questioned, something which you later rely on in court. Anything you do or say may be given in evidence.'

'Screw you, you fat pig. How's that for saying something?' she spat at Ryan but missed.

'Charming,' Alfie snorted.

'Boss,' Ryan held up his hands. They were covered in blood and so was his shirt.

'Ryan,' Alfie looked helplessly at his partner and friend. He looked down and saw the knife also covered in blood on the pavement. Jemima laughed and Alfie punched her in the face. She collapsed unconscious to the floor.

Ryan sat on the curb and coughed up blood. It trickled down his chin, 'I didn't even see it boss,' he looked up at Alfie.

'Don't worry mate, you'll be ok,' Alfie pulled his phone from his pocket and called for an ambulance. He knelt next to Ryan, put him in the recovery position and did his best to stop the bleeding. Ryan was muttering something but Alfie couldn't hear it over the noise of the cars and people around him. A sizable crowd had gathered and some scumbags were even videoing. He made a mental note to break their phones if he got the chance. Suddenly Ryan shuddered and went limp, 'Ryan,' Alfie's voice was hoarse. Ryan didn't answer, Ryan couldn't answer. He was gone and Alfie cried.

9

A few days later Alfie was going over the interview with Jemima Longbottom in his notebook. The Detective Inspector had told him he should stay away from the office and the case for a while, but Alfie ignored him as usual. He had managed to stay calm during the interview even when she kept calling him names and complaining that he assaulted her. No one defended her and every witness said she was knocked unconscious by a random bystander who could not be identified. She was a grade-A bunny boiler if he ever saw one. She had obsessed over the poor dentist for months before getting a job at his office. She even beat the previous nurse to a pulp so that she was too scared to leave her house. She lusted over her boss but never acted on it as she felt that he was far too good looking for her and the only way she'd have a chance is if he had such low self-esteem, he would be willing to give her a chance. That's all she needed, just a small chance to show him that she'd treat him like a king, serve his every need and pleasure him in ways that he could only dream about. She would show him that looks weren't everything and that he could be happy if he would just give her the opportunity.

She never meant to kill Anna, just scare her off. But when she'd confronted her in her house, the girl fought back. She'd punched her and strangled her to half-consciousness, then used a sharp dentist's tool she carried for protection to pierce through the ear and into her brain. A few of the girl's teeth had already been knocked out and in a moment of sick pleasure, she removed the rest as if she was Doctor Stubbs and he was helping her commit the gruesome act. This only made her feel closer to him and after that, the other two had been easy. She did the same thing to them, simply because the first time had felt so good. She confessed that they hadn't felt the same and she wanted to try again and see if she could replicate her euphoria.

The phone rang and he picked it up, 'Hello?' his voice was as deep and sombre as ever.

'We have the results of the DNA match between the sample you sent yesterday and the hair you found,' a woman said.

'Well?' he asked.

'They match; ninety-nine percent to be precise.'

'Email me the results,' he put down the phone. It wasn't like he needed them to put the Psycho away. She had killed Ryan right in front of him. He looked over at his partner's desk. He looked down at his hands. He could still see Ryan's blood all over them even though he knew they were clean. He had done everything he could to save his friend but no matter how hard he tried, Ryan hadn't responded to the CPR. He put his hand's palm flat on the desk.

'I'm sorry,' said the Detective Inspector as he approached Alfie's desk. He was genuinely concerned.

'What for?' Alfie growled.

'Ryan, obviously,' the Detective Inspector was trying to be patient.

'You didn't kill him, so why apologise,' Alfie stood up and walked off before the DI had a chance to respond. He grabbed his long Crombie coat from the peg where it hung and left. As he walked out into the crisp air, he decided that he'd had enough. He would retire from the police and look for a job in the private security sector. The death of his friend was more than he could take and that was the last time he set foot in the station.

Stubbs crawled over Alfie and looking for a comfortable spot. He settled on Alfie's chest and looked at his friend, 'how are you feeling?'

'It feels like I have a hole inside me, but every time Ryan dies in my story, I feel it close a little. Is that bad?' Alfie's eyes were wet with tears.

'Of course not little dude,' the spider replied, 'everyone deals with grief in their own way. This is your process.'

'I guess it's hurting less each time, but I still miss him so much.'

'And you always will, but that's a good thing. It just shows how much you love him. He will live on forever in your mind Alfie. He will live on through you,' Stubbs was wise, but that's because Alfie was. He was after all just Alfie's subconscious projecting itself in the form of his favourite animal.

'I love you, Stubbs,' he whispered.

'Love you too little dude,' Monty meowed as if to say, "me also".

Chapter 10

Carol woke and touched Gary's side of the bed. The palm her hand slapped down on the white-sheeted mattress as she searched for her husband. It took her a couple of seconds to recall what had happened the night before and when she did she touched her face as if the ghost of his hand was still on it. She wasn't bruised or hurt in any serious way physically but inside, deep inside, her mind was in an insurmountable amount of pain and distress. There she was, alone and solely responsible for an autistic child. Why had she sent him away? Why had she pushed him? It was her fault he'd gone; she'd been so stupid she thought. The phone buzzed on the nightstand next to her and it made her stomach turn. She didn't know if it was the thought of Gary ringing to apologise that had her feeling ill or that he was going to leave her for good? She touched her cheek again and swallowed, she made a strange squeaky murmur as she held back her crying anguish and picked up the phone.

'Carol, is that you Carol?' Keith's voice was shaky.

'Hi Keith,' she said softly. She lay back against the pillow and sunk into its softness.

'Carol, Gary was in the boozer last night saying you kicked him out, is that true?' he was breathing heavily as if excited and nervous at the same time.

'He hit me,' she just said it. She didn't know why. She hadn't planned on ever mentioning it to anyone, especially Keith.

'I'll kill that bastard,' he said coldly.

'Ok,' what was she doing? Why hadn't she told him to stop, think and calm down? She wanted him to fight for her, she wanted someone to care that much for her, she needed it.

'Is that what you want Carol? Do you want me to hurt him? Cos I'll do it if you want,' he didn't sound so certain and his nerve was beginning to waver at the thought of actually hurting his friend, no matter how much of an arse he was. Keith was a professional with a good job and a responsible member of the community. He had never committed a crime in his life, except for occasionally going over the speed limit.

'No, he's not worth it,' Carol said in a hollow voice, 'I don't think he meant it, it was probably my fault anyway.'

'That's a load of crap and you know it. There's no excuse for hitting you,' he was on the charm offensive again, pouncing like a leopard while the lion looked the other way.

'I don't know what to think. He's been so down lately with all the bad things happening one after the other. He was trying, I swear he was, more than I've ever seen him try before. Maybe that's what's driven him over the edge? Maybe he couldn't cope anymore?' she drifted into her thoughts and didn't hear Keith's reply.

'Carol, are you there?' he asked, panicking that she'd put the phone down on him.

She drifted back into the real world and thought to herself how easy and nice it was to be somewhere in your mind and not have to deal with real life. No wonder Alfie did it so much, 'I'm here, I'm just very tired Keith. I'll talk to you later,' then she hung up and momentarily considered what he may have said. She racked her brain and thought about calling him back, then Alfie appeared at the door and she forgot all about it.

'Hello Mummy, please may I have toast with jam for breakfast?'

'Of course you can sweetheart. Would you like some milk?' the sight of his smiling face and his SpongeBob pyjamas was enough to temporarily help her forget about all the bad things. She could just focus on him and making him feel happy.

'Yes please, Mummy,' he looked around the room, 'where is Daddy?' he asked curiously.

'Daddy went away for a while to see Grandma,' she lied but it was for his own good and she believed if he ever found out he would understand.

'Does he still hate me because I have Autism symptoms,' he didn't quite know what it was they said he had. All he knew was that he was Alfie and that something in his brain meant that people didn't like him. He didn't care about the details, he had other things to think about.

'Oh, baby no. He's just upset, that's all, and he says stupid things he doesn't mean. He loves you, we both do, just the way you are,' she held out her arms and moved her head backwards beckoning for him to come to her. Surprisingly he reacted to her, something she never thought would happen but hoped would. She kept on trying with him and this time it worked. He walked forward slowly at first, then jumped on the bed like an excited puppy ready for a walk. She embraced him and they hugged. He began to struggle though and this was followed by a cry as if he was in pain. She let go of him quickly and he pulled away from her at the same time, 'Baby, what's wrong? Did Mummy hurt you? I'm so sorry.'

'Too tight, too tight, too tight,' he repeated and curled up in a little ball, his arms wrapped around and hugging is own legs, his knees pulled up towards his chest.

She hadn't realised, in her elation, that she squeezed him too hard. The knowledge of how to be around him had escaped her like water through a sieve and she hated herself for being so stupid, 'Mummy didn't mean it, Baby, I'm so sorry. Let's go downstairs and have that toast, shall we?'

He looked up at her, his brown hair flopped over the side of his face. It desperately needed cutting, if only he would allow someone other than Ryan to do it, 'Ok Mummy, but don't squeeze me,' he spoke in a more childish voice than normal as if he'd regressed in age by three or four years.

'I won't, I promise,' she slid out of bed, her nighty hanging loosely around her undernourished frame and waited for him to uncurl himself. She caught a glimpse of herself in the dresser mirror and was disappointed to see herself looking so ill. She'd lost so much weight lately with all the stress, at least a stone, maybe more. She'd always been a little on the underweight side, Gary had made sure of that, "I'll leave you if you ever get fat" he would say if she was ever eating a piece of cake or trying to enjoy a biscuit. So, she stopped eating treats when he was around just to avoid the nasty remarks and, in the end, she just stopped enjoying food. Every bite reminded her of his discontent.

'Come on, Mummy,' Alfie was by the door waiting for her. She was still staring at the mirror and hadn't realised that she'd drifted away again.

'Yes, Sweetheart,' she said, still half in a daze, 'let's go.' The two of them went down to the kitchen and had breakfast. There wasn't any jam, but Alfie was ok with Marmite. Sometimes this caused a meltdown, but this time he was fine. Carol had an idea that maybe in the future she should always come up with two possible options for him. That way he was more likely to get the thing he was expecting. She remembered all the times Alfie would roll around on the floor or throw things in public. People would stand and stare, judging and tutting as if they could do much better at parenting him. But he couldn't help it, he wasn't a bratty child that didn't get his way, he was an autistic child whose brain couldn't cope when things didn't go to plan or when the world became too much of an overbearing place. She wished those judgmental pratts could have a day in Alfie's head, just to see what a confusing place the world was to him. It was confusing enough for her, a Neurotypical adult, let alone for a nine-year-old with sensory issues. She decided that they'd watch some cartoons, play with some Lego and bake some brownies today. Alfie loved all those ideas. She was going to get through this, she just hoped that Gary wouldn't come back now and ruin it. She wanted to put off the confrontation for as long as possible, but eventually, it would come, no matter how much she wished it away.

Chapter 11

The doorbell rang and Carol wiped her flour-covered hands on the Loch Ness t-towel they'd picked up when visiting Scotland last year. She went to answer it. A sick heavy feeling rumbled in the pit of her stomach. She wasn't ready for Gary, she didn't want the conflict. She and Alfie had had such an amazing day and she didn't want him ruining it and setting Alfie back into one of his states again. They'd watched two Disney classics and built a castle out of Lego, well Alfie did and she watched while passing him the pieces. Now they were in the middle of baking brownies and having the best of times. When she reached the door, she hesitated, her hand hung in the air, almost touching the door handle. What if she just didn't answer? Would the person know they were in? she didn't have to answer, it was her choice. She was about to put her hand by her side and walk back to the kitchen when the doorbell rang again and made her jump. 'Carol,' a voice she knew but couldn't quite place, 'Carol, it's me, Tiff,' her heart sank and she knew their fun was over for the day. 'Carol, answer the door, I know you're there, I can see your shape through the frosted glass.'

She'd forgotten about the stupid glass window next to the door. She steadied herself, breathed deeply, exhaled slowly and opened the door, 'hello Tiffany, what do you want?' She was hostile but didn't want to be, it just came out mostly because of frustration.

'I've come to make sure Alfie's ok,' she took a step towards Carol but stopped short when Carol's face contorted with anger.

'Why wouldn't he be?' she raised her voice.

'No need to be hostile, you know he doesn't like that,' she said derisively, her lips curled at either end into a sickening smirk.

'Alfie. Is. Fine,' she said through gritted teeth trying to rise above it, 'you can see him tomorrow if he wants, but you can't just turn up like this.'

'How dare you, he's my Son, not yours. I carried him for nine months...'

Carol interrupted, 'and a year later you left him and I looked after him for the remaining eight, so don't give me that rubbish,' Carol began to close the door but Alfie appeared next to her.

'Why is she here, Mummy?' he pointed at Tiffany who was grinning at him like Jack Nicholson in the Shinning.

'She's just leaving, Baby,' she tried shutting the door but Tiffany put her foot in the way.

'Hello Alfie, I just came to see you and give you a present, but Carol won't let me give it to you,' she picked up the big box next to her and showed it to him, waving it tantalisingly in the air. Bitch, Carol said to herself, then let go of the door. It swung open and strained as it reached the limit of its hinges, before bouncing back slightly and settling in a half-open position.

'What is it?' Alfie's eyes enlarged and his hands started to flap a little.

'Don't you want to be surprised when you open it?' Tiffany didn't know him at all.

'No, what's the point in hiding it when you could just give it to me, that seems like a waste of paper and trees,' he looked at her blankly and she felt silly realising that he was right. 'It's stupid that society tries to hide presents and make someone pull the unwanted coloured paper apart, just to throw it in the bin and create more rubbish in the world.'

'Just open it, Alfie, stop being rude,' she really didn't get it and Carol knew she was going to upset him.

'I'm not rude, it's not my fault that you stupidly wasted paper just so you could hide my present,' Carol almost burst out laughing but kept her cool.

'Fine, it's Lego but now you don't get it,' she was blowing it big time.

Carol could see this was beginning to upset Alfie a lot. He loved his Lego and he would be inconsolable if Tiffany took it away, 'goodbye Tiffany.' She snatched the present from her hand in a move that would have impressed Muhamad Ali, and with her other hand, she slammed the door in Tiffany's face. It came to a stop millimetre in front of her nose and she felt its wind rush across her face. She huffed and walked away wittering to herself in disbelief. 'That'll teach her to mess with my boy,' Carol winked at Alfie. She held the present steady in her grip and ripped off the blue shiny paper then handed him his Star Wars Lego set. He looked at her like a starving man would look at a steak dinner and, for the second time today, he hugged her. She remembered not to squeeze this time and they stayed there for at least ten seconds. It felt more like a blissful hour to her before he grabbed the box and dashed into the living room. She finished off the brownies knowing it would be pointless getting in between him and his "special interest" and, for the first time in a long while, ate some without feeling guilty. Maybe this was the way things should be, she'd never felt so confident in her life and she was beginning to believe that she could stand up to anything.

Half an hour later the doorbell rang again and this new reserve would now be tested. She knew it was Gary because she heard the key turn in the door, he must have thought better of it and pulled it back out. She looked at it from the kitchen and hesitated, building her confidence before facing him again. Before she could move Alfie walked up to the door and opened it, 'hello Daddy, did you have fun with Grandma?'

Gary immediately realised what was going on and reacted accordingly, 'yes mate, I had a great time. How've you been? Did you have a nice day with Mummy?' His head remained facing Alfie but his eyes looked up at her with sorrow and guilt written in them like words etched in stone.

'We watched cartoons, and I built a castle, and Mummy and I made brownies, and then Tiffany came and was mean to me and Mummy stole my present from her and gave it to me, then I played with my new Lego and Mummy finished the brownies, then the doorbell rang and it was you,' he sucked in a lungful of air and walked backwards towards Carol.

'Sounds like you had fun,' he raised his head, 'I'm sorry. I don't know what else to say. You know I didn't mean it, I just don't know how to cope lately with all this crap going on and Ryan's death. Even my boss has lost patience with me. She said, if I don't sort out my temper, she would have to take disciplinary action. I only got this last chance because they feel bad about Ryan,' he was babbling and he knew it.

Carol crossed her arms across her breasts in a statement of steeliness and held back her tears, 'it's too late Gary. I'm done,' her voice was as calm and casual as if she had just asked him if he wanted a cup of tea. Alfie looked at her confused by what was happening, he slunk backwards away from his Dad as if instinctively knowing that something bad was about to happen.

'What do you mean done?!'

'I can't take your crap anymore. I've put up with you going up and down from one day to the next for eight years and you made me feel like dirt…'

'Wait a minute…'

'NO GARY,' she elevated her voice, 'it's my turn to talk,' her eyes narrowed and her body stiffened, she was ready for a fight. 'Like I was saying, you made me feel like dirt and that I was useless and couldn't do anything right. You bullied me into submission and even made me resent our poor little boy because you convinced me that it was his fault that he behaved like that and that I was too soft on him. You blame everyone but yourself Gary Fenix, but this time, you know you messed up. Well, I'm sorry Gary,' she stretched his name out for effect, 'this time you don't get to say you're sorry and have everything go back to the way it was. This time I get to decide and I decide that you're getting the hell out of this house,' her heart was racing, but you wouldn't know it by the way she spoke. It unnerved him to see her this confident and he didn't know what to do.

'You can't kick me out of my own house,' he tightened his fists in anger. Alfie was beginning to realise what was going on. Despite his misunderstanding of social interactions, this argument between his parents was serious and his dad wasn't a nice person.

'If you don't leave now, I'll call the police and tell them what you did,' she shifted her feet slightly wider. Alfie wondered what his dad had done, it must have been really bad to make his mummy this mad, because normally she was so calm.

'Oh yeah, what are you going to show them, there are no marks on your face, I barely touched you,' Gary said in a low and disturbing tone that made her shudder.
Alfie frowned. He had hit his mummy and he knew that you should never hit someone you love.

'There will be when they get here, I'll make sure of it,' she glared at him without blinking, inside her heart was beating twice as fast.

He was in unknown waters without a life raft or jacket and he was about to sink, 'you cow, I bet you would and all,' Alfie slowly approached, 'I can't believe I didn't see it before, you're a total nutter...hey, what the hell. You little git,' Alfie was next to him and his foot was returning to the floor after kicking his dad in his shin.

'Leave Mummy alone,' he screamed and kicked him again. Carol dove forward, anticipating Gary's reaction, her blood running cold. Her parental instincts took hold of her and she lunged towards her son to protect him at all costs. But it was too late, and she wasn't close enough. The back of Gary's hand smashed Alfie across the face and catapulted him into the frosted glass window, his little body crashed through the thin glass and he fell covered in shards onto the path leading up to the house.

'BASTARD!' she cried and collided into him like a battering ram. He stumbled backwards but didn't fall. She clawed at him, her fingers curled like talons and she caught his right eye. He roared with pain and raised his hand to strike, but as he was ready to make an impact, something held it in mid-air.

'What the...' he turned to see what was holding his arm and a fist crunched into his nose. A white flash appeared in front of his eyes, and his stomach made him regret drinking three beers for lunch. Before he could get his bearings, the fist hit him again, this time the pain was even worse and sent a wave of agony across his face and head. His knees felt weak and began to buckle. The third punch was too much for him to take and he slumped down into a pile of bleeding pathetic fat and bones. He couldn't see out of either of his eyes, but he recognised the voice of his attacker and it didn't astonish him one bit.

'Are you ok?' Keith said breathlessly and cradled his aching fist in his other hand.

She didn't even acknowledge him or his heroic act, instead she pushed past him and dropped to her knees next to Alfie. She was afraid to touch him, his head and hands were sprinkled with glass shards, some stuck to him and others embedded in his skin. She trembled as she brushed the hair from his face and saw a nasty gash across his brow, 'get the first aid kit, it's in the cupboard below the sink and ring a bloody ambulance NOW,' she shouted the last word because he was just standing there stunned like a deer caught in some headlights.

'Right,' he said and turned on his toes.

Gary still couldn't see anything, his face looked like a bloody pile of mincemeat and he spat blood as he stirred. He felt a tooth come loose and spat that out too. 'Kief, you bathtard,' he slurred and tried to stand. When he realised he couldn't, the anger began to dwindle and the realisation of what he'd just done hit him harder than Keith's fist. His memory went back to the hospital room where Alfie was born, he saw his son's face for the first time as he held him proudly and kissed him on his head. He saw Tiffany's face, puffy and red, but with a smile from ear to ear as she watched her three boys all together for the first time. He saw Ryan standing next to him, looking down at his new baby brother with a look of pure adoration and love written like an open book across his face. He knew his boys would always be there for each other, he was the happiest he had ever been.

Then he saw the day his wife left him, and he was reading the note she'd left behind. The pressure of having so much responsibility was too much for her and she was sorry. She couldn't be their mother because he'd made her feel like she was useless and they were his problem now. It was his fault she went away, and he had blamed Alfie because he didn't want to admit to himself that he'd been a crappy husband, who had bullied her since the day they got married. He'd taken his misery and self-hatred out on his youngest, and the fact that Alfie acted out only made things worse. He wanted to blame him, he was looking for an excuse to blame him and poor Alfie kept giving him one. Ryan knew what he was, that he'd hit Tiffany and almost hit him. Ryan knew why his mum had left and that's why he'd never blamed her, only him. The closer Ryan got to Alfie, the more Gary hated his youngest and, after Ryan had died, he'd sunk into a hole so depressingly deep that he had no idea how to escape. Then, just when he thought he was beginning to climb out, Tiffany turned up and reminded him of the past. As hard as he tried, he couldn't stop hating poor Alfie, especially when he saw how close Carol and he were becoming. Carol was his and Alfie was taking her away just like he did with Ryan. So it came to be that he was slumped down bleeding and beaten in his own hallway, his wife cradling her injured son, his best friend pushing past him to get to her while on the phone. The baby boy that he had held in his arms so lovingly on that perfect day, unconscious and bleeding, covered in glass because he couldn't control his jealous temper.

This was rock bottom and he knew it.

'Don't worry Alfie,' tears poured down her gaunt cheeks and splashed onto his face, 'you're going to be ok,' she was telling herself as much as she was telling him. She desperately wanted to pull the shards from his face, but listened to Keith when he said to wait for the ambulance; after all, she didn't know how deep they were and she could cause more harm than good. She wrapped gauze around his head attempting to stop the bleeding, but it was soaking through and he was going very pale. Then as if hit by lightning Alfie's eyes opened and he looked at his mummy crying. She didn't notice, she had been distracted by the sound of sirens in the distance and by the time she'd put her head down to check on him he'd drifted away and she continued to sob.

The burning man

1

Alfie woke with a start as a loud bang shattered his thoughts and he lay in the hospital bed shaking in a pool of his own sweat. The lights were dim, but they still hurt his eyes and he could tell it was night by the absence of colour outside the window that was situated in the corner of the hospital ward. He looked around and saw he was in the bed at the far end of the room, the only door was at the opposite end of the ward. The bed next to him had a young man in, he was about twenty and his heavily bandaged left hand was swaying gently at the side of the bed as he slept. The thin sheet that lay over him hugged every contour of his body, that was except his left leg as he didn't have one. It was missing from the bottom of the thigh down and Alfie shuddered at the sight.

He couldn't see the next bed, but he could just about make out the bed in front of him. It was empty, or was it? He looked harder and thought he saw a person lying on top of the neatly made sheets and pillow but he was tired and confused, so maybe he was seeing things. He rubbed his eyes and that's when he saw the bandages on his own hands. His skin stung like a bite from nettles as he pushed his hands against his face. His eye also hurt, so he checked it and found a bandage on his head as well, with a gauze above his eye. Whatever had happened to him it was bad, but he couldn't remember a thing. He couldn't even remember who he was, let alone where he was or how he got there. The shadow shifted on the bed opposite, but Alfie still wasn't sure that it was actually there; the air around it seemed distorted and blurry, like watching a screen with Vaseline smeared across it. His head was throbbing and he could hear his heartbeat in his temple as it pounded against his brain like a parade marching drum. The shadow sat up. It was definitely there; Alfie could see its shape clearer now in the dull light of the room. He squinted to clear his vision, convinced that this was why the shadow was blurred. Then it was gone. Alfie stared across the room as hard as he could, but the shadow was no longer there and Alfie started to doubt it ever was. He lay back down having leaned forward to peer into the darkness and shut his eyes to help alleviate the pain in his head. He sighed, then opened them again.

A face peered down at him, inches from his own. Its skin hung loosely from the muscles of its chin and one eye was nothing more than a gaping hole. Its lips were gone and its teeth were bared in a permanent, evil grin. The gums were raw with decay and the teeth themselves were black and rotting. Its hair appeared sporadically on its head, the bald patches shined a crimson glow of burnt skin. Its remaining eye was wide and forever seeing. The lids had been melted to the top and bottom of the eyeball, holding it spread open and staring at him with a glaring menace. Pus and blood from the horrible face dripped onto Alfie. He shook his head from side to side to rid himself of the repulsive liquid. Around its face, the light blurred as if it was peering through a transparent liquid and Alfie saw it had only small black scorched cavities where its ears used to be. It spoke but with no lips, Alfie couldn't understand how it sounded so clear.

'Help me, I'm burning,' its voice scratched like fingernails scraping on a chalkboard. 'Help me, I'm burning,' it pleaded and jerked its face away. In a flash like an old movie it returned to its original position inches from him and repeated itself, 'help me, I'm burning.' Smoke began to appear, pouring out of the hole in its eye socket, then from the ones on the side of its head. It shook violently but stayed where it was. Its features went blurry and it began to glow orange and red. It stopped shaking and opened its mouth. Smoke bellowed out, choking Alfie and bringing tears to his eyes. Its skin began to melt, dripping off its face like hot wax from a candle and Alfie was catching every last drop. 'Help me!' It cried out through the smoke, 'I'm burning.' Alfie struggled and tried to get away, but his body felt impossibly heavy as if his bones were made of concrete and his muscles of lead. He couldn't breathe now, the smoke was filling his lungs and the heat was burning his skin. He felt it bubbling and heard it crackling as he slowly cooked like a roast chicken. He wanted to cry out, to call for aid, but his throat was closed-up, filled with grey and black smouldering ash. He could no longer see the face and for that he was glad, but this was the least of his worries as he suffocated to death. The smoke suddenly vanished and he gasped as he was once again allowed to breathe. The face was still there, but it was no longer a face, just a burnt soot-covered skull, floating in mid-air. It spoke, but did not move its mouth, 'help me, I'm burning.' The skull began to crack along its forehead and then all over. It started to crumble and before Alfie could reach out to grab it and stop it from evaporating, it decayed into dust and was gone.

He lay shivering from fright, but also from the freezing cold that had saturated the room. He could see his own breath, a cloud of icy carbon dioxide floating away from him. He touched his face expecting to find sticky residue, but none was left behind. His throat was clear except for the tickle of the chill. The room was quiet and all was calm. Suddenly, he was so tired and tried to fight it off. He didn't want to sleep, he wanted to already be asleep, as this would mean that he'd been dreaming the whole time. Could you sleep while in a dream? He hoped so because the harder he tried to stay awake the more he drifted away. Just as his vision faded, and the world of dreams and nightmares took him for its prisoner, he noticed a calendar next to his bed, and he swore it read November 17, 1918.

2

'Give it back, you fat, idiot, you'll get it wet!' Alfie grabbed at the small black and white photo in the rotund boy's hand and missed it by a fingertip as it was jerked away.

'Pretty little thing, maybe I'll take her to bed with me,' his chubby red cheeks, blotchy and caked with mud, wobbled as he moved and Alfie thought he'd be easy pickings for the Hun if the call to go over the top ever came.

'That's enough horsing around young Drammer, give Private Fenix his photo back,' a posh silver-spooned tone flowed from the lips of the sergeant and he plucked the photo from the boy's grip.

'Ah Sir, we were just muckin' about, Alfie knows I meant no 'arm,' he sounded like a west country farmer, and it wasn't surprising to find out his father had been one. Had been, because he'd been drafted at the beginning of the war and hadn't lasted the year. Bobby Drammer had joined two years later as soon as he'd come of age, but his maturity was that of a school child's.

'Thank you, Sergeant,' Alfie put his hand out to receive the photo, but the moustached short muscular man hesitated giving it back and instead ogled at it with a glassy look of lust in his eyes. The trenches were a lonely place for a man with needs and he scanned across the picture of Alfie's girlfriend Beth before handing it back to him. Alfie shuddered at the thought of what he might have been doing but drove the dirty thoughts to the back of his mind as he could hardly blame the man for finding her attractive. He looked at the photo, checking it for any damage, there was a slight crease in the right-hand corner but other than that it seemed to be fine. Her long, dark, wavy hair was brushed back behind one ear and on the other side, it lay, loosely covering her right eye and cheek. Her left eye had a cheeky look of love that was meant to be for him, but now other men had seen it and they imagined it was for them. He carefully placed it in his jacket pocket and buttoned it up for safety.

'You're welcome Private, but I might suggest that with a picture as pretty as that one, you keep it out of sight. The lads don't need those sorts of distractions, it might have them thinking more about girls than fighting for their country and we wouldn't want that, would we now,' his eyes sharpened and Alfie knew he was as serious as a graveyard.

'No, Sergeant Williams, we wouldn't,' he looked over at Bobby who was about to pick his nose then saw him looking and thought better of it, 'he's just a kid, he doesn't know what he's doing,' he worried that Bobby might get in trouble, the Sergeant was a no-nonsense man who wasn't afraid to lay down the law. Alfie had already seen him shoot a man who was trying to run out into No Man's, but if he hadn't, a Fritz would have or even worse captured and tortured him for information that could have put them all at risk. It hadn't been the act that had scared Alfie, more the look of nonchalance on Sgt Williams' face. Perhaps it was all for show, and he'd gone back to his quarters and cried about it? But Alfie doubted this man had ever cried even as a baby.

'The sapper stole from you, but I guess as you said, he's just got some growing up to do. That's if he ever gets the chance,' this last sentence was exactly what worried Alfie about him, he might not have been wrong, but he didn't have to be smiling behind his bushy whiskers when he said it.

'Thank you, Sir,' Alfie walked away forcing himself not to glance back. He didn't want to see Sgt Williams staring and smiling ominously. He reached his shelter, a misleading name for the step dug into the wall of the trench, barely big enough for him to squeeze into and a foot off the ground to avoid the mud and slime from soaking him as he recuperated. He avoided a huge black rat and kicked at it, shooing as he did, 'get away, filthy git.' The rat dodged his attack, then sat up and hissed. It wasn't afraid of him; it wasn't afraid of anyone. Alfie wished he could have brought his cat with him. Whisky was a huge, crossbred moggy, who delighted in killing anything furry that dared cross his path. He would have dealt with this cocky flea-infested disease carrier. He missed his home and he wondered, like most of the Tommies, if he would ever see it again. He coughed and his throat felt like he'd eaten dry sawdust with a side of woodchips. He lay on his back, on the dirty ledge and closed his eyes.

3

'Good morning,' a sweet-sounding nurse leaned over him, her white muslin cap glowed in the sunlight like a halo.

'Are you an angel?' Alfie asked still delirious from the nightmare he'd been part of during the night.

'You might say that, but most people just call me Diane,' she smiled at him so he could see her teeth, wide and beautiful, her lips were a reddish pink. She was pale and slim with blonde hair poking out the sides of her cap. Her eyes were a bright, piercing blue and he could have been lost in them forever had she not looked away.

'How did I get here?' his voice sounded to him like it belonged to another person, he didn't recognise its tone, he had no idea who he was, so why would he?

'Well, you were one of the lucky ones,' she said tenderly, 'you made it home. A little worse for wear, I will admit, but considering everything you lads have been through…' she glanced fleetingly at the one-legged man in the bed next to them, 'you came out alright.'

'I don't remember anything,' he reached for the water beside his bed, but he couldn't quite get to it.

'Let me help you with that,' she gently forced his hand back to his side and picked up the glass. 'Your name is Alfie Fenix,' she carefully put the glass to his lips and he sipped the room-temperature liquid down into his sore throat. 'You came here a few nights ago, but only woke up this morning. Truth be told…' she lowered her voice to a whisper, 'the doctor thought you weren't going to make it, but I had a feeling a strapping lad like you would pull through.' She touched his shoulder and he felt warm, like he'd swallowed hot soup and the heat rushed through his body relaxing him. Then she absentmindedly removed it.

'I don't know who Alfie Fenix is. All I remember is the guns, the terrible noise of the guns as they bombarded our trench and the foul stench of blood lingering in the air, rotting corpses on top of me, crushing me, making me wish I was one of them,' he began panicking and tried to get up.

'Alfie, calm down, it's ok,' she touched his shoulder again and he calmed.

'Nurse Davies you are needed in the south ward, please kindly finish your duties and leave this poor man alone,' Doctor Richards walked over to them holding a chart and looking down at it through his spectacles.

'She's been helping me remember,' Alfie said.

'That may be Private Fenix, but that is not her job,' he stood over her, a tall, elderly, gaunt man, whose top lip sported a thin white moustache and his hair ran away from the centre of his head, gathering at its side.

'Sorry Doctor Richards, I've finished now,' she didn't look at her superior, but managed to wink at Alfie without the old man seeing, gathered her tray and carried on with her daily tasks.

'A treat for the eyes,' he said looking back at Alfie, after gazing after the nurse as she left.

Alfie didn't like men like this, who thought they were better than others just because they had a better education or richer parents. He was beginning to recollect his likes and dislikes, but who he actually was still evaded him, 'she's kind, not everyone is kind. It's not a kind world,' he said.

'Fair enough,' the Doctor ignored his melancholy mood and looked at his chart, 'I must admit, Private Fenix...'

'Alfie is fine if that's my name.'

'I must admit Alfie I had my doubts about you. You were in a catatonic state when they brought you home. You hadn't spoken or reacted to anyone's presence since they found you in that trench. You must have been there for days, thank God the War ended and you were rescued,' he spoke as though he'd been there and it had been him that had hauled the bodies off him and by chance found him alive. That was one more memory that just came back to him, a memory he would rather forget.

'Why can't I remember who I am?

'There are a few reasons, but the most likely is that you have slight brain damage from the bang to your head. Your mind might return, but you might just have to accept that you may never remember exactly who you were,' he didn't seem to be the least bit sympathetic.

'So that's it then, the War's over,' he didn't know this until the doctor just mentioned it, 'Just like that, one day we're all killing and dying, ending the lives of men the same as each other just with a different language, a different uniform, a different set of murderous blood thirsty fools in charge of innocent men.'

'Now, now Private, let's keep the potty mouth in check, shall we. This War was a bad one, we can all admit that but there is no excuse for bad-mouthing one's superiors,' there was that word, "superior". How were they superior to anyone else? What gave them the right to use men like waves breaking on rocks, trying to wear them down while they died by the thousands. He didn't have the strength to argue with this stupid man and instead closed his eyes. 'Now you've woken up would you like us to call anyone? We checked your records and saw your parents are both deceased and your brother is MIA. You have no wife or children either, do you have anyone else we can notify?'

He kept his eyes closed, the darkness was better than the glare of the conceited doctor. He racked his brains trying to remember. I couldn't recall any of his family, which hugely frustrated him. What about the photo in his dream? Who was the girl? he knew her name but didn't know her, 'Beth,' he said jadedly.

'Beth who?'

He struggled to stay awake, the sandman coming to sprinkle him with sleep, 'Beth,' he wasn't saying her name for the doctor now but remembering her fondly and wishing she was there. He drifted away.

'Too much for the poor begger,' Doctor Richards wrote something on his chart and went about his business starting with the patient next to Alfie, 'how are you today Private Stubbs?' he said not missing the amusing irony of the man's missing leg.

'Get lost,' the Tommy snarled.

'Charming,' the doctor retorted.

'If you want me to charm you, you'll have to buy me diner first,' Stubbs smiled and winked.

'Indeed,' replied the doctor without an ounce of humour in his tone.

'SERGEANT,' Alfie called as loudly as he possibly could over the deafening sound of the German artillery forebodingly close to their trench line. He was running back to the support trench but could barely see or hear anything helpful in the rainfall and the din. 'SERGEANT WILLIAMS!' he bellowed once more, sliding around in the mud, grasping at more mud trying to keep his balance. Another explosion shattered through his bones and he fell to the wet sodden sludge with his arms over his head.

'Well, that won't stop you from dying, will it Private?' the oddly relaxed voice of Sergeant Williams was barely audible, but its unnerving sense of calm made it somehow stand out in the chaos of the moment.

'Sir, the north side of the trench has collapsed and men are trapped in the landslide, I think some are dead,' he took the Sergeant's hand and he was lifted to his feet.

'That's the war I'm afraid Son. We'll pray for their souls when it's done, but until then let's concentrate on digging the others out without our arses getting well and truly smacked shall we,' his reserve was cool and his steeliness unmatched. The two of them made their way to the stores to grab some shovels and more Tommies to help.

Alfie woke with a start and once again he was drenched with perspiration and thirstier than an alcoholic at happy hour. He thought he'd made a loud noise when he awoke and checked to see if anyone else had risen from their slumber. From his position, he could still only see about two feet in front of him. Had he really seen the melting man? No, he dismissed the idea from his mind no sooner had it entered it. He had brain damage that's all, just his head playing tricks on him like a schoolboy prankster. The room was quiet except for the low hum of the lights in the hallway just outside the door and the ticking of a clock that he couldn't see. Tick, tick, tick, it repeated in a perfect pattern as the second hand raced around the face trying to prove it was better than its slow, short, fat sibling. He wedged his elbows into the mattress and pushed himself up into a more upright position. He could see the clock now, it was white and hung above the door. There were seven beds on each side of the room, fourteen in all but only five of them were being used. He couldn't make out the faces or even the sex of his fellow hospital residents just their shapes.

He stared at the door, he thought that out of the corner of his eye he'd seen the light disappear, only for a fraction of a second but it was enough to draw his gaze. He looked intently at it, expecting it to do it again thinking that it had been a faulty bulb or some issue with the wiring but the light held strong and didn't flutter. He looked back at the clock to check the time, realising that he had just watched it and not taken note of where the hands were, just that they were moving. Ten past one and the hallway flickered again. His eyes dashed back to the open gap and the light was bright and unfaltering. He was doubting everything at his point even whether he was awake or not, then the hairs on his arms began to rise as if they were being sucked up into the sky by an invisible power.

A freezing sensation caught every bare bit of his skin. The corridor went black and this time stayed that way. Alfie could hear something moving along the floor outside. It shuffled along one foot dragging behind the other and what might have been a hand slapping against the wall, keeping it upright. Alfie wanted to turn away as it approached the door but his neck wouldn't budge. He wanted to close his eyes and wake up in the morning knowing this was a bad dream, but his eyes wouldn't shut. There was an orange glow beginning to break through the blackness as the noise approached. Alfie tried to get out of bed but he was too weak and too injured to move. All he could do was stare at the rectangular hole at the far end of the room and hope that nothing appeared in it while he was still awake. He urgently tried to shut his eyes, they were weary and wanted to send him back to sleep, but something was keeping them open and, as yet, he couldn't see what. Scrape, clump the shoes of the visitor went as the gap was getting closer. The orange light was strong and Alfie could tell it was getting stronger by the instant, 'who's there?' he asked barely able to speak due to a mixture of fear, tiredness and possible brain damage.

'Help me,' it said as if it were next to his bed, 'I'm burning,' he looked from side to side, his neck suddenly mobile, imagining the melting man was there but saw nothing.

The orange glow was at the door now and every muscle he had tightened so much it was painful, 'is that you Alfie? Are you awake?' Nurse Davies, Diane to her friends and family, was stood holding a candle cradled in her hands like a precious new-born chick, 'the power went out so I came to check on you... I mean everyone... I mean the patients in this room,' she stuttered her words as they bundled out from her sumptuous lips.

He breathed a sigh of relief when he saw her candlelit face and not a burnt skull floating in the air, 'yes I'm awake and everything's fine,' his voice was as confident as a small child's the first time it jumps off a high diving board.

'Are you sure, you don't sound fine,' she entered the ward and made her way over to him, 'you're drenched Alfie, what happened?'

'Bad dream I'm afraid. I get them a lot,' he didn't want to share the details, as he wasn't entirely clear on them. All he knew was that he'd been in the trenches, bad things had happened and now he was here. The details were sketchy and maybe that was best. He was already having waking nightmares, he feared what might happen if he thought harder about the horrors that took place in that filthy disease-ridden ditch he had called home. Nothing good would come of it, he was sure of that.

'I'm sorry to hear that, I wish there was something I could do to magic them away but I'm afraid I don't perform miracles,' she smiled ever so slightly, not confident that it was the correct time to do so but also not wanting to be too serious because he might think she was unfriendly.

'I'll be fine. Thank you for coming to see me.'

She at first avoided his gaze but then turned back, her hair moving beneath her muslin cap. She sat down on the chair next to his bed and leaned over to him putting her lips an inch from his ear 'help me,' she whispered, 'I'm burning.' He pulled away from her, jerking his head as if he were trying to dodge the words but it was too late, he had heard them and coming from this sweet, beautiful angel made it all the worse.

'Are you okay?' her usually blue eyes, now shimmering orange with dancing flames from the flickering candle she held, were wide and stunned, 'what's wrong Alfie?' she was desperate to know what had made him react this way, perhaps he was scared of her being this close? or perhaps it brought up bad, repressed memories best left forgotten.

'What did you just say?' he quivered.

'I said I'll help you through this and then the candle got close and I said sorry I almost burnt you. Maybe I should go? I must check on the other patients,' she rose from the chair and pulled her dress at the knees with her free hand to straighten it out.

'Sorry,' he said peering up at her, 'I don't know what's going on at the moment. My head's all over the place.'

'I understand, no harm was done, you've had a rough time of it that's all. Go back to sleep and I'll see you in the morning,' with this she walked away with a bouncing light guiding her every step. He lay silent in the dark, his mind a mess of confusion and fear and another sensation he hadn't felt for some time: lust, desire, needs, possibly a sexual infatuation. He closed his eyes and fell asleep dreaming of the angel nurse.

5

Morning came and Alfie woke again but this time he had not dreamt of death and cold and disease and hatred, instead had dreamt of a girl. She had long dark wavy hair and she sang to him as he slept. He had huddled up against her breasts as they lay beneath an oak tree, watching the clouds drift slowly by. She had told him that she loved him and he had asked her to marry him. She had said yes and they had kissed under the trunk of the ancient woodland giant. He had never been happier and he would never be that happy again.

'Alright pal,' Alfie looked to his right to see where the words had come from, 'cheer up, at least you got all ya limbs eh.' Alfie tried not to look down at the dismembered leg under the white sheet, but his gaze shifted over and remained for a fraction of a second too long. He felt ashamed that he had stared, 'don't worry about looking mate, I can't stop staring meself. I still feel it ya know? Still keep trying to wiggle my toes,' he smiled, a smile of genuine happiness and friendship. He seemed glad to be alive, even if not in one piece.

'How'd it happen?' Alfie didn't bother with the polite avoidance of the obvious question, after everything they'd seen it seemed pointless and idiotic.

'Shell went off as we were making our advance. Killed both me mates and the bastards thought they got me but they didn't know who they were messing with, cos I'm still here and they're running for the hills,' his face contorted between looking sad for his friends and happy he had got one over on the Hun, but Alfie suspected that the former was the real feeling and the latter was desperately trying to hold him together. Alfie knew this look, it was the look every Tommy wore when faced with their own mortality. Why am I still here? What did I do to deserve a second chance? What did the others do wrong to deserve to die? Who they would ask these questions to was a matter of personal belief and faith, but they all asked the questions even if they no longer believed in anything.

'All that bloody waiting,' Alfie said to himself, but the words left his lips.

'All that God damn waiting,' Stubbs repeated lost in his own recollection of the trench.

'All that time thinking we were making a difference, then all those men lost with barely a whimper. There are some lost souls out there who'll never find their way home, most probably don't even know their dead,' Alfie was still speaking as though to himself, softly and thoughtfully. He faced his head towards the ceiling and pictured the Sergeants lifeless face laying on top of him, his soulless eyes staring at him as if to say, "you lucky git, how are you alive and I'm the one who copped it?" Alfie will never forget him, he'd be dead if it wasn't for his bravery.

'Jesus,' Stubbs moaned, 'if I'd wanted to be depressed, I would've asked them to leave me on the battlefield.'

'Sorry,' Alfie said, 'It's all a bit fresh in my head. I only woke up yesterday and not for long and before that, all I remember is being buried under…' he stopped and couldn't carry on, the nightmare of it all overwhelming him.

'It's ok Alfie,' he overheard the conversation last night and wished the nurse had shown him half the amount of concern she'd shown this soldier, but he wasn't bitter just a little disappointed.

'It'll never be ok; it might be better than this, but it'll never be ok.'

Stubbs thought about this and his mood dropped, the mask fell from his face and his true mood was revealed. He was sad. Sad, lonely and missing his friends, his brother who'd died two years ago and his leg which he'd been very fond of. It was his kicking leg, and he was a pretty decent footballer. His life, his world and his future had been gravely affected by some men pushing pieces around on a map, making decisions with no care of the individual consequences to human lives. Alfie was depressing but only because he was right. They didn't speak the rest of the day but remained in a state somewhere between sleep and wake, self-reflecting and wishing they were somewhere else.

6

'WAKE UP,' Alfie screamed in the ear of the young Tommy who lay limply in his arms, 'COME ON YOU BASTARD, come on,' he knew the boy was gone but he couldn't let him go, not just yet.

'Come on young man, let the boy rest. God has him now,' Sergeant Williams knelt beside him, his hand rested on Alfie's shoulder a small comfort amid such heartache.

'He was just telling me how much he missed his Mother, he was just talking to me then...' he trailed off and his hand tightened grabbing the dead boy's curly hair, blood staining the blonde, his life force dripping into the mud and disappearing forever.

'Let go now son, Private Hale will look after him now,' he gently but physically persuasively pulled Alfie away by linking his arm under Alfie's and drawing him backwards. Alfie went limp and provided no resistance, his hand eventually falling away from Bobby's, dirty, crimson red face.

Awake again this time his own sobbing stirring him from his rest. His vision was blurred and he blinked away the tears resisting the temptation to use his hands as he knew it would hurt. Something passed his hazy sight and he bristled, 'is that you Stubbs?' he asked hopefully. There was no answer, but he hadn't in all honesty expected one, his right hand wavered and tremored as he pondered whether to wipe his tears. A shadow moved and a faint smell of burning drifted up Alfie's nostrils making his hairs tickle. 'Nurse Davies, Diane are you there?' he whispered hoping that she might hear but nobody else. He could hear breathing, laboured and wheezy like an old man who smoked forty a day.

'They told me I was going to be fine. They told me not to worry,' the rasping voice spoke but it was as if Alfie was remembering a conversation rather than hearing it first-hand. It coughed long and painful exhalation of air and Alfie strained his eyes in the dark through the indistinct watery vision, but it wasn't good enough. It spoke again but this time the voice was louder as if it were next to his bed, no wait not next to but underneath it, 'they lied to me, all of them. They lied to you too Alfie,' it said his name and his heart raced. It knew him, it chose him. All of a sudden it was more than just a waking nightmare, it had become reality and he shook with fear. He could make out a light shuffling coming from beneath him then it began to get warmer. He wanted to cry out, wanted to scream for help, but his cries were trapped inside him, bubbling at the surface ready to explode. He strained from the force and his mouth opened but still, no sounds were made. Exhausted he sunk back into the pillow his neck tender from arching, 'Help me,' it coughed, 'I'm burning.' A split second later it was as if the bed was on fire but no flames appeared around him. He could smell his flesh sizzling like a Sunday afternoon barbeque, the sensation of crackling agony encircled his body and still, he couldn't scream. 'I'M BURNING,' it was inside his mind tearing away, ripping his brain, burning his consciousness. Thick black smoke was everywhere; he couldn't see a thing. His eyes watered not from sadness but stinging blindness. He inhaled and his lungs filled and emptied harshly. This isn't real he thought but the burning man was part of him and his fear and his anger controlled Alfie and the sensation was too much to bear. His heart stopped and pulsed no more.

A light appeared and Alfie felt hope. The pain was gone and he knew this was the end. He could feel air rushing into him and something beating on his chest, 'come on man, don't you dare die. Not after everything you survived, you're not dying today.' Alfie felt as if he was floating, his spirit leaving his useless carcass, his very being free and alive again. He felt euphoric and hopeful and not in the least bit afraid. It was his time and he had accepted that, but someone was dragging him back, 'no you don't,' the voice said, 'no you bloody don't,' Alfie blinked and a blurry shape peered down at him, 'thank Christ soldier I thought you were a gonna,' Stubbs was lent over him breathless and sweating.

'What the…' Alfie whispered, his throat was tender.

'I just saved your arse, my friend,' he sat back against the frame of his bed, exhausted from keeping a fallen comrade alive.

'But I was free,' he sounded disappointed.

'Oh, well next time I won't bother,' Stubbs said sarcastically, his chest rapidly rising up and down.

'Sorry, I didn't…'

'Not to worry, I was glad to help. You would've done the same for me,' Stubbs hoped that he wouldn't as he longed for the sweet release.

'How?' Alfie wheezed.

'You fell out of bed and crashed on the floor writhing in agony. Then suddenly you went still and that's when I dropped down and started saving your life,' he emphasised the last three words.

'Yes, thank you,' Alfie pondered whether he was thankful then saw Nurse Davies appear by his side and her face made him positive he was glad to still be there to appreciate her beauty and kindness.

'Alfie,' she said touching his face, 'are you alright? What happened?' she faced Stubbs, 'Private, your leg!' she panicked. Alfie raised his neck and saw he was wincing with discomfort, then he saw why. The bandage around the nub of the missing leg was soaked through with blood. It was even dripping onto the floor, forming a red puddle that looked like spilt wine.

'Bloody hell,' Alfie remarked.

'It's nothing I haven't had before,' he smiled through the pain.

'What have you two been up to? I can't leave you for one second before you're all rolling around playing silly sods,' her attempt at lightning the situation was a success and both men looked at each other and laughed, then grimaced because laughing hurt like hell. She firstly helped Alfie back into his bed where he rested, sitting on the edge like a perched canary then went to get help as she couldn't lift the one-legged hero by herself.

'Seriously,' Stubbs said in a low voice as if whatever he was about to say was only for them to hear, 'what happened? When I woke you were convulsing on the bed holding your throat with your mouth open trying to breathe, but your grip was so tight you couldn't, I thought you were going to strangle yourself,' he shifted his good leg to gain better balance, 'that's when you fell off the bed. Did you have a bad dream or something?'

'You could say that,' Alfie was thinking hard about what he remembered as it was all very obscure.

'What do you mean?'

'I dreamt there was a man, I think it was a man, I couldn't actually see it, I just heard it. It called out to me for help, it said it was burning, then all of a sudden I was burning and there was smoke everywhere. I couldn't breathe, couldn't see, couldn't speak, only feel and hear the man's terror and agony like it was my own,' he shuddered at the memory.

'Jesus, maybe you do have brain damage,' Stubbs said concernedly.

'I don't think that's it.'

'What makes you say that?'

'I saw him the first night I woke here, he was sitting on the bed over there,' he pointed with his head, 'he appeared above me and his face turned to flame then melted away only inches from my face,' he held his hand flat up to his nose to emphasise the distance the man was from him.

'That sounds exactly like brain damage, why don't you think it is?' asked Stubbs.

'I can't explain it, it's just a feeling that's all. I don't think it wants to hurt me, I think it wants me to feel what it felt so I can help it. He keeps asking me for help but I don't know how, Christ I didn't even think that it was real until just now when I said it out loud, but now hearing me say it to you should sound crazy but it doesn't.'

263

'That's a matter of opinion mate,' Stubbs looked doubtfully at his fellow Tommy. Before Alfie could argue Nurse Davies came back followed by one of the other nurses, a beefy older woman with rolled-up sleeves and a slightly different uniform. The two of them approached Stubbs and took him by an arm each. Together they hoisted him up onto the bed and he roared.

'Come on now, you're a tough soldier aren't you?' the older one asked rhetorically.

'Nina, you can see he's hurt,' Nurse Davies was more sympathetic in her approach.

'These boys don't need pampering Diane, they're soldiers not puppies,' she began unwrapping the drenched gauze and Diane prepared the fresh one. They dressed the wound and Alfie caught a glimpse. He had seen it all before but would never get used to it, at least he hoped he wouldn't.

After they were done with Stubbs they helped Alfie lay back down and Nurse Davies checked him over fully while the older nurse cleaned up the sticky mess on the floor, 'what happened to your neck?' she asked, his red handprints were still partly visible.

'I don't know,' he lied.

She glanced at Stubbs who had his eyes closed trying to will away the pain then leaned into Alfie's ear, 'he didn't hurt you did he?' It was a reasonable assumption.

'God no,' Alfie spluttered, 'he saved my life.'

'Then how did you hurt your neck?'

He had to be careful how he answered as he didn't want her thinking he was suicidal, 'I had a bad dream that a German soldier was strangling me. When I woke I had my own hands around my throat and was so shocked I fell out of bed. I think that's when I passed out and stopped breathing. The brain can make you do funny things it seems,' he added the last bit just to help explain it away as if he knew anything about how the brain worked.

'You poor man!' her eyes were ocean blue and he could have swum in them for days, 'I can't even imagine what you must have been through. Don't you worry I'm not going to let anyone hurt you ever again,' the words just slipped out. She hadn't meant them to, especially in earshot of her colleague but they were the truth and she had no regrets.

'Ever again?' he repeated questioningly.

She wanted to tell him that she was falling for him. She couldn't explain why, there was just something about him. She felt safe around him, her heart raced when she stared at his handsome features and his heroism in the face of danger also helped. She wanted to kiss him and be touched by him, but this was neither the time or place so she just said, 'well at least while you're in my care,' and smiled as if it were a joke.

He smiled back hoping she'd been serious as he too felt a burning desire to be with her but couldn't even imagine a woman like this ever wanting a disfigured, brain-damaged wretch like him, 'obviously,' he said.

The rest of the day had been uneventful after that. He and Stubbs hadn't been able to go back to sleep and had instead played cards. The other patients who'd been woken, not by his almost dying, but by the loud older nurse, had all except one gone back to their dreams. The only one not to was a middle-aged, averagely built man who according to him was a butler for a very wealthy family named the Roundtree's and they had driven him there themselves when he had collapsed while serving them tea on their veranda. Alfie thought him to be snobbish and hadn't wanted him to join in but Stubbs had invited him without a seconds thought and the snotty-nosed, dark but greying haired man had pulled up a chair on the opposite side of Stubbs' bed to Alfie.

The three of them had played various games from Rummy to a not so friendly game of poker, in which they used matches instead of money. Alfie had never seen so much fuss made of little flammable sticks and wondered why it had meant so much to him to win. He'd forgotten he was competitive and wished he hadn't remembered as he was behaving like quite the arse. They'd decided that after Alfie had thrown a handful of matches at the butler who he called Butler rather than his actual name which was Harry, they would call it a day. Alfie apologised like a reprimanded toddler but didn't mean it and it showed. Butler had returned to his bed and Alfie was glad to have his new friend to himself. 'That wasn't called for ya'know,' Stubbs scolded him, his tone was that of a school teacher, his posture like an angry parent.

'The guy was a snob,' Alfie retorted like he had a leg to stand on.

'He fought in the same war as we did, he just got lucky he won't have any scars, not on the outside anyway. We all got scars on the inside, there's no hiding that.'

Alfie thought about this for a moment and realised that the guy had just wanted to be friends but wasn't very good at it. He was hardly endearing the way he boasted about how rich the Roundtree's were and how he was one of the family. He was kidding himself if he thought that, Alfie pondered to himself. He had met upper-class families and through all their fake teeth smiling when they met you he knew how they felt. They were the chosen, they were the privileged and the rest of us were just there to serve and be sent to war. We were cannon fodder for their safety and that's all. This deluded butler was wishing with the fairies and Alfie had said so out loud which was when the hostility started. 'He thinks that stupid family love him. They don't love their servants, they just depend on him. They only drove him here because they want him fixed up as soon as possible so he can get back to serving them tea. They don't care he was sent to die for their war, they don't...'

'Enough Alfie, stop going on about the bloody war as if it were us versus the aristocracy. The classes are there whether ya want em to be or not and I for one can accept that even if I don't like it. You need to get off this pedestal of yours and concentrate on making yourself better and stop giving me a blooming headache. The Hun were the ones killing us and I for one would like to hate them if it's all the same with you,' he closed his eyes in frustration knowing the annoying git was right, but he didn't want to hear it. He just wanted to get better and move on with his life.

'Sorry,' Alfie leaned over to face Stubbs, 'I just get so angry, but that's no excuse.'

'It's not me you need to apologise to,' he snapped still feeling the heat inside him.

'You're right,' he replied and swung his legs over the side of the bed, 'I know you think I imagined the burning man, but I swear he was as real as you and me,' he didn't wait for an answer and walked over to Harry's bed.

7

The night came and Alfie sat up straight desperately trying to stay awake. Half of him thought he'd seen the burning man the other half thought he'd also seen it but it was because he wasn't right in the mind. If he was real, what did he want? He knew he wanted help but how was he supposed to help him if he didn't say how? All he did was cause Alfie agony but if there was ever a reason to help someone, stopping that pain from happening again seemed worthy enough. He looked over to Stubbs who had refused to stay up with him, he still thought Alfie was imagining the burning man and didn't want to encourage his friend with his unhealthy fantasy. Alfie had thought about asking Harry but the man had only begrudgingly and out of noble politeness excepted his apology earlier that day so he wasn't the best choice for backup in this situation. Alfie had wanted to ask the other patients if they'd seen the phantom but changed his mind when Nurse Davies entered with their lunch and told him off for getting out of bed in his condition. He'd retreated hastily to the confines of his mattress prison and not moved since.

Now there he was, staring into the darkness, occasionally glancing at the open door expecting the light to flicker or at least see something out of the ordinary, but nothing stirred. His eyes wavered and drooped closed but he forced them open again. She was on his mind again. The dark-haired beauty under the tree. Who was she? Why hadn't she come to see him? Were they still engaged? Why couldn't he remember? His fists clenched and he hit the mattress with the right one, 'Crap,' he said out loud as the stinging shock shot up his arm. He forgot his hands were mangled and wondered how bad it was. It hurt like hell but the doctor hadn't seemed overly concerned last time he checked on him and if Stubbs didn't complain about his leg, he wasn't going to fuss over his hands. His eyes drooped again and this time they remained closed.

8

The whistle blew, it was a sharp bone curdling noise they had both feared and looked forward to hearing. This was their moment; this is what they'd come here for. They were about to give the Hun a beating they would never forget. They would all be heroes and everyone back home would cheer them as they returned. They were invincible, they were warriors sent from God to right all the wrongs of the world. They didn't believe the propaganda, they knew the Germans were just the same as them. They had heard the stories of the football games on Christmas day and how the enemy was no worse or better than they were. They wanted to villainise them, to hate them and to loath them but inside they knew why they were here. Here in this filthy, rat-infested swamp of a ditch. Hungry, sick and covered in lice.

The whistle continued to blow and Alfie's stomach churned. From young boys to middle and even ageing men they scrambled up the ladders and disappeared over the lip. One man, George from Horsham in West Sussex who Alfie knew well, reached the top and in an instant, his body went limp and tumbled back down into the trench. Alfie ran to his side and turned him over. His face was no longer there, just a hole and bits of the skull remained of the married dad of three. He jumped back, dropping the corpse which splashed into the mud. He began to shake and walk backwards until his foot caught on something solid and he fell on his arse. He looked over his knees at what had tripped him and saw another well-known Tommy lifeless beneath him. He scampered backwards using his hands to pull himself along until something grabbed the back of his collar and hoisted him to his feet. He swayed unsteadily, but there was no sympathy for his sickness only the ear-splitting screams of Sergeant Williams as he pointed a pistol at Alfie's head, 'GET UP THAT LADDER OR I WILL BLOW YOUR HEAD OFF!,' the dangerous end of the gun was pressed into Alfie's temple just to emphasise the point, he got the point, there was no way he didn't get the point. But no matter how much he got the point, his feet would not move and fear had immobilised him. 'NOW!,' bellowed the Sergeant, but this just made Alfie even more afraid. The next few seconds seemed to last minutes as everything around him slowed to a fraction of the speed. The bullets flew through the air above them, their intricate detail visible to the naked eye moving faster than the speed of sound. The Sergeants voice was hollow and sluggish, every word spread out thin like butter on bread. Alfie's heartbeat boomed in his ears with long gaps spaced between them. His fellow braver Tommies ran past at walking speed, hurriedly making their way to their impending deaths. The grenade floated through the air like a balloon caught in a midday breeze. All the men looked up, then down at it in unison as it landed by their feet. The Sergeant dropped his gun and in his final act on earth pushed Alfie away. Time resumed its normal fast pace and the grenade exploded. A flash of fire and death blinded Alfie. Bodies mutilated and inert, flew in every direction with several of them landing heavily on him. The Sergeants back had been eviscerated and all that was left was barely recognisable. He tried to lift the dead men off him but had little to no strength. He struggled for a while before blacking out and waking up in the Hospital.

He woke with a start, a sensation that he was beginning to tire of. He was back in the hospital, his mind now fully recovered. He remembered everything and he was ashamed. If he hadn't got scared and had done his duty, the Sergeant might still be alive. But if it wasn't for the grenade, would the Sergeant have shot him? He would never have moved, he knew that now. As much as he wished things had been different and he'd been brave and heroic, he knew now that he was nothing but a coward and he didn't deserve to be alive. Why had they rescued him? It all came flooding back now, he recollected wishing he would die as he lay beneath the pile of rotting corpses he had once called friends. The room shuddered, or was it him? All thoughts left his mind and he focused his sniper-like attention on his current predicament. The walls shuddered, they rippled ever so slightly like a pond disturbed by a fly. Instinctively he stared at the open door as if he knew what he'd see there. He wasn't wrong, though he wished he had been. The burning man was standing, silhouetted in the doorway. He was staring straight at Alfie before he walked away, disappearing from Alfie's sight. He quickly jumped out of bed ignoring the pain in his hands from swinging himself around and raced to the door. He stopped as he reached it hesitating only for a second before sticking his head out into the hallway and looking up in the direction of the phantom. He saw him standing at the end of the corridor next to a door watching Alfie, waiting for him to follow. He didn't need to say anything, didn't need to beckon or gesture in any way. Alfie knew what he wanted and reluctantly put one foot in front of the other. The lights flickered as Alfie walked beneath them as if they were reacting to his presents, but that's impossible he thought, well maybe not as he was following a ghost around. He neared the burning man who moved towards the door and stepped through it as if it wasn't there. Alfie reached the door and his hand reached out to touch the handle, 'where do you think you're going?' he recognised the beefy nurse's voice from the night before.

'I have to go through here,' he said, not knowing how or why he'd said it.

'Oh no you don't, you need to get back to bed and sharpish before I drag you there,' her stance shifted to a more bullish one as if she was preparing to tackle him like a rugby scrum-half.

'I have to go through here,' he repeated still unable to control himself as if someone else was speaking for him. The lights above her flickered and the burning man appeared behind her. He was stretched thin rising above her looking down on her head, his arms reaching up to the ceiling. He wanted to tell her but as before his voice was lost to him and his words stuck in his throat. Had he been able to release them he would have warned her of the figure looming above, menacingly swaying from side to side like a snake ready to strike. But instead, he stood there as helplessly as that day in the trench, unable to prevent the inevitable demise of a fellow human being. Nina who'd just turned forty and was one shift away from going on holiday to Brighton with her Sister and Mother, felt the hairs on the back of her neck rise to their full extent and a feeling of dread filled her from head to toe. The phantom arms shot down and grabbed her. She rose in the air, her legs and feet flaying about trying to kick something that wasn't there. She opened her mouth to cry but like Alfie she had become mute and not even a whimper was heard. He lifted her up sharply smashing her skull against the ceiling. A gash opened up on her forehead and blood trickled down her face. The crimson liquid entered her mouth and she spat it out instantly like a boxer in the corner of a ring between rounds. In an instant she was forced downwards at a startling speed, her legs pummelled into the ground with such force every bone shattered and the noise echoed up the hallway and assaulted Alfie's ears. Dazed and confused and writhing in agony the nurse reached out to Alfie as if only he could stop this repulsive display of horror. He wanted to, he tried to, but he was pinned and forced to watch as the hands of the burning man came hurtling down upon her head, knocking her unconscious.

He sunk to his knees but felt hands grab him under his arms and lift him. He knew who it was and with no control over his movements, he was forced through the door into the stairwell. It was on fire; the heat should have been unbearable but Alfie felt nothing. He was standing in the blaze but no flames touched him. It was as if he had an invisible bubble surrounding him that repelled any heat away and the flames bent as he approached. He walked up the stairs to the next floor then out of the door into another hallway. This one was identical to the one below and the burning man stood by another door halfway along it. Alfie moved, too fatigued to struggle control of his own will from the grips of the phantom. The burning man went into the room as Alfie approached. The door was ajar and he pushed it open to reveal a small room with a single bed. The light was off, but no sooner had he noticed this it turned on to shed a light on exactly what the burning man had wanted to show him.

9

Carol sat beside his bed holding his little hand as gently as she could with one hand and stroking his hair, avoiding the bandage around his head with the other. Her Baby had been out cold now for over seven hours and the Doctors had just put it down to shock. "Sometimes when people, especially children, experience something traumatic their brain shuts down for a while to protect itself" she'd been told by a paediatrician whom she could have mistaken for a student if it weren't for his uniform and name badge. She hadn't left his side, even when the police came to interview her. They took her statement in the corner of the room despite the protests from the nursing staff. Keith had a word with them on her behalf and they'd finally understood why she wouldn't move.

Gary was arrested and didn't even put up a fight despite the police being heavy-handed with him after they'd seen what he'd done to his own nine-year-old son. It enraged one officer in particular, who had a son of his own just a bit older than Alfie and he'd recoiled at the thought of a man doing this to a child. He'd slammed Gary up against the wall, knocking down a commemorative plate from the wall, it landed with a thump on the carpet but luckily hadn't broken. The other officer who was also angry but more level headed had gently pulled her partner away and taken over the arrest, tightening the handcuffs one click more than they needed just to make sure the bastard was uncomfortable on the way to the station. They let Keith follow the ambulance but told him they needed a statement from them both and they would come to them at the hospital so they could check on the boy. Carol had gone in the ambulance. She cried uncontrollably when they placed the breathing apparatus over Alfie's mouth, purely as a precaution they said but that was no comfort to her. Now there she was holding his hand, stroking his hair, praying to any God, Unicorn or fairy that would listen to her desperate pleas, to help her little Boy. His eyelids fluttered and her heart skipped a beat, 'Baby, it's Mummy,' this had happened on several occasions, but he hadn't woken. His dream disturbing his slumber and tricking the poor helpless woman who sat heartbroken by his side.

10

The man in the bed was covered in bandages. Alfie couldn't see an ounce of flesh showing through the white wrap. He looked like an Egyptian Mummy and he half expected him to rise with his arms outstretched, but he didn't. He lay there, his chest rising up and down slowly then quickly then slowly again. The burning man stood on the other side of the bed looking down at the man and Alfie heard his voice inside his head, 'they told me I would be fine, they told me not to worry. I told them to kill me, I begged for them to let me die. They didn't stop trying to save me. That bitch downstairs kept me alive. I wanted them to stop. They wouldn't stop. Help me,' he sobbed, 'I'm burning.' Alfie suddenly felt his skin on fire, the sensation crippled his mind. 'This is how I feel all the time, but they won't let me die. What would you do to end this pain, Alfie? What would you do?' Alfie would have done anything, even kill the nurse downstairs but would have hated himself afterwards. This thought was heard by the burning man 'I wanted to kill her, but I couldn't do it. But I had to stop her or she would have stopped you. The pain is too much, I have no control over myself. Stop me before I hurt someone else, end my misery please,' it sounded more human this time, more like a sad creature mangled beyond all hope, begging to be put down. But humans don't put down each other, that just isn't done. All life is precious that's what they're taught in Sunday school and church when they're older. That's why this poor soul was trapped here on earth searching for someone to release him, someone who would understand, someone who had done it before. He had done it before, he remembered it now. It came back to him like a sledgehammer to his gut.

Sergeant Williams hadn't been dead, he was still alive when he landed on Alfie but his legs no longer worked and his spine was hanging out of him like a piece of loose string on a rope. 'Let me go, Alfie,' his Sergeant had begged, 'end it, I'm ready.' Alfie had granted the man who saved his life one final kindness. With his only free hand, he put it over the Sergeant's mouth and nose and watched as his eyes went blank. He didn't know if it had been him or the horrific wounds that had finally finished him off, but it hadn't mattered, it was him that had caused the whole thing and him who had suffocated a brother in arms. He had blocked the memory from his mind, trying to save his sanity but now the truth was forced upon him and he withered at its vulgarity.

'Alfie,' oh God no, he shot back into consciousness at the sound of her voice, 'what are you doing?' he looked down at his hands which were gripped onto a pillow, which he was forcing down on the face of the bandaged man. He went to pull away but couldn't, his hands were frozen in place, his decisions no longer his own. She jumped towards him but was knocked back by the burning man who appeared in-between them. She landed by the wall, dazed but alive. He lurched over her his arms raised threateningly.

'NO,' Alfie cried, 'LEAVE HER ALONE,' he forced the pillow down, this time of his own accord. 'Die and be free,' with a judder the man died and the burning man faded. In his place stood a tall man in a dirty grey waistcoat, brown trousers and loose-fitting green shirt. He was older than Alfie and he stood with his hands in the waistcoat pockets as if he was out for an afternoon stroll. Alfie recognised him immediately. It was his brother Ryan. How could he have forgotten him? He had been told by the Doctor he was MIA, but couldn't recollect ever having a brother until now.

'Hello little Brother,' he smiled at Alfie.

'They told me you were MIA,' Alfie was confused and angry.

'They thought I was someone else, they thought I was a Lieutenant named Barnes. But he was killed and I survived, well if you call that surviving,' he pointed to the body, lifeless on the bed.

'But I couldn't remember you, why did I forget you?' Alfie's voice broke.

'You didn't forget me little Brother, you let me go. You need to let me go again,' Ryan began to fade slightly.

'No, wait. Please don't go. I can't do this without you,' Alfie reached for Ryan.

'Yes, you can, you are stronger than you think, look at what you have done in all your adventures, Alfie. You are a hero, you are an amazing little dude,' Ryan suddenly faded away, then immediately came back. But this time he looked like Ryan from the real world. The Ryan that Alfie knew. Alfie looked around him. The room had also transformed. He was now standing in his own room in his house. He was no longer a bandaged soldier, but a nine-year-old boy again, 'I miss you so much Ryan,' he sobbed.

'I miss you too little dude, but you have Carol now and she will take care of you. I'll never be truly gone; I'll always be in your memories,' he knelt on one knee as he had done so many times before and opened his arms. Alfie ran into them and squeezed tighter than he had ever done.

'Will you visit me?' Alfie asked.

'When you need me to, I'll be in your adventures from time to time. But it's time you concentrated on yourself. You have a long journey ahead of you little dude and you now have the strength and resolve to battle it head-on. I'm so proud of you, never forget that and never forget how remarkable you truly are,' Ryan pulled away and stood.

Alfie stood tall to show how brave he could be. He was determined to prove his Hero right. He would never give up fighting for what he believed in; he would always protect others who needed his help, 'I love you, Ryan, I won't let you down.'

'I know little Brother. Thank you for being the best part of my life. I'll never forget you,' before Alfie could protest, Ryan faded away again, leaving particles of light which then also faded. He stood staring into the space that had once been his brother for what felt like hours.

Stubbs the spider appeared on his shoulder, 'he's right you know, you are remarkable.'

'I know,' said Alfie without any doubt in his voice.

'That's why I love you, Alfie, you're so very humble,' the spider laughed and nearly fell off Alfie's shoulder.

'Silly Spider,' they laughed together until he woke.

He opened his eyes, 'Mummy, I said goodbye to Ryan.'

'Oh baby you came back to me,' she hugged him, too overjoyed to register what he had said and he squirmed free 'sorry, sorry,' she said hastily, 'I just missed you so much, I was so worried,' she wanted to squeeze him till he popped but restrained herself barely and just touched his arm gently.

'My head hurts,' he lifted his hands to touch it and saw they were bandaged just like in his adventure. He paused for a moment wondering if he was still imagining things but he was awake because his Mummy was there and she was never in his adventures.

'It's ok Sweetheart you have a cut on your head and some little grazes on your hands, but other than that you should be fine,' she tried to smile but instead grimaced at the thought of him falling through the glass, 'do you remember what happened?' she cursed herself for bringing it up. How stupid was she that she would make him relive the terrible moment in his fragile mind? "stupid, stupid, stupid", she thought.

'Not really Mummy, I just remember you and Daddy were arguing then I kicked Daddy because he was mean to you and then I was in a hospital,' he meant the World War One hospital but she assumed the real world one.

'You fell through some glass next to the door,' she should tell him the truth, he would appreciate that more, but she just couldn't make him hate his father, he was hated enough as it was.

'Can I go home now Mummy? I want to go home,' he squirmed into a seated position and looked at her pleadingly.

'I don't see why not, let me go and find a nurse and I'll ask,' she got up pushing herself out of the chair using its arms for assistance as her knees had gone stiff from sitting down too long. She stretched holding the base of her spine.

'Mummy,' he said, she turned around, 'I love you,' he wasn't looking at her when he said it but it meant the world all the same.

'I love you too Baby, now let's get you home to your Lego.'

Chapter 12

Gary sat in the plain simply designed police cell with his head in his hands, sobbing uncontrollably. The police desk Sergeant had told a duty officer to keep an eye on him and double-check him for anything he could use to harm himself. They'd removed his belt and taken everything out of his pockets. They'd even taken the shoelaces out of his trainers for christ sake. It wasn't as if he was going to strangle himself with shoelaces, not unless he was a pixie and the last time he checked they weren't real so he was ok on that front. They'd sent for a medic to clean him up before taking him for questioning.

He'd barely spoken when they brought him into the cramped room with its single desk and four chairs, two on each side and had instead begun mumbling about how much he hated himself and how he wished he could take it all back, "take what back?" a WPC had asked him repeatedly but got nowhere fast or slow for that matter. His solicitor despaired when he'd nodded his head and muttered yes when they'd asked him if he'd hit his son, then the grey-suited representative did the same when they asked Gary if he'd tried to hit his wife and he admitted to that too. They told him he would be charged with GBH and took him back to his cell. The small metal window in the cell door lifted open and a bald man with droopy eyes looked through, 'you alright?' he asked with a tone that suggested he cared about as much as a Tiger did for the deer it was eating.

'No, now get lost,' Gary barked hating himself even more for winding up the police as if his situation wasn't bad enough.

Whatever,' the officer replied nonchalantly and slammed the little window shut.
Gary knew his life would never be the same, this is what he deserved, this was justice for all the times he had lashed out and hurt those he loved. He never understood why he did it but that didn't matter anymore, he'd done it and there was no going back. He continued to cry and hate himself even more.

Chapter 13

At last, they were back home. Alfie was upstairs in his bed trying to play with his new Indiana Jones Lego set Keith had bought him as a present when he picked them up, but finding it a challenge with his hands still bandaged. Alfie was already fond of Keith, but this act of kindness made him infallible in his eyes. Carol and Keith sat in the living room drinking cups of tea. Carol held hers like a small child would hold a bottle and Keith sighed inside at how sweet she looked. A plate of chocolate biscuits sat on the knee-high coffee table in-between the woodchip coasters and Keith placed his Rose patterned mug down and picked one up. He shyly bit into it and crumbs dropped onto his lap, he looked down at them and smiled a nervous grin, melting chocolate covered his teeth.

'What am I supposed to do now?' Carol said dejectedly and slumped into the cushions.

'Whatever you want, you're free of him,' he was trying to help but knew he was blowing it.

'Thanks to you,' she raised her soft stare to meet his gaze and her heart felt giddy and weak,' you saved both of us.'

'I did what anyone would have done,' he said modestly staring back at her with the same week feeling in his heart.

'No Keith, they wouldn't and they didn't,' she leaned closer to him, his hand stopped as it reached for another biscuit. She put her drink down missing the coaster, her eyes not leaving his, 'do you love me Keith?' she craved his approval, his want for her, even if she didn't match his enthusiasm. She needed to be loved, she wouldn't be able to cope on her own and here was a good, stable, loving, sort of handsome man who could look after her and more importantly Alfie.

'Yes,' he said with total confidence, 'ever since I met you.' She leaned forward and their lips met. They passionately kissed, hard and franticly. All her anger and fear expressed in one sexually charged act.

'Wait for me in the bedroom while I check on Alfie,' she gasped, her heart beating recklessly.

'Okay but only if you're sure,' even now he was gentlemanly.

'I've never been more sure of anything in my life,' and she hadn't. She was in control now, she was taking charge of her life and she would be the one to choose how it panned out. They kissed again and rushed upstairs, her hand pulled him as they climbed. He went into her bedroom and she went to Alfie's. He was asleep, knocked out by all the excitement of the day. They'd been out for a meal at a Harvester because Alfie liked the salad bar but she had to fill his bowl up because it was too crowded. He hadn't stopped playing with the Lego since they got back and she admired the huge structure he'd built despite his bandages, leaning up against the wall in the corner of his room. Little Lego Indiana Jones with his yellow head and plastic brown hat stood on the steps of the colossal tower, holding his stationary trademark whip in the air. She closed the door quietly, but not before Monty darted in, meowing his disappointment at almost being shut out. She stood for a moment gathering her thoughts then entered her room, nervous but happy.

'Are you awake Alfie?' asked Stubbs. 'I've got a great idea for the next adventure,' he looked over at the Lego tower.

Alfie smiled in his sleep, he was always ready for another adventure.

Epilogue

The greatest adventure

'Sweetheart.' Alfie stares blankly down at his toast. The edges are slightly burnt but he doesn't care because he'll just leave those. There was a time when he would freak about something so trivial but nowadays he's way more zen. 'Alfie, sweetheart are you with us, or are you away with the fairies again?' He looks up and smiles, bits of peanut butter stick to his teeth like desperate men clinging to the side of a mountain. His eyes soften when she smiles back. 'Don't forget to call your Mum, she wanted to wish you luck with the new job. I still can't believe your head of the department. My sexy science boss. We're all so proud of you,' Sylvia looks over at Ryan sitting in his high chair. The baby's covered in the mornings' breakfast. He bangs his tiny plastic spoon on the tray in front of him as if to cheer on his Daddy.

'Thanks, Babe, thanks little Dude,' Alfie picks up a slice of toast and takes a bite.

'Keith will be over later to help fit those shelves you promised to put up, so don't worry about that. I know your minds been on other things,' she attempts to wipe Ryan's face but he ducks and weaves like a lightweight boxer, avoiding her at all costs, 'fine, don't be a handsome boy,' she gives up and puts down cloth. She sits down opposite Alfie and giggles.

'What?' he says.

'You almost have as much mess on your face as your Son,' she picks up the cloth again and leans over. She wipes his face and sits back down, 'I remember a time when you would hate that.'

'I did, I just know how to keep calm that's all,' he throws her a sly look, 'you're the only one who'd get away with it.'

'Of course, I'm the only one who should be wiping your face, I am your wife after all. I hope you don't have some hussy come over and wipe your face for you when I'm not here?' she pouts but it only lasts a second before both of them snigger.

'Did my Dad ring?' he straightens his face.

'No, sorry,' she looks away avoiding the disappointment on his face, 'but Tiff sent a text wishing you luck.'

'That's cool, maybe she could come over and see me, oh wait a minute of course not she lives in Australia,' he grits his teeth.

'Come on sweetheart we talked about this. She loves you no matter where she lives, besides if we want to go on holiday there we'll have somewhere to stay,' she smiles again cheekily.

Alfie stands and tucks his chair under the breakfast table. He rolls his eyes dramatically, deliberately overemphasising the gesture to show he's playing around. His communication skills have improved so much since he met Sylvia and with her and his Mum's help he was able to finish University and get a degree in Zoology. Today he would start his first day as head of the Care of endangered animals department at London Zoo. He was the youngest person ever to be given the position and this was all down to his hard work and socialising with his colleagues, something he never thought possible twenty years ago as he hid under Mrs Honeywell's desk. He thought about that day and his old friend. He wished sometimes he could go back and tell that scared little boy that it would turn out alright in the end and not to be sad even when bad things happen. Stubbs was long gone, but never forgotten and he would make many appearances in the stories Alfie would make up and tell his infant son when he put him to bed. Ryan was the light of his life and he vowed the day he was born that he would never let his difficulties affect him as a Dad. Life was almost perfect except when it came to Gary. His Dad had been in and out of his life for the last two decades but had never hung around long enough to establish a bond between the two of them. Alfie never gave up hoping though and would refuse to blame him for it. Keith had been an amazing substitute and a wonderful husband to Carol, but he wasn't his Dad and never would be. He lived twenty minutes drive from them and they would meet up as often as possible. He loved Keith but mainly because he loved his Mum, and he was good to her.

'Are you alright sweetheart? You drifted away again,' she was used to him doing this.

'I'm great actually, I was just thinking how proud Ryan would be of me,' he looks down at his shoes.

'I know baby, he would have been so, so proud of you,' she walks over to him and embraces him. They hug tightly for over a minute, then kiss.

'Now, now Babe we don't want to make all those ladies waiting for me at work jealous, do we?'

'Your right sweetheart, because you're such a catch.'

'You thought so.'

'I was drunk at the time,' she giggles. She loves playing these games.

'You took advantage of a mentally different man you saucy harlot,' he points at her.

'Fine, you win. I couldn't resist your inability to not tell me a million facts a day and that my hair was looking a bit windswept,' she flicks her hair to emphasize her point.

'Actually, it was a million and one facts and your hair often looked windswept and sometimes I didn't tell you and you complained about it because you looked like a plonker,' he reaches for his jacket that hangs on a peg next to the door. They kiss again, uplifted by the banter. Sylvia was so good at taking his mind off things. She knew he was apprehensive and expertly acted in accordance.

'Have a great day handsome,' she touches his face with her hand and stares deep into his eyes. He holds her gaze.

'I will,' he says and because of Carol, Sylvia and Ryan, he does.

About the Author

Joe James is an Autistic / ADHD adult and Neurodiversity advocate from the UK. He is an Award winning landscape photographer and published poet. He is married to his wife Sylvia James and together they have two Neurodiverse children.

Joe is proof that although difficult at times, being Neurodivergent can be a great asset to his life and helps him achieve all that he has, including writing this book.

Printed in Great Britain
by Amazon

61023546R00169